Fighting Fate

A Redwood Pack Novel

By
CARRIE ANN RYAN

Fighting Fate

With her blue-black hair and striking green eyes, Cailin Jamenson is the epitome of beauty and the exemplar of strength. She has fought the enforced boundaries of being the lone Jamenson daughter and Redwood Pack princess, but it is the potential future with the dark wolf in her path that threatens everything she thought she desired.

Logan Anderson's own darkness provided the reasoning for his abandonment of his former Pack, the Talons. Now, newly accepted into the Redwood Pack, this jade-eyed wolf and all she represents could be his own undoing.

In this final installment of the Redwood Pack, unimaginable tragedy strikes, and the two wolves who have fought the longest for their independence now face the uncertainty of fate and the epic battle that could end the war... and their lives.

Dedication

*To the fans of the Redwood Pack. It all started with a
blind date with a werewolf...and look where we are.
Thank you.*

Acknowledgements

I honestly have no idea how to start this. Fighting Fate is the final full book in the Redwood Pack series. Oh, there will be more novellas and a full set of eight novels in the same world with familiar characters, but Cailin is the last Jamenson to find her mate.

Each book took an army it seemed to finish and as the series progressed, as did my need for my writing friends, readers, support, and family. I couldn't have done any of this without each and every one of you.

Thank you Lia for working with me on each book in little ways (and sometimes large ones). You're by my side no matter what and I love you for it. Charity Hendry, you rock girl. You totally understood the Redwood Pack and jumped right in. Thank you for helping me work out *that scene*. Without you listening to my breakdown, I don't know if I could have written it. To Devin, Saya, Lillie, Fatin, Scott, Donna, and Michelle, thank you for each of your hands in this series and helping me get Fighting Fate to where it is now. And to Rebecca Royce, thank you for asking me to write An Alpha's Path so long ago. Who knew we'd end up here?

And to my readers, thank you from the bottom of my heart. I never thought I'd get to live this dream. I hope you enjoy Fighting Fate and the rest of the Redwoods, Talons, and other books I have to come.

You guys are amazing.

Redwood Pack Characters

With an ever growing list of characters in each book, I know that it might seem like there are too many to remember. Well don't worry; here is a list so you don't forget. Not all are seen in this exact book, but here are the ones you've met so far. As the series progresses, the list will as well.

Happy reading!

Adam Jamenson—Enforcer of the Redwood Pack, third son of the Alpha. Mate to Bay and father to Micah. Story told in *Enforcer's Redemption* and *Forgiveness*.

Anna Jamenson—late mate of Adam.

Bay Jamenson—new member of the Redwood Pack. Mate to Adam and mother to Micah. Story told in *Enforcer's Redemption* and *Forgiveness*.

Beth—member of the Redwood Pack. Aunt to Emily.

Brie Jamenson—daughter of Jasper and Willow.

Cailin Jamenson—Only daughter of Edward and Pat.

Camille—deceased former member of the Redwood Pack.

Caym—demon from Hell summoned by the Centrals. Lover of Corbin.

Charlotte Jamenson—half-sister of Ellie's. Will be raised as a daughter by Ellie and Maddox.

Conner Jamenson—son of Josh, Reed and Hannah. Twin to Kaylee.

Corbin Reyes—new Alpha of the Central Pack. Lover of Caym.

Cyrus Ferns—deceased former unit teammate of Josh's.

Donald—member of the Redwood Pack.

Edward Jamenson—Alpha of the Redwood Pack. Mate to Pat. Father to Kade, Jasper, Adam, Reed, Maddox, North and Cailin.

Ellie Jamenson—Daughter of the former Alpha of the Central Pack. Mate to Maddox and mother to Charlotte. Story told in *Shattered Emotions*.

Emily—young member of the Redwood Pack. Orphan and niece of Beth.

Emeline—elder of the Redwood Pack. Lost her mate in the first war with the Centrals.

Finn Jamenson—son of Kade and Melanie. Future Heir and Alpha of the Redwood Pack.

Franklin—deceased former member of the Redwood Pack. Camille's lover.

Gina Jamenson—newly adopted daughter of Kade and Melanie. Her birth parents, Larissa and Neil were killed during an attack.

Hannah—Healer of the Redwood Pack. Mate to Josh and Reed. Mother of Conner and Kaylee. Story told in *Trinity Bound* and *Blurred Expectations*.

Hector Reyes—deceased former Alpha of the Central Pack. Father to Corbin, Ellie, Charlotte and Ellie's twin.

Henry—Redwood Pack member and store owner for 60 years.

Isaac—deceased member of the Central Pack.

Jason—member of the Redwood Pack and one of the Alpha's enforcers.

Jasper—Beta of the Redwood Pack. Mate to Willow and father of Brie. Story told in *A Taste for a Mate* and *A Beta's Haven*.

Jim—hot dog vendor and one of Josh's former friends.

Joseph Brentwood—deceased former Alpha of the Talon Pack.

Josh Jamenson—former human Navy Seal. A Finder and partial demon. Mated to Reed and

Hannah. Father to Conner and Kaylee. Story told in *Trinity Bound* and *Blurred Expectations*.

Kade Jamenson—Heir and future Alpha of the Redwood Pack. Mate to Melanie. Father to Finn, Gina, and Mark. Story told in *An Alpha's Path* and *A Night Away*.

Kaylee Jamenson—daughter of Josh, Reed and Hannah. Twin to Conner.

Larissa—deceased member of the Redwood Pack. Witch and friend to Melanie. Mate to Neil and mother of Gina and Mark.

Lexi Jamenson—former Talon Pack member and new Redwood Pack member. Mother to Parker and sister to Logan. Mate to North. Story told in *Hidden Destiny*.

Logan Anderson—former Talon Pack member and new Redwood Pack member. Uncle to Parker and brother to Lexi.

Maddox Jamenson—Omega of the Redwood Pack. Mate to Ellie and father to Charlotte. Story told in *Shattered Emotions*.

Mark Jamenson—newly adopted son of Kade and Melanie. Her birth parents, Larissa and Neil were killed during an attack.

Melanie Jamenson—former human chemist and mate to Kade. Mother to Finn, Gina and Mark. Story told in *An Alpha's Path* and *A Night Away*.

Meryl—Redwood Pack Elder.

Micah Jamenson—son of Adam and Bay.

Mrs. Carnoski—elderly customer of Josh's when he was human.

Neil—deceased member of the Redwood Pack. Mate to Larissa and father of Gina and Mark.

Noah—member of the Redwood Pack and former lover of Cailin's.

North Jamenson—doctor in the Redwood Pack, son of the Alpha. Mate to Lexi. Story told in *Hidden Destiny*.

Parker Jamenson—new member of the Redwood Pack and son of Lexi's.

Patricia (Pat) Jamenson—mate of the Alpha, Alpha female, and mother to Kade, Jasper, Adam, Reed, Maddox, North, and Cailin.

Patrick—disgruntled member of The Redwood Pack.

Reed Jamenson—artist and son of the Alpha of the Redwood Pack. Mate to Josh and Hannah. Story told in *Trinity Bound* and *Blurred Expectations*.

Reggie—deceased former member of the Central Pack.

Samuel—deceased former member of the Central Pack.

Willow Jamenson—former human baker and now mate to Jasper. Mother to Brie. Story told in *A Taste for a Mate* and *A Beta's Haven*.

PROLOGUE

Death came in many forms, but in the end, the lack of breath, the lack of existence was all Caym craved.

Sometimes waiting was the only way to ensure the success of a well-laid plan. Sometimes death was the only way to give rebirth. The act itself would take a piece of him so far away, break it into so many pieces he'd never recover it. That didn't matter though.

No, only the blood and deaths of those who would soon fall mattered.

He fingered the line of text on the yellowed page of the book that lay in front of him and grinned. Yes, the Centrals had been on the right track, but they hadn't had his vision. Hadn't had his promise. They'd used this spell before, and now he knew how to make it his own.

It would come as a clash of Titans.

Caym would rejoice and win.

And, in his victory, Caym would be benevolent.

He would grant the mercy of death to the defeated.

He was a demon, after all.

CHAPTER ONE

The couple looked so in love, so at peace, that Cailin Jamenson thought she might break out in hives or a cold shiver at the thought of them. Her palms itched, and a line of sweat trailed down her back. She licked her lips, trying to keep her mind off of the rabbit hole of heartache her thoughts would eventually find. It wasn't that she was upset her brother North had finally found his mate, Lexi. Just like it wasn't that she was sad that the rest of her brothers had found their mates as well.

No, it was something much worse.

She was jealous.

Like angry-green-monster, wolf-howling-rage jealous.

Jealous and refusing to do anything about it because once she did...well, once she did, everything she'd fought so hard for would have been for naught. It had taken years, but she finally felt like she was worth something more than the title—at least in her mind. Going down the path where her wolf begged to be led wouldn't accomplish anything but pain and rapid denial.

The wind picked up, knocking a strand of hair out of place and she tucked it back behind her ear. She could hear the sounds of her Pack, her wolves, sniffing, murmuring, and paying attention to the ceremony. The noise mixed with the sounds of nature, the birds chirping and the leaves rustling in the breeze. None of that centered her though. No, she only knew of one way to do that. One way she wasn't ready to face.

Her wolf might crave the dark wolf with rough edges who haunted her dreams, but that didn't mean the woman inside would succumb.

She was stronger than that.

She was Cailin Jamenson.

Redwood Pack princess.

Lone daughter of the Jamenson clan.

Younger sister to six over-protective yet loving brothers.

Aunt to countless nieces and nephews.

The Beta's assistant.

And lost.

So *fucking* lost.

She knew what the others saw when they looked at her, the raven-black hair, the light green eyes. So many others had told her she was one of the most beautiful people they'd ever seen. What a load of crap. Even if they weren't just saying that because of who she was, she wouldn't take it at face value. She'd seen true beauty in the selfless acts of her sisters and friends. They were the beautiful ones. Cailin usually responded to those who spoke only of her looks that they hadn't seen that many people. Most didn't see beyond the surface, beyond the blood in her veins.

Someone murmured something behind her, and she blinked, forcing her attention to what was going on in front of her rather than wallowing in the shames

3

she should have buried. Shames that weren't really shames at all, not in the grand scheme of things. She'd always tried to be so strong for others, and in turn, hadn't treated those she now loved with the respect they deserved. She'd tried to fix that over time, but she wasn't sure she was worth it. Others worried so much for her and her safety, she knew they weren't taking care of themselves like they should. She needed to stop acting so self-centered, so hurt and broken when it was her own doing.

When her father, the Alpha of the Redwood Pack, put his hand on North's shoulder then did the same to Lexi's, solidifying their bond and mating in front of the Pack, Cailin sucked in a breath and pasted on a smile.

She was happy for them, she really was.

She hated herself for wanting what they had and what they were just beginning.

North cupped Lexi's face, kissing her so softly it looked as if it was barely a whisper. Their gazes never left each other, though Cailin knew North couldn't see Lexi. He'd been blinded in their last battle with the Centrals, but that didn't stop him from living his life to the fullest. Cailin swallowed hard, burying her own pain. Her brother looked so in love, so *whole* after being alone for decades, hiding his own darkness until Lexi came along and found what Cailin and her family had missed.

North had needed his mate, his Lexi.

Had needed her more than anything in the world.

He needed their son, Parker, and the bonds that came with mating and fatherhood. Those grounded him and kept his wolf calm.

Cailin would never allow the love and connections to settle her.

She vowed she wouldn't. At least, that's what she'd told herself over and over, what she said to herself the moment she'd laid eyes on Lexi's brother.

Her gaze met that of the other man at Lexi's side, and she raised her chin. She wouldn't have him. Couldn't have him. She just needed to remind her wolf that.

Remind everyone who thought so much of her of that fact.

He gave her a small nod, and her wolf brushed against her skin, a soft caress. A plea for submission, dominance, mating, and everything in between.

Logan. Lexi's brother.

Cailin's potential mate.

No, she wouldn't be mating with him. She'd lived her life with seven dominant men—not even counting the others in the Pack who'd watched her grow up— telling her what to do, how to act, how to behave. She'd vowed to herself long ago she wouldn't be following the same routine for eternity tied to a man she felt was even stronger than her brothers.

Even darker than her brothers.

The wolf wouldn't be able to stop himself from dominating her, and that wasn't what she craved, what she *needed* in order to survive whole.

Logan narrowed his eyes, but Cailin didn't miss the promise in his gaze. Promise of something far greater than the anticipation and trepidation she'd been burying deep inside since she'd met him. Damn it, she'd run out of time. She'd been dancing on the fine line of temptation and playing hide and seek for far too long when it came to the wolf standing across the aisle. The wolf wouldn't wait for Cailin's cue anymore. No, he'd take what he thought was his. What he thought the Pack and she herself wanted.

Cailin's wolf, though she panted as well, sneered. Well, he'd just have to wait an eternity for that, wouldn't he?

Cailin wasn't some weak-kneed little girl. She'd fight for her freedom—just like she'd always done.

"Stop growling, little sister. You're scaring the children."

Cailin winced at her brother Maddox's words and tried to smile again. It came out more like a grimace, but at least it was something. "Sorry," she whispered. She'd let her emotions get the best of her and let others know what was going on inside her mind when she hadn't wanted them to know too much. Not the best way to observe a mating ceremony while trying to remain stoic and happy at the same time.

Maddox put his arm around her shoulders and pulled her close. Her wolf calmed down from the storm Cailin wasn't even aware was brewing. She didn't sigh or relax, even if her wolf was ready to bare her belly for her brother who seemed to know just how to make her feel loved and cared for. This was why wolves were such tactile creatures. The barest touch and her wolf felt cemented, loved.

Her brother bushed his lips over her temple. "The ceremony is over, Cai. You can go stand in a corner and hide from the big bad wolf if you'd like. No one would fault you." Though his words were teasing, the meaning behind them held the hints of truth she wasn't ready to face. And having her brother call her meekness out filled her with a rage she knew wasn't fully on his shoulders.

He would bear the brunt of it anyway.

Cailin turned and faced him, her claws scraping along the insides of her fingertips at the taunt. She lifted her lip and bared a fang. Maddox only laughed, the scar on his face tightening as he did so. Her heart tugged at the sight. She despised that damn scar and all it represented. The now-dead Central Alpha, Corbin, had carved him up years go. The bastard had tortured her brother because of a prophecy that hadn't even been about Maddox to begin with.

No, it had been about North.

The same North that had killed Corbin anyway.

The prophecy had been correct, and Corbin had scarred the wrong brother.

The fact that she couldn't kill Corbin again enraged her and she had to push that familiar feeling back. No good would come from what-ifs.

Her brother bopped her on the nose, that smile on his face infectious. God, she loved this Maddox—the Maddox that smiled, laughed, and looked *happy*. His mate, Ellie, had done that, and Cailin would always be grateful.

Taking a deep breath, she forced her hands to relax. Instead of beating her annoyingly astute brother up, she patted the scarred side of his cheek, something she hadn't done in the past because of her fear of hurting him. She'd been an idiot, and the lack of touch had only pulled him deeper into himself, away from his family and those that loved him. Now she tried to make sure he knew that she loved him, scars and all.

"Thank you, big brother, but I will not cower." She refused to. There would be no hiding from the wolf that haunted her dreams...and now her days. She might not want to deal with it, but she wouldn't run away with her tail tucked between her legs. That wasn't who she'd been her entire life, and she wouldn't resort to becoming that person now.

Maddox raised a dark blond brow. "If you won't let me beat Logan up, or at least maim him a bit, then you'll have to do something about him."

Cailin rolled her eyes. "Stay out of it, Mad."

Maddox traced a line down her cheek, and she sighed. Her wolf brushed along the inside of her skin, settling under her brother's touch. "I don't know that I can, Cai. Your wolf isn't happy, I can feel it. The woman isn't that happy either."

Her wolf rumbled, agreeing with the man. No, she wasn't happy. She wouldn't be without a certain dark wolf.

Damn them both.

Her brother was the Omega of the Redwood Pack, meaning he could feel the emotions of every Pack member other than his twin, North. He had once been unable to feel his mate, Ellie, before they'd bonded, but now their mating bond was stronger than most. His role was to ensure the emotional needs of the Pack were met and they were healthy from the inside out. It also meant he took in each pain, hurt, and overabundance of happiness right into his soul. Cailin just thanked the moon goddess he had Ellie now to share that burden.

His role as Omega, though, didn't mean Cailin liked having her brother intrude on her feelings. It wasn't that he was reaching inside her through that fragile bond that connected him with the Pack on the emotional level. No, when she was this angst-filled, she was apparently blasting her emotions clear and far. She was usually much better at hiding everything having to do with that and erecting a shield from his nosy wolf.

"I'm fine. Butt out, Maddox."

Maddox growled a bit but put his hands up. "Deal with it, Cailin. You're on edge, and this isn't the time to have your wolf weak because she's not getting what she needs. We're Pack animals, Cai. We need touch. We need that connection."

She ignored the last part of his statement, concentrating on the part that dug deep. Cailin lifted her chin. "I'm not weak. Despite the fact that I don't have a penis, which you Jamenson boys think one must have in order to be strong, I can and *will* fight for my Pack."

Maddox lifted a lip, his eyes glowing a soft gold. "First, don't say penis. You're my baby sister. You're innocent and pure."

Cailin snorted. Her brothers kept saying that. If they only knew...

No, she didn't want to give them all heart attacks. Or go attack her ex, Noah...or hurt Logan for playing some key parts in her dirtiest fantasies.

And it was time to get her mind off that particular track.

"Second, what the hell do you mean about women being weak? Have you seen our mates? Do you really think any of the six of us consider our mates weak? If that's what you believe, you aren't looking close enough, and it's fucking insulting. Get your head out of your ass, Cailin, and fix this. Find a way to deal with Logan. Either mate with him or let him down. Running away and hiding behind your need to find another way to live isn't helping anyone. We're at war. And even if we weren't, you deserve to be happy."

Chastened, she took a step back, her heels digging into the ground underneath her. "I'm sorry. I didn't mean that the way it came out." Oh, she did, but only when it came to the way they thought of her, but that was another matter. "I'm going to go get some air." Maddox raised a brow, and she shook her head. "I know we're outside, but I need different air. Jamenson-free air."

Maddox pulled her into a hug then kissed the top of her head. "I love you, little sister. I'm sorry for pushing, but you're so bottled up I'm scared for you. Something's coming, something darker than we've ever faced before, and I want to make sure you're as ready as you can be for it."

She had the same oppressive feeling as Maddox and the rest of her family. There wasn't any way to tell what the darkness was or what danger it might bring, but she knew it was coming.

They all did.

Cailin cupped Maddox's face and leaned forward. He was a full half foot taller than her, but in heels she could rest her forehead on his scarred cheek. "I love you, Maddox. I'm sorry. You won't have to worry about me. I promise. I won't let you down."

Maddox squeezed her. "You could never let me down."

She pulled away with a small smile at his lie, then turned toward the line of trees, needing space. Maddox might have said she could never let him down, but she knew that wasn't true. She'd been letting everyone down around her for years. Her brothers were all around seventy years older than she was and had practically helped raised her along with their parents. Kade, Jasper, Adam, Reed, North, and Maddox didn't know how *not* to be overbearing and protective.

It was just their way.

They, however, all had roles within the Pack, whether it be powers blessed from the moon goddess herself or roles they'd created for themselves so they were worth something.

Cailin had always been a step behind.

She hated it.

What worried her more than all of that, though, was the fact that her brothers didn't trust her to take care of herself. No matter how grown up she thought she was, she'd always be their baby sister, too weak, too frail to fight in the war with the Centrals.

They'd been at war for almost four years.

Four. Years.

Those years didn't even include the tension and pain they'd experienced for decades before the Central Pack summoned and teamed up with a demon named Caym. The other Pack had sacrificed their own princess, Ellie's twin sister, and brought forth hell into their world. One by one, year by year, Cailin had watched her brothers not only fall in love but fight for their lives against the cruelty that was the Centrals.

Now, though, the war was coming to an end.

At least that's how it felt to Cailin.

The Centrals had lost two Alphas in those four years, Hector and his son, Corbin. Now Caym ruled them with an iron fist. His own dose of dark magic prevented the Redwoods from being on the offense, forever on the defense and trying to scramble the protection needed to survive.

Oh, she'd fought by her family's side when they let her, when there was no other way to hide her behind closed doors. God, she hated sounding so ungrateful for her family's worry and care, but the smothering had to stop.

And mating with Logan would only intensify that feeling. She was sure of it.

She took long strides toward the tree line, nodding at other Pack members who stared at her as if they knew what her innermost thoughts were. Her innermost fear and insecurity. Knowing the way she couldn't seem to hide anything today, she wouldn't be surprised if that was actually true. No one called out to her, telling her to come to their side and join them in the celebration.

She was alone.

Just like she'd always thought she'd be.

Just like she'd forced herself to be.

"What are you doing out here all alone?"

The deep timbre went straight to her core, her body shaking at just those words alone. Words that didn't mean anything beyond the fact they were spoken by the one wolf she'd truly tried to hide from.

Cailin stopped moving, her hand pressed against a tree as she prayed for composure. It wouldn't do well to bite and snap at him or, worse, press her body up against him and rub her scent all over him. She turned to face Logan and tried not to swallow her tongue. No matter how hard she fought her attraction to him, her wolf ached for the man in front of her.

The woman wanted him as well but tried to hide it.

Damn it.

Those hazel eyes bore into her, the dominance held within them not begging for her wolf's submission—only the woman's. Within those eyes she could see the man and the wolf, two halves of a whole. Two distinct ideas and desires. One wanted her submission, the other wanted her by his side. That was the difference between him and the other wolves who might have laid claim to her.

The difference she wasn't ready to accept.

The difference she wasn't sure she understood.

Her hands ached to run through his dark hair that he'd recently shorn so it lay close to his scalp. At five-five, she wasn't the shortest of women, but next to Logan's size, she always felt small, fragile.

And that's why she would never mate with him.

She needed to be strong, not weak—not how she felt around him. How she feared he'd make her be once she gave into the yearning both she and her wolf craved.

"Following me now like a lost puppy?" she sneered.

Logan pinched her chin, forcing her gaze to his. She narrowed her eyes, but her damn inner wolf wouldn't let her move back. No, the annoying canine wanted to rub up all along the man and make sure all those women eyeing him at the ceremony kept their paws off of him.

Not that she'd been paying attention to them.

No, but she had felt their gazes digging into her back and on the tall drink of water in front of her.

If her mind had been making any sense at all, she should have been happy other women wanted to lay claim—if only for an evening. Instead, she battled within herself so much her head ached.

"You should be with your family," he said, his voice low, *tempting*. "It's a day of light rather than the darkness you've been fighting for far too long."

"You say that as if you aren't a Redwood." She held back a wince. Damn it, she did not want to get into a conversation with this man. Not when she needed to breathe, to feel like she had a choice in the matter.

Logan rubbed her chin with his thumb before pulling back. Cailin immediately wanted his touch back, the loss almost overwhelming.

Her wolf whimpered.

Freaking whimpered.

"I might have the bond with the Alpha, but we both know that finding your place within a Pack is more than a bond and a promise."

She blinked up at him, surprised at his insight. That sliver of connection to the man in front of her she'd tried to ignore thickened just enough that she had to hold back a gasp. Her wolf wanted that bond, badly.

13

They stared at each other for a few more moments, though it felt like longer before she shook her head, clearing thoughts of forever and a promise she'd never intend to keep.

"I should get back. They'll be wondering where I am." And wondering how to fix her because everyone knew something was off, that the broken parts within her were fragmenting even more.

"I'll walk with you," Logan said, his voice low, enticing.

Stop wanting him, Cailin. Don't give in.

"I don't need a chaperone, Logan. I'm a big girl."

His gaze raked over her body, and she fought the urge to wrap her arms around him and never let him go.

"I know who you are, Cailin. I never forget that."

She glared. "You know nothing. Don't follow me."

She stormed off, knowing the wolf prowled right on her heels. Damn him. Damn fate. Damn everything.

Someone stepped on a fallen branch in front of her. A deliberate action alerting her to his presence. Her wolf stood at attention, ready to run toward the sound. Toward the comfort.

"Cailin, come here, baby girl."

Her head shot up at her father's words, and she went to his side, wrapping her arms around his waist and burrowing into him. Her wolf immediately calmed, their Alpha soothing hurts she hadn't known she'd had—or maybe known all along but ignored for far too long. The daughter, though, needed her father, and the feeling grated. She was an adult, yet she wanted her father's hold to make it all better.

Maybe her brothers were right and Cailin wasn't ready to grow up.

The doubt ate at her, but she ignored it, inhaling her father's crisp scent of forest and home, letting it wash over her so she could breathe again.

People milled around them and she could feel their looks, but ignored them. Apparently when she'd run from Logan—or rather, walked quickly away— she'd made it back to the celebration in the field without even realizing it.

"Feel better?" her father asked, his voice so low she knew that his words were just for her and no one else.

She pulled back so she could look up at him but kept her arms around his waist. "Yes, thank you, Dad. I didn't know I needed a hug so much."

Her father cupped her face, and she leaned into him. She was a daddy's girl at heart, and everyone knew it. "You crave touch, darling girl. And not the touch an Alpha provides. Your wolf is restless."

She knew her father was treading the line on the subject of Logan, but she couldn't speak about it. Not then. Maybe not ever.

"I'll try to hang out with the pups more often."

Her father raised a brow. "As much as we all love how much you care for your nephews and nieces, we both know that won't be enough. That's not the type of touch you need."

She blushed hard at her father's words. "I'm so not talking about this with you."

"I really don't want to talk to you about this either. I'd rather your mother handle it, but I'm here and I care. If you won't do anything about Logan, then what about that wolf you were secretly seeing, Noah?"

Cailin closed her eyes, wishing there was a hole to swallow her up and take her away from this conversation. "Noah and I are just friends now. And if it was a secret, why does everyone seem to know about it?"

Her father patted her back. "We're a Pack, darling."

Meaning there were no real secrets. Not anymore. Not that there ever were. "I'll figure it out," she said after a few moments of silence.

He cupped her cheek and smiled. "I know you will, baby girl. I know I don't say this enough, but I'm so proud of the woman you've become. You're so strong, Cailin. I know between me and your brothers you sometimes feel like you can't breathe, but it's only because we love you. I love you, Cailin. Never forget that."

Tears filled her eyes, and she hugged her father hard. He knew the exact words to say to make her feel better. She didn't know what she'd do without him.

"I love you too, Dad."

A chill washed over her, and she pulled away, her hand on her father's arm, not wanting to lose his touch. The trees seemed to freeze in the wind, their leaves rustling no more. The birds had stopped chirping, their song of silence a warning of what was to come. The hairs on the back of her neck stood on end and she inhaled the scents around her, trying to discern what was wrong, what had changed.

Her wolf bucked, rubbing along her skin, ready to break free and find the danger that had arisen out of nowhere.

"What is it?" she whispered.

"Something's coming." Her father didn't sound like the warm man who had just comforted her then. No, he was the Alpha.

Everyone around them quieted, their wolves going on alert. Cailin straightened, her senses going out, trying to feel what was out of place.

Her father stiffened then looked over his shoulder at his Pack. "Grab the children and run!" He turned to her, his eyes gold, Alpha. "The Centrals are right outside the wards."

The others didn't waste time, grabbing their pups and moving at their Alpha's command. Cailin focused on the clearing in front of them, her wolf ready to howl. She wouldn't run with the others, she would stand and face what was coming. The maternal wolves and submissives would take the pups and do what they were born to do—to protect what was theirs.

Cailin would do what *she* was born to do—to *fight* for what was hers.

Then a sharp pain slammed into her, her knees going weak. The connection she had with her den snapped and bile rose in her throat. Her father gripped her elbow, keeping her steady.

"The wards," she whispered.

"I know, they're gone. The Centrals have come to us. Fight well, baby girl. Fight hard."

She met her father's gaze and nodded, pride filling her, warring with the fear. She looked out into the clearing again and swallowed hard.

Dozens of Central wolves in wolf form prowled into the clearing, ready to kill, to fight. That wasn't what scared her.

No, the demon who led them brought forth the fear to end all fears.

The demon with dark hair and chiseled features gazed in her direction and smiled. The chill shooting down her spine made her want to retch. She pulled her gaze away, instinctively searching for the one person she had to be sure was okay.

Logan stood by her mother, his fists clenched. He met her gaze and nodded.

Immediately, a small trigger relaxed within her and she lifted a lip, baring fang as she turned toward the demon. She was ready. Caym gave her one more slow smile, then nodded.

With Caym's nod, the Centrals attacked, teeth and claws bared.

The battle had begun.

The war had come to the Redwoods.

It was time.

CHAPTER TWO

Today was not the day he wanted to die. Logan Anderson raked his claws down the Central wolf's side, digging deep and ending its life before it could even snap at him with its fangs. The Redwoods mostly fought in human form against the Central's wolf forms. His Pack was strong enough to use their claws and strength in a partial shift that gave them the dexterity and movement of a human and deadly abilities of a wolf at the same time.

Pat, the Alpha female, fought by his side, more fierce than he'd ever thought she'd be. The woman was all soft curves and smiles to most, yet, right then, he knew why others feared her in battle.

The woman was a machine.

Another wolf attacked him and he growled, his vision going dark.

Fuck. Not now.

He threw head his back and howled, the adrenaline coursing through his veins putting him in overdrive. His wolf went on autopilot, taking over his body as he killed four more wolves in quick succession.

Logan just prayed they were Central wolves and not Redwoods.

When the darkness took over him like this, he was never sure.

He howled again, using whatever inner strength he had to pull himself to the forefront, pushing his wolf back. Blood coated his arms and chest, while dead Central wolves lay at his feet. Their tattered remains evidence that Logan had lost control once again.

He couldn't even feel relief that he hadn't killed his own Packmates at his utter loss of control due to the blood running in his veins. He shook his head, pushing those thoughts to the back. He'd deal with that later. He always did.

"Logan! Down!" Pat yelled over her shoulder, and he ducked, trusting her implicitly. She used his shoulder as a launching point, putting her foot down and jumping so she could attack the wolf on his other side.

He rolled off as she jumped, giving her more momentum, then got to his feet again so he could take down the next wolf. He and Pat fought in tandem, killing wolves as a unit. Out of the corner of his eye, he could see the other dominant Redwoods fighting as well, working in pairs and kicking ass. They were all closer to him than the one wolf he truly wanted to protect so he could see them better. Pat gripped his arm and they fought their way to the first set of wolves of her family.

Kade and Jasper, the Heir and Beta, fought alongside one another, kicking ass and killing wolves left and right. Kade looked over at his shoulder at Logan and nodded, his eyes pure gold, the control over the strength of his wolf intimidating. Logan took down another wolf at Jasper's feet and the Beta helped him end its life quickly. Pat fought at the women's sides, her body low to the ground as she helped eliminate those who came at her daughters. Kane and Jasper's mates, Melanie and Willow, also fought together, their skills far superior to what they'd had when Logan had first met them. Everyone had been forced to train to improve their skills, and it was clearly working.

Out of the corner of his eye he saw another pair fighting against twice as many wolves and he pulled Pat toward them. Adam and Bay fought together, Bay doing most of the low-to-the-ground work as Adam's prosthetic leg didn't allow for that. But the Enforcer and his mate knew how to fight as one unit, their mating bond stronger than most because of everything they had lost in order to make it. Logan helped Bay take down a wolf quickly as Pat stood by her son's side, aiding him where she could.

Beside them, Reed, Hannah, and Josh also worked as a unit. The men stood on either side of Hannah, protecting her as much as they could. She didn't fight hand-to-hand, making her seem weak to those who didn't know the power that ran through her veins. Hannah's power as a witch made her just as deadly as any wolf with sharp teeth and ready claws. Each time Reed would take down a wolf with his claws or when Josh would rip apart another wolf with his immense half-demon strength and blades the former human kept on his person at all times, Hannah would call up a wall of earth and slam the wolves down and push them away.

They'd clearly been practicing.

Logan pulled away from the group quickly, running toward the Omega and his mate as a wolf tried to come up behind them. It was for nothing though as Maddox turned on his heel, taking down the wolf who would have hurt his mate without even blinking. The Omega gave Logan a nod before going back to the fight. Maddox would take down a wolf with his strength, and Ellie killed it at her feet. He knew the pair could read each other's minds and send messages through their mating bond, so that's how they were able to fight without speaking aloud and giving away their plan. Neither of them were fighters by nature, but they would protect their Pack and their families with their lives.

Pat pulled him to another set of Centrals that were coming up along some of Edward's enforcers. He and the Alpha female raked their claws along the other wolves' sides, ducking out of the way of vicious bites and snarls.

North and Lexi fought close beside Pat and Logan, North's wolf stronger than most of the wolves on the field even without his sight. Lexi would tell him where to attack and then help him in every way possible. Lexi could fight in human form better than any of the other women out there because she'd *always* fought in that form when she'd been younger because of her latency.

Unable to help himself, Logan risked a glance at Cailin. Her blue-black hair blew behind her as she fought off another wolf. His own wolf begged to fight alongside her, protect her from those who would dare harm the woman he craved. Doing so would only put more distance between them. Not only could she fight for herself, but the Alpha fought next to her. Edward battled just like his wife, all out, yet making it look effortless.

There was a reason they were the Alpha pair.

Knowing Cailin would be safe in her father's hands, he turned to the Central wolf in front of him, killing it quickly.

Too quickly.

It was as if the fifty or so Central wolves attacking them were mere cannon fodder.

Something was wrong.

He went to Pat's side, instinctively checking her for injuries while looking out for the next attack. "Why are we killing them so quickly?"

Pat shook her head, her attention on the horde coming at them. "I don't know, Logan. We've always been stronger than the Central wolves, but not to this degree. These look like their weakest fighters, and yet Caym brought them to the front? Why is that?"

"I'm not sure I want to find out," he answered honestly.

She met his gaze, and he swallowed hard. There was something going on here that they didn't understand. The unknown was a deadly enemy, one they couldn't fight.

Caym stood on the other end of the clearing, his arms folded over his chest, that annoying smirk on his face. Kade and Jasper each tried to make their way to the demon, but the bastard's power pushed them back. No matter how hard any of them tried, they couldn't get close enough to Caym. Though the claw marks on his face, courtesy of Logan's sister, Lexi, stood out, reminding him that the demon *could* be hurt under the right circumstances.

Logan and Pat fought off more wolves, the Redwoods effectively neutralizing at least eighty percent of their enemy. It wasn't enough though. When it came to Caym, it was never enough.

His attention kept straying to Cailin, his wolf not backing down until they could be fighting at her side.

"Go to her," Pat said from his side. "You're distracting yourself because you can't be near her."

Startled, he looked down at the mother of the woman he wanted to be his mate. "What about you?" he asked.

Pat growled, kicked a wolf out of the way, and then sighed. "I'll go with you. Edward is by her, and my wolf needs him just as much as your wolf needs my daughter. Mating isn't easy, Logan."

He nodded then began to fight his way toward the two people he and Pat needed most. Logan wasn't about to argue with the woman about the fact that Cailin hadn't accepted his mating. That would come later. Right now, the battle roared around them, and that sickly feeling in the bottom of his stomach wouldn't go away.

He needed Cailin.

Now.

Just when he was ready to move, more wolves came out of the clearing. He cursed, pissed that he couldn't get to Cailin; the enemy in front of him needed his attention.

These weren't like the wolves from before. No, these were the stronger wolves. Caym's sentinels. And from the way these new wolves only surrounded two sets of fighters, Logan knew the game plan had been revealed.

The Central wolves weren't going for any of the other Jamensons. No, their focus was on Edward.

And Pat.

Logan pivoted, helping Pat with the seven stronger wolves who had come at her. Edward had twice as many, and Logan knew Cailin was at her father's side, helping.

It seemed Caym was after the Alpha mated pair, and only death would be the answer.

Logan clawed at the nearest wolf, growling as the bastard bit down. Luckily the Centrals couldn't contaminate others with their demonic taint by tearing flesh. Pat killed two more, but unlike those wolves Caym sent in as cannon fodder, these newer wolves had the strength and power to fight back and possibly win. Each blow hurt like hell and he knew that if there were any more of these wolves out there, the Redwoods might not prevail.

Logan could see the others trying to make their way to them and the other stronger wolves, but the opposing force grew in numbers.

They were cut off but not out.

He dug his claws down another wolf and pulled its lungs through its rib cage. The wolf looked startled for a moment before collapsing. As a unit, he and Pat killed the remaining stronger wolves, blood soaking their clothes. He finally looked up at Cailin and saw she and Edward had killed their last sentinel.

All of them carried cuts and gashes, oozing blood.

That had not been as difficult as it had been in the past, but it was far from easy, and he had a feeling that was not the last of it.

Logan had taken two steps toward the woman he craved when a flash of light seared his eyes and his body flew back twenty feet. A sharp pain lanced up his arm, blood trickled down his arm, sprinkling on the ground as he slammed into it.

He coughed, rolling over to reach for Pat, making sure she was unharmed. "Pat?"

"I'm fine," she rasped. "Get to Cailin. Now. There's something wrong. Even more wrong than what's happening. Logan. Please."

He nodded and forced himself to his feet, pulling Pat with him. Smoke, fire, and debris filled his vision, but he took it step by step, trying to find his way to the one person who could soothe his wolf. He wiped the blood from his brow, grimacing at the crimson stains on his arms. The blood was not just from the wolves that lay dead at his feet and he wished he could wash it off his wounds, not wanting to contaminate himself with whatever the Centrals held within their bodies. The others might say the taint of being connected to the demon couldn't be passed on that way, but that didn't mean he wanted to take the chance.

"What happened? Was that an explosion?"

Pat coughed and squeezed his arm, her gaze going around the clearing, straining to see through the smoke. "I think Caym blew up that copse of trees over there...seven...eight...oh thank the goddess, all my babies are okay."

Logan clasped her hand. He had no idea how she could cope with the thought of losing her immense family. Every single son and daughter was there, their mates by their sides. The grandchildren, at least, were back behind the groups of houses, the maternal wolves caring for them.

"We'll get them out of here," he promised, not knowing if it was a lie or not.

Pat nodded, her face set, determined.

He and Pat fought off two more wolves and were almost to Edward's and Cailin's side when Caym's voice stopped them in their tracks.

"Sacrifices will be made for the greater plans. Fall to your knees now and pledge your allegiance. If you do this, then you might survive the battle. If not...well, the time has come. Choose."

"Never," Pat shouted at the same time as Edward.

Logan threw his head back and howled, the Jamensons and other Redwoods joining in. They were Redwoods, fighters. They would not bow down to a demon from hell. They would not lose.

Caym smiled, the scars on his face tugging as he did so. "So be it."

He turned toward Cailin and Edward and held out his hand.

"No!" Logan screamed, trying to get his feet to move faster, trying to reach her in time.

He'd be too late though.

He couldn't lose her.

Not now. Not like this.

"Cailin!" he shouted, but he wouldn't be fast enough. He could hear others around him shouting, feel Pat beside him, taste the salt on his tongue from the tears he hadn't known had fallen.

It happened so fast, yet Logan saw every detail, every breath, every movement as if it was in slow motion.

Cailin turned to Logan at the sound of his voice, her eyes wide, her body trying to move out of the way. He saw the understanding in her eyes, knowing she'd never make it, knowing this was the end.

Edward moved faster than all of them, faster than any wolf should have been able to and pushed Cailin out of the way. He growled, facing the demon and his power head on as Cailin hit the ground.

Caym screamed in delight, and Logan looked over to see the demon's palm light up. Lightning shot out, arcing and heading directly toward where Cailin stood.

The lightning hit their Alpha straight in the chest, the strong man's body lifting off the ground, flying a few feet before slamming back down again in a pile of smoking limbs and broken dreams.

For a moment, Logan couldn't comprehend what he was seeing, what he was hearing.

In the breadth of silence that followed, the bonds of his Pack flared, the moon goddess's powers breathing new life where one was lost.

Pat screamed beside him, dropping to her knees.

In front of Logan, beyond where Edward lay, Kade's knees buckled, the mantle of power slamming into him.

Out of the corner of his eye, Logan saw a small boy run to his mother. Melanie ran to him, picking up the little boy who screamed, clutching at his chest.

Wolves howled around him, mourning and anger warring and threatening to consume them all.

All of this, the new Alpha in Kade, the new Heir's powers in the little boy, Finn, the immense pain and loss radiating from Pat told Logan what he already knew.

Their Alpha was dead.

Edward was no more.

Sacrificed to save his daughter.

Logan pulled Pat to her feet, needing to get to Cailin's and Edward's sides. The former Alpha female stood on shaky legs and gripped his hand.

Before they took their next steps toward Edward's body, Pat stopped and faced Caym. She raised her chin, the power within her coming from deep inside, the dominant wolf not backing down.

"Fight until your last breath, my wolves," she said, her voice eerily calm. "Fight. We will not fall."

The Redwoods howled, their pain so thick Logan had to swallow hard to breathe.

He pulled Pat toward where Cailin sat, her father's head in her lap, tears streaking down her face, her body shaking.

The Central wolves had either died or had gone behind their master. Dead bodies lay in a grotesque, macabre tableau, their blood staining the earth, the den itself. Central wolves, weak, dying, and long forgotten by the Redwoods, scurried away, their tails tucked between their legs even in the sight of the immense failure of the Redwoods. He could sense his own Pack trying to get at Caym but not succeeding. The demon's personal wards and powers—despite been used in such an immense show of power just then—were too strong for them. They wouldn't be able to. Not now. They didn't have the power to defeat the demon.

Logan looked up at the demon as he shifted his stance, facing *him*. Caym grinned, the sheer sadistic delight in his eyes making Logan want to retch. The demon held out his arm one more time and Logan cursed, the lightning arcing toward him at a remarkable speed.

With one last glance at Cailin, he knew this was the end, knew that he'd lost it all before he'd ever had a chance to hold the idea of something more in his hands to begin with.

Small hands from a wolf that smelled like pain, warmth, and kindness, pushed at him with a force he didn't know they possessed. He slammed into the ground, shouting as Pat screamed above him, her body glowing white-hot before falling on top of him, the weight feeling a frail shadow of what had once been.

Caym disappeared in a cloud of smoke as others ran to where Logan lay. Tears streaked down his face, but he ignored those as the others came to his side, sitting up so he could cradle Pat in his arms.

Her body shook, and her eyes were open. She hadn't died as quickly as Edward, but from the wounds on her chest, he knew not even the Healer, Hannah, would be able to save her. He pressed his palms over the wounds, trying to staunch the blood to no avail.

"Why did you do that?" he cried. "You can't leave them. They need you."

Pat gave a weak smile, a small trail of blood seeping from her lips. "She needs you more." She coughed, a spray of blood catching Logan in the face. "Take care of her. Take care of my baby."

The last flash of light seeped from her eyes, and she stilled in his arms. He clutched her close, knowing Cailin did the same to her father only a few short feet away.

Others gripped at him, screaming, trying to get to their fallen mother, leader, savior, but he couldn't let go.

He squeezed harder before throwing his head back, letting an inhuman wail rip through his throat.

Edward and Pat had died for those they loved...for Cailin...

Logan wasn't worthy. He'd never be.

The Redwoods were losing a war they had no hope of winning, and they'd just lost the most important part of their soul.

Logan couldn't breathe.

The end was near, and this time, he didn't see a way out of it.

Not alive.

CHAPTER THREE

Silence.

That's all Cailin could hear.

Silence.

She blinked once. Twice.

Yet the silence remained.

The nothingness.

How could there be anything else when the world had ended?

Maybe she would wake up from the nightmare, pinch herself and find herself tangled in her sheets. Maybe then she could run to her parents' home and find them there.

Alive.

Breathing.

Not dead.

Cailin opened her eyes, not remembering when she'd closed them.

Her parents wouldn't be there.

They'd left.

Her mother and father were dead.

And Logan wasn't here.

She swallowed hard then shook her head. She wouldn't think about Logan. Not yet. Not when she could barely breathe, barely think.

"Cailin."

Maddox sat next to her on the couch, pulling her into his arms. She sank into him, using his warmth, letting her wolf settle with her Omega. But she didn't cry.

She'd cried on the battlefield, but she wouldn't cry in Kade and Melanie's living room. Not when the world had shattered around her, and she knew she had to be the strong one.

She didn't have another purpose. Not anymore.

With one last sigh, she sat up straight, pulling away from Maddox's arms.

"What can I do?" she asked, her voice oddly hoarse. Only it wasn't so odd now that she remembered the screaming, the pain. Her body shuddered, but she pushed it away, pushed it deep down to a place she prayed she'd never have to see or deal with again. No, she wouldn't think about that. Not now. She wouldn't break down.

Her brothers and their mates needed her to be strong. They'd be able to grieve with each other soon, hold their babies, and try to find a reason to go on.

Cailin would go home.

Alone.

She stood on shaky legs, wiping her clammy palms on her jeans. She froze when she noticed the blood and dirt on them. Though she'd killed many wolves on the field, she knew whose blood soaked her skin. Soaked so deep she knew she would remain stained, tainted.

Her father's blood would mark her for all eternity.

Bile rose in her throat, and she ran to the bathroom, pushing a pale Reed out of the way as he exited. By the time Cailin finished retching, Hannah was at her side, sitting down next to her on the floor, a cold washcloth in the Healer's hands patting Cailin's forehead.

So much for Cailin being strong for others.

Cailin took the cloth gratefully and wiped her face, pressing it against her cheeks to cool the heat and her aching head. She leaned against the bathtub while Hannah ran a hand down her arm.

"Go with Reed and Josh and the twins," Cailin whispered, forcing the tears back. She might not be strong enough, but she would not cry.

Not anymore.

Hannah shook her head. "I'm a Healer, Cailin. I...I don't know what to do, but right now what I *do* know is that we need to get you out of these clothes and cleaned up. Mel has things that can fit you. Okay?"

Numb, Cailin nodded then stood. Hannah helped her strip off her clothes, the bloody items piling up on the floor.

Hannah looked down at them, her face oh-so-carefully blank, then gently pushed Cailin into the tub. "I'll take care of it, darling." Hannah and Cailin might have been the same age, but right then, the woman seemed so much older, so much more in tune with what was needed.

Cailin turned on the water, the cold a shock as it woke her up before it warmed. Hannah left the room, and Cailin scrubbed her skin, still trying to get the blood off, even though the water cleared after the first few minutes.

"Here, honey," Hannah whispered. "I have clothes for you. The others think you're just taking a shower and handling it all." Cailin met the other woman's eyes, the pain in them so potent Cailin could almost feel it through the numbness. "They won't know you needed help. They won't know anything. But, honey, even if they did, it wouldn't matter. You aren't weak for needing to lean on someone." Her voice cracked at the end, and Cailin shook her head.

She turned off the shower and stood for a moment, putting on the shield she'd worn so long it was almost a second skin.

Bitchy Cailin would make it through the day.

Broken Cailin would have to hide.

"Thank you for your help," she said, her voice wooden. She got out of the tub and dried off before pulling on a pair of Mel's yoga pants and a shirt. Hannah had taken care of Cailin's bloody clothes. Where the other woman had put them, Cailin didn't know. She didn't want to know. Never wanted to see them again. "Now go out and cuddle your mates and your babies. They need you."

Just as much as you need them.

She didn't say that last part aloud, but she had a feeling Hannah knew it anyway.

Hannah nodded once, and then left the bathroom, hopefully going back into the living room where the rest of her family was.

When the smoke cleared after the demon left, things had happened quickly. Or maybe it was in slow motion. Cailin wasn't even sure anymore. Her brothers had come to her side as well as Logan's. They'd looked as broken as she'd felt.

The rest of the Pack had come as well, helping her family deal with the aftermath that none of them had been prepared for.

Edward and Patricia Jamenson were not supposed to die. They were supposed to lead their people in the final battle, their heads held high, their wolves in perfect, exceptional form.

They were not supposed to die for their daughter and the wolf her own wolf craved.

She shook her head, clearing those thoughts. She'd deal with Logan and what her own guilt meant later. Right then, she needed to *do* something. Her parents' bodies—hell, she couldn't believe she was thinking that—were with her father's enforcers. They were going to take care of them for the family. While she knew she and her brothers could have pushed through and handled it, the men who fought and put their lives on the line for her mother and father needed their closure as well.

The Jamensons also needed to regroup and find a way through the mess that was their lives.

Cailin went into the living room and sat on the floor beside the armchair where Adam sat with Bay on his lap. He whispered into his mate's ear, and she snuggled closer, their son Micah against her chest, Adam's hand on his little back.

Kade stood at the fireplace, his back to the family as Mel ran a hand down her husband's back before holding him around the waist. Not leaning into him, more like showing him she was there for him.

It surprised Cailin how strong Mel was, knowing the woman had been human when they'd first met and a very analytical human at that. Cailin hadn't welcomed Mel with open arms, and though her doubt in the woman's ability to become a leader had faded, Cailin still didn't feel like she knew this Mel.

The Alpha female of the Redwood Pack.

Goddess, Cailin didn't know how the other woman could do it—take Pat's place and lead their wolves into blessed peace after battle.

Mel was stronger than she for sure.

The rest of her family sat on various couches and chairs in Kade and Mel's large living room. The children were scattered about either on laps or on the floor. There would be no hiding this from them, not this time. They were just as much Pack as the rest of them were, and now one of the babies held a power that Cailin couldn't even comprehend.

It was odd to be here for a meeting rather than at her parents'...

Cailin swallowed hard.

No, she wouldn't have been able to make it there, and she didn't think the rest of her family would have been able to either.

"Where do we stand?" North asked his gaze unfocused, while his son Parker sat between him and Lexi.

Cailin wasn't sure when her brother would be able to see again, *if* he'd be able to see again. She knew he fought well because of his other senses and the fact Lexi had been by his side, but it couldn't have been easy. Her brother was a doctor, and yet now, he couldn't practice his profession. He could only stand by and help Noah, Cailin's friend, step in and try to take care of the Pack's health.

"Lost?" Reed asked then leaned into Josh's hold. Reed was part of the triad with Josh and Hannah. He was also the softest of her brothers, if that made any sense. Oh, he could fight, kill, and stand for his family, but other than Maddox as the Omega, she thought Reed *felt* more than the rest of them. Being an artist helped him have an outlet for that, and having two mates and twin children helped too.

Jasper shook his head, his mate, Willow, on his side, their daughter Brie on his lap. "We can't afford to be lost. We need to be strong. Now more than ever." Brie patted his chest, and Jasper leaned down to kiss her tiny head.

Cailin swallowed hard and nodded. Though it hurt to think about, she agreed. The Pack needed them to be strong, to be their center. Their Pack had lost their Alpha today. In some ways that crushed her even more than losing her father.

Her wolf howled, needing to be held, but Cailin couldn't handle that right now—not without breaking.

Again.

Cailin cleared her throat. "I...I don't remember much after...well, just after." Her family looked at her, the pity and grief in their gazes almost her undoing. "What happens now? Hierarchy-wise. The Pack will need to know. The structure will help our wolves focus."

Kade gave her a sad smile. "You're right, Cai." He took a deep breath, straightening his shoulders. Mel bent down and picked up Finn, holding him close to her chest. The three-year-old looked pale, his eyes wide and full of knowledge no child should have to bear.

"When...when the bond broke with dad, I felt the Alpha bond slam into me at the same time the Heir bond severed. Jesus. The pain. I...it was like a jagged blade in some respects but quick and white-hot at the same time. The loss...I don't know what you all felt but...I can barely think." He looked down at his son and sighed. "Finn's too young for the responsibility of Heir. We all know this."

Mark, his adopted son, spoke up, "Then you'll all help him like you did us. I know Gina and I aren't blood, so we didn't get the Heir powers, but when we get older, we can help Finn. We can help him now."

Cailin sucked in a breath, fighting off tears. Those kids had already been through so much, and now they'd lost their only grandparents as well.

37

Kade dropped to his haunches and ran a hand through his son's hair. "You and Gina are my rocks. Both of you. I know you'll help Finn. That part I'm not worried about."

Jasper cleared his throat. "I'm still Beta, if that helps. I can still feel the bond within the Pack. The moon goddess passes Alpha, Heir, and Beta by blood only, but the rest are up for grabs when the next generation gets older."

Adam jumped in. "I'm still the Enforcer because I can feel the tenuous bonds. Although since I couldn't sense the danger until it was too late, I'm not sure what my role is anymore."

Cailin reached out and patted his arm. "Stop it. You've been on edge for years because right now there's *always* a threat to the Pack. There's only so much you can do."

"He's right," Maddox added in. "Yes, I'm still the Omega. That's not going to change for a long time, but while my wolf is screaming to help everyone in this room, we need this pain, this idea of what was lost to take the next steps."

Though it hurt to hear, Cailin agreed. She wouldn't let Maddox take her pain. Not now. Not ever. She needed to feel it through the numbness that had become who she was since those moments on the field.

"What are we going to do?" Ellie asked, her hand on Maddox's knee.

Kade's mouth firmed. "I don't know. I'm not ready to be Alpha."

Cailin stood quickly and stalked toward her brother. She punched him in the chest and kept her fist there. "Stop it. You have the power and knowledge to be Alpha. What you aren't ready for, what none of us are ready for, is living without them. I know this more than anyone." Her voice broke, and she sucked in air through her nose, pushing her emotions back.

"You can't be weak in front of the others. You can't show that you want to scream and sob and try to make sense of what is going on around you. None of us can. We need to be strong for the Pack, or all else will fail. We can grieve, but we can't back down. We can't show the Centrals that they've won. Because they haven't. Don't let what happened be in vain. Please." She rasped out the last word, and her brother's gaze bored into hers.

"It wasn't your fault, Cailin," Kade whispered, far too much knowledge in his gaze.

She backed up a step, knocking into Charlotte, Maddox and Ellie's daughter. Her niece wrapped her arms around her legs, and Cailin centered herself.

Or at least tried to.

Not her fault? Her father had *died* for her. She hadn't been fast enough and had watched her father die when it should have been her body on the ground. Then she'd watched the same thing happen between Logan and her mother.

No one would understand how she felt.

No one but Logan.

Her wolf cried out for him, and Cailin knew she wouldn't be able to hold it back much longer. She needed to leave the room, leave the people that surrounded her who all had babies, mates, and a future.

She had *nothing*. Nothing worth saving, and yet her father had died for her.

How was she supposed to live with that?

Maddox let out a pained groan behind her, and she closed up her emotions tight. She wouldn't put the burden of her pain on her brother's shoulders.

She'd done enough to her family as it was.

"Cailin, it wasn't your fault," Kade repeated.

She backed up fully until she stood by Adam's chair again. "He was aiming for me and Logan," she finally said, her voice void of emotion. "I didn't miss that, and I don't think the rest of you did either."

"Why would he be trying for you two in particular?" North asked. "Does Caym know something we don't?"

Cailin closed her eyes. "He knows so much more than we do it seems. Why Logan and me? I don't know. That's something we have to find out."

Kade raised his chin and took Mel's hand. "Go home, all of you. Sleep, grieve, and find some form of peace. Anything that you can put over yourself so we can function tomorrow."

Tomorrow.

The funeral.

There would be no waiting. Not when the Pack was at war.

"Emeline is still researching," Adam put in before everyone got up. "She said she might be onto something with the dark magic. We can tell her about Logan and Cailin to see if that helps."

Emeline was an elder wolf who helped when she could. She wasn't as sheltered as the rest of the elders and had tried to integrate within the Pack more.

Right then, though, Cailin needed space. She needed to breathe. "I'll help tomorrow," she whispered before turning away from her family.

She walked out the door while the others said their goodbyes, their heartbreak so heavy she could feel it in the air all around her. Her wolf begged for touch, but Cailin knew she couldn't ask the family for it. She didn't want to be their burden to bear while they had so much else on their plates. Her family could go to their individual homes, hug their families, and let their wolves howl for the loss and pain that seemed never-ending.

One wolf hadn't been there.

One wolf with so many ties to her family that he was practically part of it already.

She hadn't failed to notice his absence, and she knew the others hadn't either.

He wasn't a Jamenson, wasn't her mate, wasn't anything but a Pack member.

And that angered her.

Shamed her.

She'd fought the mating so hard, and now, when she needed someone the most, she didn't have them because she'd been too prideful, too selfish. She didn't even know how Logan was feeling, how she could help him.

How he could help her.

Her wolf craved a mate, and the woman within her was too broken to think past the pain, past the thought that having someone to hold her might make it go away...at least for a little bit.

Logan could help her.

He had to.

If he didn't...well, she'd already shattered into a million pieces; she didn't think she had anything else left to break.

She just prayed she wasn't wrong.

CHAPTER FOUR

Sometimes being a wolf sucked.

Not being able to get drunk when he needed to was at the top of Logan's list at the moment. No matter how much whiskey he poured down his throat, he'd never get more than a buzz. Well, that wasn't quite true. If he drank a few bottles in a row he might be able to get drunk enough. According to Pack gossip, Adam had done that when he'd met Bay a couple years ago, and their mating had progressed from there.

Logan wasn't sure he needed to be *that* drunk.

Lexi, his sister, and the Jamensons were meeting at Kade's home. He didn't know how long they'd be there, nor did he know if they'd tell him what they'd discussed. He wasn't part of the inner circle. Not really.

He set the bottle down and ran a hand through his hair, the short strands sliding through his fingers. It needed to be cut, but he couldn't really care at the moment. He wasn't equipped to deal with what was going on inside of him, what was going on within the

Pack. No one should have been ready for what had happened.

Pat had died for him.

It made no sense.

He wasn't worth the sacrifice. Everyone knew it. He'd left his old Pack because he hadn't been strong enough to keep Lexi and Parker safe. The old Alpha of the Talons had made it clear that if Lexi stayed within the Pack, she would have been killed. It wasn't her fault she'd been forced into a partial mating with Corbin, the sadistic, and now dead, former Alpha of the Centrals, but the old Alpha hadn't wanted her taint to infect their precious Pack. Logan hadn't been strong enough to protect his sister or the baby in her womb, so he'd left with her. He'd vowed to protect her from the evil that surrounded them, though he hadn't been enough to save her from Corbin's clutches in the first place.

She had North to take care of her and Parker now, though since she'd found her wolf, she was strong enough to protect herself.

Logan wasn't needed.

Again.

He knew he wasn't good enough for Pat's last words, last actions.

Cailin, the woman who could be his mate, wouldn't even look at him. She'd left the battlefield, tears drying on her cheeks, her eyes wide and dark on a pale face, and hadn't looked back. He'd known she'd been pulling away from him, little by little, but what had happened earlier had cemented their break.

It wasn't as if he deserved her and the alluring brightness that came from the green-eyed woman he'd thought he'd one day love.

Cailin was not alone in the way she treated him, though. Most of the Redwood Pack members kept their distance, their wariness of the darkness in his soul justified.

He'd lost control for just a moment on the battlefield. That moment could have ended so much worse for those who fought alongside him. It was a twist of fate, a stroke of luck, that he'd only killed Centrals in the first place.

Yet, Patricia Jamenson had jumped in the line of fire for him.

Logan had no idea how he was supposed to repay that, if there even *was* a way to repay that. Even if he could, he wasn't sure the Redwoods, and the Jamensons in particular, would want him to.

Would take what he had to offer.

Logan Anderson wasn't a normal werewolf. No, he was even darker than North, the one Jamenson brother who thought he had a grasp on the darkness that had almost claimed him. But while North had to deal only with a wolf who craved the violence of the beast, Logan had another power to overcome. He'd left bouts of anger, control issues, and death in his trail over the years, and he'd fought to overcome it.

He'd been blessed by the moon goddess.

No, that wasn't right.

He'd been cursed.

While most wolves knew the story of the first hunters—humans who had been given the soul of the wolf to learn the value of taking a life—Logan was not like them. The moon goddess had been the one to grant the human hunters the power when she'd walked amongst the mortals.

According to Logan's father and legend, the Andersons were the first of that line.

That was why Lexi had been given the strength of the moon goddess to fight Caym in their last fight with the Centrals. Without that, the demon would have killed his sister. Lexi hadn't known the connection, the power, the fear. It hadn't surprised him. He'd had it all his life.

That was why he had an extra curse from the goddess herself. He'd been born for something more, something he didn't understand. That was what his wolf told him and what his father had told him long ago. The extra strength, the extra adrenaline that came with the darkness of his wolf made it harder for him *not* to act Alpha.

Though not all could feel the presence of the difference of Logan's wolf, Edward did. He'd watched Logan like a hawk and hadn't let him gain too much power in the hierarchy. Logan had never blamed the Alpha for that. In fact, his own wolf had liked the fact that another wolf had been ready to take the reins and allow him to follow a new path.

Oh yes, that new path had been the Alpha's daughter.

Hence the other reason for watching Logan closely.

No one was good enough for Cailin Jamenson.

From the way Cailin avoided from him, he had a feeling she knew that as well.

It didn't matter now anyway. Her mother had died for him. There was no way he'd ever be good enough for her...be what she needed.

At this point, *he* didn't even know what *he* needed.

The moon goddess had cursed him for a fate he didn't understand.

Fate had allowed him to find his mate, one he could never have.

Fate fucking sucked.

He wanted no part of any of the judgments. No part of a destiny that took him for granted. Nothing.

No matter the path it put him on, he'd fight. He was through with the world as it was, the battles, the war, the torment. He wanted peace. And waiting for Cailin to find him wasn't working anymore.

He wasn't good enough for her, and everyone knew it.

Disgusted with himself and his train of thought, he shook his head, pounded back the last of his drink, and stripped his shirt off so he could go for a run. Maybe if he went wolf and let his beast run wild, he'd burn off the anger.

Burn off the shame.

He stripped quickly then walked naked into the backyard. When they'd first moved to the Redwood den, he, Lexi, and Parker, had taken one of the smaller guest houses on the Jamenson property. While they could have stayed in any of the empty houses within the den, the Jamensons had wanted the Andersons close.

Not only had North wanted Lexi near, but Logan had a feeling the Alpha wanted them near. The other members of the den hadn't been too keen on allowing outsiders, and Logan hadn't wanted to deal with them anyway. He was more lone wolf than Pack most days, and sometimes there was no fixing that, no changing the fact that he'd lived with the curse of his wolf for his entire life, hiding who he was.

Once outside, he let the moon's light tingle on his skin before pulling on the bond with his wolf. The change came over quickly, slower than an Alpha but faster than most dominant wolves. Soon, instead of two feet, he stood on four paws, his wolf on the prowl, ready for the hunt. Contrary to popular belief, werewolves did not need the moon to change. It certainly helped, and during full moons, some of the less dominant Pack members needed to shift so they could burn off their energy.

He shook his head, letting his wolf take over so he wouldn't have to think, wouldn't have to feel. The pads of his paws hit the ground hard as he ran with all his endurance, pushing himself to the limit so he could feel the burn. The sounds of prey—rabbits, deer, and other mammals—got further away. Prey skittering off, their fear radiating off of them. They knew a predator was in their midst, and though Logan wasn't in the mood for blood, he would take the chase, the dominance.

He ran for twenty minutes or so, knowing that the Jamenson meeting might be ending soon. He wanted to be there in case Lexi or anyone else needed him. The ache in his muscles didn't hurt but rather let his mind focus on his body, rather than in his heart. He shifted back so he stood naked in his backyard, sweaty, chest heaving from running too fast, too hard, and still he needed to find the will to become the man who would survive and make it through the day.

With one last deep breath, the fresh scent of the forest not enough to clean his lungs, he strode back into the house, heading toward the shower. He needed to wash the grime off, the sweat and memories that he knew would lay on his skin like a film no matter how many times he showered.

Jets of hot water pounded onto his back, and he closed his eyes, not wanting to think even knowing it would be a lost cause. He filled a loofah with some of the flowery crap Lexi had left in the shower since he didn't have anything else. He'd been too busy dealing with helping the Jamensons to worry about things like soap. As he scrubbed down his body, the image of a particular Jamenson filled his mind, and he lowered his hand to his cock, unable to stop himself.

Cailin's green eyes gazed at him in his vision, and he soaped up his length, his dick filling quickly where it lay heavy in his palm. He dropped the loofah and cupped his balls, rolling them in his hand as he imagined them in her mouth, one at a time as she sucked on them like candy. The groan escaping his lips filled the room, and he let go of his balls so he could use his hand to lean against the shower wall. Bending forward, he let the water wash down his back as he gripped his shaft firmly, sliding up and down. He imagined Cailin on her knees in front of him, her hands submissively behind her back.

No, that wouldn't be his Cailin. She'd never submit fully to him, and he wouldn't want that. He wanted to dominate her but have her fight back with the intensity he knew she possessed—had witnessed.

Instead, he imagined her raking her nails down his thighs as she sucked him down her throat. He'd wrap her hair around his fist and fuck her face hard, fast, exactly what both of them would need.

He let his thumb trace over the precum at the tip of his dick and slide over the slit, imagining her tongue doing the same as he blew him. With that image on his brain, he grunted, increasing his pace until his balls drew up, tightening. He shouted her name as he came, spurts of come hitting the shower wall, sliding down to mix with the water now cooling in the bottom of the tub.

With one last quick rinse, he got out of the shower and toweled off. Coming might have taken off a slight edge, but he was still running hot.

There was only one person who could help with that, and he knew, at this point, it would be a lost cause. He couldn't even go to her to help her grieve. He was one of the reasons she was in pain as it was, and from the way things had been since they'd met, he knew he wouldn't be the company she wanted. He might never be the company she needed. That was just one more thing he would have to learn to deal with. There was no way he'd inflict his presence on her. Not anymore.

Just as he pulled on his jeans, his wolf scented her. He didn't bother buttoning up his jeans or pulling on a shirt, his wolf—and the man—needed her beyond all rationality. He was already walking toward the door before he could rethink his decision and try to keep away. She hadn't knocked but stood on his porch, her head down, her shoulders slumped.

"Cailin," he breathed, not knowing what else to say.

What else could he say to the woman he wanted more than anything and knew he could never have?

Her head lifted, and she blinked up at him. Once. Twice. His wolf nudged him, begging for their mate. He could get lost in those eyes, the deep pools of green pulling him in and never letting him go.

Logan held out his arms, not knowing if she'd come to him, but honestly, she'd already come to his door. If she needed to take the extra step, he'd open himself to her. He might have told himself he'd back away, unable to deal with the pain and rejection, but he'd been an idiot.

He could no more walk away from Cailin than he could walk away from his wolf.

"Come here," he ordered.

He didn't know if it was the right thing to say, but he was beyond waiting, second-guessing.

Cailin licked her lips then took two steps, resting her head on his chest while wrapping her arms around his waist. He pulled his arms in, holding her close as they stood in the doorway. He could hear other wolves around them, scent their presence, but the others

49

were too far away to see what was going on. They were all in their homes, grieving as they should be. They shouldn't care that the Redwood Pack princess was at his door, in his arms.

The others had watched him and Cailin dance around each other yet hadn't pushed them. A mating was a private thing, despite the fact that, as wolves, others would be able to sense a change in them, sense the hint of connection.

Cailin wasn't his mate, though his wolf already thought of her as that, and he'd slipped up a few times in his head as well. She was a potential. One of the few—and sometimes even the *only*—whom he could mate with and create a true bond. The mating bond would connect their souls in a special and unique way. No two matings were the same.

However, both parties could ignore the mating urge if they needed to, if they didn't have the right chemistry in their human forms.

It would hurt.

It *had* been hurting with Cailin, but he'd take the pain for just a moment with her in his arms.

Fuck, he was a sap when it came to the green-eyed princess clutched to his chest.

They stood there for a few more moments before he pulled away, but he didn't let go of her completely. He led her into his home, closing the door behind them. His wolf liked her scent mingling with his, her presence in his home. His wolf also wanted to lock her up and never let her go.

Sometimes his wolf just had to deal with not getting what he wanted.

"Tell me what I can do, princess," he said, his voice low.

Her eyes widened at the word spoken as an endearment, and he held back a curse. He needed to dial the need and desire back if he had any chance of comforting her tonight. Though for all he knew, she was there for a fight so she could blow off steam and let out her own form of aggression and deep-seated anger.

Of course, he'd help her with that if that's what she needed.

Anything to take away the darkness and grief in her eyes.

"I...I don't know why I'm here," she whispered.

He narrowed his eyes at her. Oh, she was lying all right. Either to him or to herself. She knew why she'd come, but maybe on some level, she didn't know why she'd *needed* to be on his doorstep. He wouldn't have blamed her for never wanting to talk to him again. The only reason he had a feeling that wasn't the case here was that she'd come willingly into his arms.

He wasn't counting his chickens though.

Logan licked his lips and held back a groan at the way her eyes followed the movement. This was not the time to indulge in the fantasies that had plagued him since he'd first seen her when he'd come to the Pack.

He tucked a strand of her hair behind her ear, his wolf clawing at him when she moved her cheek into the gesture. He cupped her face and brought his forehead to hers. They'd never been this close, not really. Oh, when he'd been hurt when he and North had fought the demon stupidly on their own, Cailin had come to his side and tended his wounds, but she'd kept her distance.

It was as if her wolf required her to help him, but the woman hadn't wanted to put down roots. He understood that. It hurt like hell, but he understood. They were together often, helping the children, helping Jasper or Adam with their duties, but the tenderness she showed him now, and he showed her, hadn't been like this before.

"What do you want me to do?" he asked.

"I...I just need you," she whispered, her eyes filling. "Please, just make the pain go away."

He brought her to his chest then, picked her up and cradled her to him. She wrapped her arms around his neck and sighed into him, tears soaking his skin.

"You couldn't cry before, could you?" he asked as he brought her to his room. It was the only place big enough for him to hold her close and make her comfortable.

Or at least as comfortable as she could be in his bed.

It would have to do.

Cailin hiccupped into his neck and shook her head.

"It's okay, baby. Cry it out." He got into the bed and laid back, rubbing his hand down her back, his own eyes filling.

God, it hurt so fucking much to watch her like this. His strong, vibrant Cailin broken and hurting in his arms. There wasn't anything he could do. No matter how strong he was, how strong his wolf was, he couldn't bring her parents back. Couldn't stop Pat from dying for him...Edward from doing the same for Cailin.

While she broke down, he murmured to her, knowing nothing he could say would make it better, but he'd try anyway. His wolf howled for her, wanting to kill anything that could harm her, that could make her do this, but there was nothing to do but hold her close and let her break down.

Finally, after an hour or so, she quieted, her body shaking.

She leaned away from him and shifted so she was fully on his lap while he sat against the headboard.

"Thank you," she croaked.

He kissed her temple then moved her so she lay on the bed. "No thanks needed, princess. Lie right here and let me get you some water. You need to rehydrate." She nodded, her eyes red-rimmed and puffy but looking as beautiful as ever.

He cupped her check once more before leaving the room and padding to the kitchen where he quickly filled a glass with water and found a couple herbal tablets Hannah had left for him. Wolves couldn't take normal medications since their metabolism worked too fast, but there were some herbs that could be used as pain relievers.

Cailin would have one monster of a headache once she finally settled. In fact, she probably already had one.

When he got back to the bedroom, he willed his cock to stand down at the sight of her in his bed. This wasn't the right time to be thinking about her like this, not when she needed to feel safe. Or at least as safe as she could be.

"Take these and drink the whole glass of water," he ordered.

She nodded, the usual spunk and quick commentary he loved from her nonexistent. The Cailin in his bed right now was just the shell of the woman he knew he'd love one day. He vowed to himself he'd do all in his power to ensure the old Cailin came back.

Or at least a Cailin who held the fire in her eyes and in her veins.

He wasn't sure any of them would come back from what had happened and be the same.

When she finished the water, he took the glass from her and set it on the nightstand before getting back into bed. Her eyes widened slightly as she stared at his still naked chest and undone jeans, but she leaned into his hold anyway when he held out an arm. She fit perfectly against him, her head on his chest, her hand rubbing small circles over his stomach.

His cock hardened at her soft touches, but he ignored it.

"My parents are dead, Logan," she whispered.

He closed his eyes at the pain in her voice and squeezed her tightly. "I know, princess. I'm so fucking sorry." His throat closed, and he coughed, trying to breathe again. "I'm so, so sorry about it all. Damn it, your mom shouldn't have done that."

He winced at his words, but the truth needed to get out. It would only fester between them if he didn't tell her what he thought, didn't explain what had happened on the field.

Cailin turned so she sat and faced him, her touch never leaving his body. "I'm all cried out, Logan. I don't know if I have anything left in me." He ran a hand up her arm and cupped her face, needing her.

"You can't blame yourself, princess."

That fire he'd missed in her eyes flared back for a moment before dying again. That was at least progress.

"Who else do I blame, hmm?"

He growled, low and full of promise. "How about the fucking demon who started it all?"

Cailin lifted a lip and bared fang. "You don't think I blame him as well? But my parents *died* because of me. Sure, Caym dealt the deathblow, but if I had been stronger, faster, *anything* more than I am, my father wouldn't have had to push me out of the way. He'd still be alive."

Logan pulled her onto his lap so she straddled him. Her breath hitched, and he knew she felt his dick against her pussy, but he didn't care. He just needed her.

"I don't know what I'd do if your father hadn't done that." She opened her mouth to speak, but he pressed a finger against her lips. "I'm not saying that I'm not torn up over what happened. I'm saying that I don't know what I'd do if I'd lost you. I know we haven't talked about what we are to each other because we're not ready. In fact, I'm not even going to mention that right now—again. But I will say that what I feel for you means that without you in this world, with me or not, I'd be a broken man."

"Logan..."

When she didn't say anything else, he sighed. "Your mom died for me, baby. I...I don't know if you can ever forgive me for that. I don't think you should. But I also don't think you should blame yourself. This is the fucking demon's fault. Not yours."

She shook her head. "I don't blame you. God, no. My mother..." Her breath stuttered. "My mother died for you because of what you could be for me. She also did it because you're a Pack member, and my mom is, *was*, one freaking strong woman who would have done anything for her Pack. And she *did*."

Logan growled and pulled at her hair so she tipped her face up to him. Her eyes darkened for a moment before shutting down to that grief again. "Don't you dare blame yourself for what your mother did for me. Do you understand? You are not. To. Blame. You get me?"

"Then you can't blame yourself."

He sighed, knowing they were at an impasse. No matter what either of them thought, the wounds were too raw, too new for them to deal with the ramifications.

"You need some sleep, princess, and so do I. It's been one long fucking day."

She suddenly looked far too innocent, too scared to be where she was, so, for this moment only, he took control. He quickly pulled her off of him and stood up, bringing her to her feet.

He licked his lips and met her gaze. "Just sleep, princess. Let me care for you. I need that. My wolf needs that. And I think your wolf does too."

"I'm not a submissive wolf, Logan."

He shook his head. "I know that, and I'm damned glad of it. My wolf needs a dominant wolf to hold him steady."

"I...I don't know if I'm ready for calling your wolf mine and vice versa. I thought I might be, but I...I don't know anything anymore."

He held back a grin. At least she was thinking about it. "Just sleep, Cailin. I want to hold you tonight, and I think we both need it."

She nodded. "I don't want to be alone. Not tonight. Not when everyone else has someone and I have nothing."

He tilted his head, a thread of anger sliding through him before he pushed it away. "Are you here because you have nothing else?" he asked, unable to hold the question back. He needed to know where she stood, at least for the moment. If she was only there because she felt she had to give in because she had no hope, then he'd have to find a way to deal with that.

"No, I mean, not like what you think." She closed her eyes and groaned. "I don't know what I'm saying. I think you're right, and I just need to sleep."

He studied her face for a moment longer before nodding. "Let me get you comfortable and under the blankets before I join you." He helped her take off her shoes and stripped off the sweats that didn't hold her scent so he knew they had to be borrowed. From the way her nipples poked hard against her shirt, he knew she wasn't wearing a bra, so she would be comfortable in that.

He could scent her arousal, and it made his dick even harder, but he ignored it, knowing they both needed to be held, not fucked. Not just then. As soon as she was tucked in, he went to his drawer, pulled out a pair of sweats and went to the bathroom to change. As a werewolf, normally he wouldn't care about nudity, but Cailin was different.

Cailin was always different.

When he came back into the bedroom, she was already turned on her side with enough space for him to join her. He turned off the light and slid in behind her, wrapping his arm around her stomach and pulling her close. His cock pressed against her ass, but neither of them made any mention of it. She sighed quietly and tangled her fingers with his before lifting her head so he could wrap his other arm around her. When she lifted one leg, he moved his own between hers so they were as close as they could get, their wolves panting, soothing, their human halves grieving and taking comfort.

After all this time, Cailin Jamenson was in his arms, in his bed.

Yet the torment surrounding them made it a bittersweet moment.

She'd come to him.

Come to him when she was hurting and knew he could take care of her.

He'd hold on to that feeling forever, knowing he'd need it in the future.

The war was exploding around them, and the mating that could be with the woman he held in his arms was only beginning.

It was time.

CHAPTER FIVE

The warmth behind her sizzled down Cailin's spine, and she snuggled closer, wanting more. A large hand moved up and cupped her breast. Her nipple pebbled against the palm, and she opened her eyes.

She looked down at the sexy, tan hand palming her breast, and stiffened.

Logan froze behind her, but that wasn't the only thing stiff in his bed. She licked her lips and thought about rocking back into that very large cock to see how fast she could get off, but then she remembered *why* she was in bed with him.

The memory was like a splash of cold water, and she cooled down before moving so she could sit up. He let her go quickly but kept his hand on her back, as if afraid to let her go completely. Honestly, she and her wolf loved it. Her wolf preened, ready for their mate, but the human part of her still had reservations.

No, that wasn't the right word.

She wanted the man in front of her. In fact, she'd come to his house, searching him out deliberately. She might have come for a full mating at first, but in retrospect, mating that night would have been a mistake. No, she just needed to be held by someone who wasn't family. Someone who didn't have others to comfort.

She needed Logan and only Logan.

Cailin Jamenson didn't like to *need* anyone.

Was that what mating was supposed to be about? Needing and relying on others? She didn't know if that's what she wanted. Maybe *if* they found themselves in a mating bond, they could find a way to work together because she didn't want to lose herself to it.

That had been her worse fear.

It didn't even make sense in some respects. She'd *seen* her brothers mate and create a bond that looked as if it was equal between them. Her parents had shown her that mating could work and provide a strength she wasn't even sure she'd been aware of at first. Yet she was so afraid to lose herself that she created a fear in her own mind that might not even manifest at all. She was afraid to lose the self she hadn't yet found.

Well, the fear *had* been her worst. She'd already faced the fear she never thought she would face and lost. Without Logan there, she wasn't sure how she'd come out of it. She'd broken down in front of him, and he hadn't judged, just picked her up and held her. He hadn't told her everything would be okay, because it wouldn't. She'd lost her parents, and there was no changing that, no coming back from it. Not in a way that would make her feel whole again.

But he'd been there for her.

"Cailin? Princess?"

She blinked at Logan's voice, warming on the inside at his endearment. When once he'd used the title princess to sneer, to taunt, it held a different meaning now—like he wanted to be closer. Like he'd cherish her and treat her like a princess.

Not that she necessarily wanted that.

She'd love to be treated like a princess who could save her own ass.

If Logan could be the man who could do all of that, be the man who could treat her like she thought she needed, then she'd have the mate she so desired.

Only time would tell.

Cailin turned so she could look down at him, his mussed dark hair making him look even sexier than usual. *Damn that wolf.* He tilted his head, his hazel eyes seeing far too much.

While part of her loved waking up next to him, an equal part of her was downright terrified. She didn't like being terrified. No, she *hated* it. That was one more reason she stayed away from Logan as much as she could.

Even if she failed at it more often than not.

"Thank you," she whispered. He'd held her and had done exactly what she'd needed. She might have no idea what she really wanted, but she wouldn't be ungracious.

He sat up, reaching his arm out for her. Without thinking, she leaned into him, letting his hand cup her face. She closed her eyes and sighed, her wolf needing the touch more than she'd thought.

"Anything, Cailin. Anything."

If only.

"I need to go get ready," she finally said after a few moments of silence. Her heart ached, and she had to hold back a shiver at the thought of just *why* she had to get ready.

Today they would bury her parents and say goodbye.

There would be no waiting, not when the Pack needed to stand together now more than ever. They needed to see Kade and Melanie in positions of power and grace. The other wolves would feel more at ease, feel that connection to their new Alpha if they could see them, grieve with them.

They also had to let go of the past. No, they wouldn't forget, goddess no. But without remembering and *celebrating* the lives that were being lived, the Pack would dwell on the lives that had been *lost*.

Cailin knew she had to be the strong one, just like she'd always been. The Pack would be looking to her, the lone daughter, the princess, and act accordingly.

She'd be the only one standing up at the altar alone. The others would have their families, their mates.

With a quick intake of breath, she shuddered. "Stand with me today," she whispered, surprised she'd voiced the words.

Logan's eyes widened, and he nodded. "Of course, Cailin." He sat straighter, removing his hand from her face. She immediately felt cold at the loss but pushed it aside. "I'll stand up with you." He frowned for a moment.

"What is it? You can tell me."

"Aren't you worried about what others will think? I'm not, and I know you aren't usually. That's one thing I like about you. I just don't want you to have to deal with the additional burden of what others might infer from me being by your side."

She shook her head. "I don't care. You're right. People will talk, and frankly, if it gives them something to talk about other than what happened, I think that will be a good thing."

Logan narrowed his eyes. "So you're doing this to take the focus off the pain and hurt?"

She swallowed hard then shook her head again. "No, that's not what I mean. If the fact that they think about something else works, then that's a bonus. I'm selfish enough to say I need you by my side, even if we haven't mated."

He nodded then ran a hand through his hair. Her gaze followed the movement, taking in the definition in his arms.

"We're going to talk about that last part soon, Cailin." His gaze met hers, and she froze, prey in a predator's path. "It's beyond time we at least discuss it, but right now I know we both need to...breathe."

He stood up, his erection tenting his sweats, but he ignored it. He held out a hand, and she took it, standing close to him. So close she could scent the wolf, power, and sin radiating off of him.

Logan cupped her face and stared down at her. She licked her lips, knowing this wasn't the time to want him, but when *was* the time?

"I'm going to kiss you, Cailin," Logan whispered. "Think of this when you're trying to decide if you want to be my mate. Think of this when you find yourself on your own and in need of comfort."

"Okay," she breathed then inwardly cursed at the stupidity of that answer.

With a quick grin that faded before she could blink, he lowered his head, the intensity in his gaze making her belly clench. His lips brushed hers, once, twice, before pressing harder. She closed her eyes, letting the sensation of his mouth against hers wash over her.

His lips were firm, soft, with just the hint of pressure to exude his dominance. Oh, she wasn't his submissive wolf. No, she'd kiss him back.

Hard.

She opened her mouth, sliding her tongue against the seam of his lips. Oh, he might have been the one to say *he'd* kiss *her*, but she'd be part of this. Relish it.

He groaned against her, opening his mouth to her. He moved his hands so they held her lower back, pressing her to his chest, his erection hard, demanding against her belly. Cailin thrust her fingers in his hair, panting as she deepened the kiss.

Their tongues tangled, fighting for dominance as they kissed each other, their chests heaving.

Finally, she pulled back, taking two steps away so she could think. He'd made her dizzy, drunk, addicted. Damn his taste, his...everything.

"Go home, Cailin," Logan grunted. He gave her a sad smile before tucking her hair behind her ear. "Get ready for what needs to be done, and I will be there by your side. I won't leave you."

She nodded, emotions clutching at her. She needed to breathe, to think.

To grieve.

Cailin quickly dressed and made her way home. Logan had left her at the door, and she could feel his gaze on her as she moved. While she had a feeling he wanted to come with her and not let her leave his sight, he must have known she needed the time alone to compose herself.

As soon as she got home she quickly showered, trying to prepare herself for the day. Logan's scent had leeched into her skin, and her wolf didn't want to wash it away. Only the fact that the man would be by their side soon seemed to calm them both.

She could still remember the first time she'd seen Logan. He'd been covered in blood, her brother's blood. North had almost been killed by Corbin during an attack on the Jamensons' property, and the

Andersons had saved his life. Lexi and Parker had been holding North's chest together as he bled while Logan had driven into the den, not knowing if either of them would die or not—North from his wound and Logan at the hands of the Pack.

After all, at the time they'd been outsiders in the middle of a war. But they'd risked it all to save North. Logan's actions were proof to the Alpha and his family that the Andersons could be trusted. That and the fact that their wolves readily submitted to a new Pack.

Cailin had been so scared for her brother, scared she'd never see him again. Yet even then, her attention had drifted to the large man with the darkness covering his appearance and build so deeply it seemed like a second skin.

That danger attracted her like no other.

Neither had made a move, even though they both knew the potential for mating lay between them. There hadn't been time, not really. And when things finally calmed down, she'd run. She'd pushed him away, not ready to bare herself and give up what she'd tried so hard to attain her whole life—freedom.

Now that she'd lost the two people she held most dear, she knew she'd made a mistake keeping him away.

She wanted to mate with Logan Anderson.

Cailin just hoped Logan still wanted her.

Oh, he might have said he'd never leave her, but she'd pushed him away for so long his wolf might have stopped the mating dance—a painful process she didn't know if she herself could survive.

Logan was strong though.

Stronger than most

Stronger than her.

She shook her head, clearing her thoughts of mating, strength, and a bond that would come later—

she hoped. Her heart lay heavy in her chest at what she was about to see, about to do. She quickly put on the black dress she kept in the corner of her closet. She'd worn it only once, and after today, she'd never wear it again.

The woman in the mirror wasn't her.

It couldn't be.

That pale face, lank hair, and dead eyes. No, it couldn't be her. She didn't look like the strong wolf she needed to be for her people, her family. She closed her eyes and shook her head, trying to gain the courage she needed to walk into the Pack circle and say goodbye to her parents.

She wouldn't cry in front of her Pack. She'd done that enough.

Only the thought of Logan being by her side helped her step into her shoes, the loose skirt around her thighs shimmering.

The knock at the door startled her, but the scent behind it calmed her.

Logan.

He'd come for her so she wouldn't have to walk alone.

Goddess, she could love him.

When she opened the door, she held back a sigh. Long legs in dark pants and a shirt that molded to his build quite nicely. Maybe if she focused on Logan, she wouldn't have to think about what was coming.

He seemed to understand she needed something...else, so he lifted her chin with a finger before leaning down to brush a tender kiss against her lips.

"Ready?"

"No," she answered honestly.

He nodded then held out his arm. She closed the door behind her and tucked her arm into his. As they made their way to the circle, Pack members joined their trek, heads lowered, wolves in pain. No one spoke—there was no need to.

Nothing to say until they found themselves in the circle.

Logan's arm on hers steadied her as she raised her chin, trying to show the others that they could be strong. It was her job as a Jamenson—a role she held with pride.

Her brothers, their mates and children were standing at their places in the circle. The raised platform would soon be too small for her growing family, but the absence of the two people who meant the most to her was stark in its evidence.

Each of her brothers noticed her in turn, their eyes narrowing slightly at Logan before schooling their features. This was not the time to deal with big-brother bullshit.

She glared, and each of them turned away, their mates leaning into them. As she stood beside Maddox, she tried to let go of Logan, only to have Logan grip her hand and squeeze. Her wolf calmed, needing the man near them.

Her brother Kade, her new Alpha, rose to stand in front of the Pack. Melanie and their three children stood off to the side, still visible but allowing Kade to speak first.

"We've lost an Alpha, a wolf, a father, a friend," Kade began.

Cailin swallowed hard, keeping her head high, leaning slightly into Logan, not so much that anyone would notice, but *he* knew. Her head pounded, creating a roaring in her ears. She could see Kade's mouth moving, could see the others in her family standing tall, grief on their faces, tears staining some of their cheeks.

The other Pack members openly wept, their emotions so strong she could taste them on her tongue. She would not cry. Not then, maybe not ever again.

Kade spoke once more, and the others in the Pack howled.

She threw her head back and joined them, Logan's howl a sweet harmony to hers—the first thing she could hear.

She could feel others' gazes on her and Logan, but she didn't care. Her heart hurt too much and the confusion in her mind too tangled to unravel. The reason they were all here was because of her parents. Not who was with whom. What mattered in her heart was that she and Logan shared a connection beyond mating.

They were the reasons her parents were dead. Not that she'd ever blame Logan for that.

No, the blame lay solely with her.

When the enforcers came to take her parents' bodies—already covered in silk—she held back a shudder. She hadn't looked down into the circle, she couldn't. Goddess, her parents were *right* there...yet so far away.

So far out of reach.

Logan let go of her hand, only to wrap his arm around her side, squeezing her other hip. He didn't pull her close, didn't pat her and tell her everything would be okay.

He knew exactly what to do to help her.

The others started to leave, their own mourning taking place quietly and in private. Cailin followed her brothers back to Kade's house for another meeting. Only, unlike the last time, Logan wouldn't be leaving her side. It might be selfish, but she needed him.

As soon as they were in Kade's living room, she knew something was coming that she wouldn't like. From the firm set of Melanie's mouth, she had a feeling her sister-in-law, the new Alpha female, didn't like it either.

"The battles are on our land," Kade said. "We need to ensure the children and submissives are safe. In doing that, I'm going to follow the plans Dad set in motion."

Cailin frowned. She hadn't known her father had any such plans. But she wasn't the Heir to the Pack, so she wouldn't have been privy to all information.

"You're going to evacuate some of the Pack to the safe zones," Logan said.

Kade started then narrowed his eyes. "And how would you know that?"

Cailin growled, not liking Kade's tone. Logan squeezed her hand, and she settled. For now.

"All Packs have places set for evacuation," Logan said calmly. Much more calm than she was. "Places that only a select few know about. The Pack isn't safe under the wards, and Caym knows that. You'll have to send them out in small groups."

Kade relaxed somewhat and nodded. "Yes. Father's enforcers..." He coughed. "I guess they're my enforcers now."

"You can choose your own men to join you in the future, Kade," Jasper whispered. "Those of Father's men who want to stay, and you get along with, will fight for you. Others will fall back and allow you to make changes. It's the way of the Pack."

Melanie hugged Kade's side, and he wrapped an arm around his mate. "We can talk about that later. Like I was saying, the enforcers have started the process." He let out a breath. "I want our mates and children to go with them."

The response to his words was loud, clear, and vehement.

"No," Cailin said above them all, her voice steady, dangerous.

Kade's eyes met hers. "I want my family safe."

"Then the children go with the submissives, maternals, and enforcers," Cailin argued. "They'll be safe there. But don't send away our family. At least the adults. You can't do that now. You all mated dominant fighters. For god's sake, Reed married two of them."

Hannah gave a small smile, and Cailin nodded at the earth witch who could move soil and bury her enemies quickly.

"We're not leaving you," Ellie whispered, her hand held tightly in Maddox's.

"None of us are," Bay said from her perch on Adam's lap.

"You can't hide us away," Willow added in.

"We're wolves, witches, and half demons. We're stronger than you think," Lexi said.

"You've never treated us as less before, mate of mine, don't start now," Melanie said from his side.

Kade lowered his head. "I just want you safe. I know you can fight. I've seen you all do it. This Alpha thing...I don't know what to do."

Cailin growled. "Yes. You. Do. You're our Alpha, Kade Jamenson. Start acting like it."

Logan squeezed her hand when Kade growled back.

"You need to go with the submissives at least, Cailin," Kade said.

"Why? Because I'm all alone? Because I'm the one who doesn't have a mate to fight alongside?"

"She's not alone," Logan said from beside her, and her wolf howled in triumph.

Each of her brothers growled in response, but their mates shut them up with small pinches and looks.

Cailin stood, tired of this. "I'll help the submissives pack up and get ready to go. I know you're sending some of your fighters with them, but it won't be me. I'm going to find a way to kill that demon no matter what. You can't take that away from me." She spread her arms out to encompass the others in the room. "You can't take that away from any of us."

With that, she stormed out of the house, Logan on her heels. She made it all the way to Logan's door before she thought better of it.

"Cailin, talk to me," Logan purred from beside her as they walked into his living room.

She turned on her heel and threw up her hands. "He was going to send me away, Logan. Send me with the others where I could be safe and cosseted. Even when he would have let the other women stay, he was going to send me away because I have no one to rely on. No one to come home to and heal.

"I have no one."

The words fell off her tongue before she could take them back, the pain in her heart spreading out, numbing her hands, making her dizzy.

"You have me, Cailin," Logan whispered, his voice low, promising. "You'll always have me."

CHAPTER SIX

Logan held back a curse at the fear in Cailin's eyes at his words. He'd moved too fast with his declarations, but fuck, they hadn't been moving fast enough as it was.

"Why?" she whispered. "Why am I worth it?"

He growled low and stalked toward her. Her eyes widened, and she froze. When he cupped her face, she let out a gasp but still didn't move.

"You are worth everything and more, Cailin Jamenson. And you know that. You're just in a dark place right now, or you wouldn't be saying anything like that at all. Even if my wolf didn't feel that pull toward you telling me you're my mate, I would have found you. And you know why? Because of the way you hold yourself, the way you fight for your family, for yourself. You're stronger than you think you are. No, that's not right. You know *exactly* how strong you are. You've just forgotten for the moment. And with what just happened? You get a pass for this self-doubt. But in the future, I don't want to hear you say anything derogatory or demeaning toward yourself. You got me?"

She narrowed her eyes. "You tell me I'm strong and worth it, then give me an order?"

Logan grinned, liking the fire in her eyes. "See? That's the Cailin I know and want."

"I can't believe Kade wanted me away from the den and tucked away safely so quickly," she whispered.

"Because he's scared for everyone." Though he'd wanted to punch the bastard for making Cailin feel like she'd be a hindrance, not an asset.

"It's not like he hasn't seen me fight before."

Logan nodded. "You're strong. And I'm going to fight at your side. Why? Because you're a fucking Jamenson. A Redwood Princess. You're stronger than most of the dominants I know. Hell, you *are* a dominant. I won't hold you back from your revenge or your justice. But that doesn't mean you get to go at it alone. Oh, hell no. I'll will fight by your side, have your back. Hold the fucking bastard down while you cut his heart out. I want the warrior in front of him, not the cosseted princess others might think you are. And if your brothers weren't so shaken, broken, they'd see that too. They have seen it in the past. Just give them time."

Her eyes went wet for a moment, and he cursed himself for making her cry. She'd had enough of that in the past forty-eight hours, and he didn't want to be the cause of it again.

Logan brushed her cheek with his thumb and sighed. "I didn't mean to make you cry."

Cailin gave him a watery smile. "It's okay. I think I feel comfortable enough to cry only with you anyway."

Touched, he lowered his head, getting closer. Even when she was in her heels, she was still too short for him to touch without bending, but right then, he just needed her scent. That icy temptation of roses that washed over him and made him want to howl.

"I'm a typical guy in that I hate seeing women cry, but the idea that you can open yourself up to me and show your feelings makes me feel...needed." He swallowed hard, not used to revealing himself just as he knew it was difficult for Cailin.

She lifted a shaky hand and cupped his jaw. He leaned into the movement, his wolf practically purring.

"Thank you."

He turned and kissed her palm, forcing a gasp from her lips. "Thank you for letting me in."

Logan swore the temperature in the room rose ten degrees with just the heat in her eyes, and he stepped back, knowing they both needed to calm down. Mating, marking, and throwing themselves at each other wasn't the answer. Not yet. They'd just come back from her parents' funeral, for fuck's sake. He couldn't jump her bones when she was in mourning.

"Let me feed you," he grunted. There was a large wake going on with some of the Pack members who wanted to be part of one. He and Cailin had needed time alone for more than one reason. Others would eat with each other and mourn; he needed to feed her to keep her strength up. The thought of feeding her something he made with his own hands excited him as well as surprised him. He never knew he was such a romantic. Or a caveman. "Do you want to get out of that dress?"

He winced as she raised a brow.

"I have a pair of sweats that Lex left here that'll fit you. Plus you can wear one of my shirts." Yes, he liked the thought of her covered in his scent. Caveman much? "I figured you didn't want to sit around in that dress for too long."

Though the lace and silk thing looked hot as hell on her, he knew it would carry memories she didn't want to deal with.

She nodded, and he went to get her the clothes. While he might have wanted to stay and watch her change, he pulled himself away, knowing they both needed space.

He didn't know what was going on between the two of them. They'd spent months tip-toeing around each other, not acknowledging the other in terms of the mating bond, though they'd both known. He'd never pursued, instinctively knowing that, if he had, he'd lose her before he even had her.

Logan muttered to himself and his dick while he took out the makings for steak and potatoes. He knew how to cook the basics because he'd been a single man for decades before he'd been on the run with Parker and Lexi. If he hadn't learned to cook, he'd have died of starvation long ago.

It wasn't lost on him that he was over thirty years older than Cailin. However, they were wolves, not humans. While being a man in his sixties mating with a woman in her twenties would have been frowned on—or downright taboo—in the human world, he wasn't human. It was normal for the age gap. In fact, every single one of the Jamensons had a larger gap in ages with their mates than he and Cailin did with each other.

Once a wolf reached majority in their early twenties, their mating instincts kicked in and a bond could be made. Sometimes it happened earlier if both partners were the same age, but that was rare.

Wolves could be near others for years, and then one day, it was like a two-by-four to the head when the mating scent washed over them, and their wolves demanded more.

He buttered and salted the potatoes before putting them in the oven to bake. They'd take a bit to cook, but he'd make a salad or something to start with. Women liked vegetables.

Jesus, he sounded like some twenty-something kid with no experience. Logan had experience, plenty.

He'd just never eaten a meal alone with Cailin before.

Never fed her food he'd made and sat closed up in a room saturated with her scent. Sure, she'd fed him soup when he was healing from an attack when he was out alone with North, and he and Cailin had eaten many meals in the company of others.

But this time was different.

His wolf loved it.

He got the other things ready for dinner, then stood in his kitchen sipping on his beer while he waited for Cailin to come back. She took her time and he knew she needed to.

He scented her before he heard her. Like a true warrior, her steps were quiet, almost silent. He didn't think she did it on purpose; it was just her nature.

His wolf approved.

Not that he'd ever tell her that. She didn't need his approval—something, on a better day, she'd understand. When she padded next to him, her bare feet on his tile floor, he turned to her, lifting his arm so she could snuggle close.

She leaned into him, burrowing herself into his side. Logan held her close, craving the intimacy of these small touches. They stood there for a few moments before he pulled away to bring the meat to the grill.

"Salads okay to start with?" he asked as Cailin stood in the center of the room, looking somewhat lost, but gaining that strength he so admired second by second.

"That sounds great. Let me help."

He nodded, knowing she needed to do something with her hands. "You can make the salad. Everything is in the fridge. I like anything, so put whatever you want on it. The steaks will take only a little bit to cook since I know we both like them bloody." He grinned, and Cailin rolled her eyes.

What could he say? They were wolves.

"The potatoes should take another ten minutes or so. You want sautéed mushrooms for your steak?"

Cailin closed her eyes and moaned. He had to shift his stance at the sound, his cock pressing against his zipper.

Fuck, he couldn't wait to peel her out of those clothes and taste every inch of her. To kiss, touch, and caress until she was panting underneath him, begging him to fill that greedy pussy with his cock.

Her eyes darkened, and her throat worked as she smiled. "Go cook your...meat. I'll take care of the salad."

Logan barked a laugh. "I'll keep my meat to myself and off the grill."

"Gah, that was a horrible joke."

He shrugged, heading to the porch but leaving the door open so he could hear her. "Give me time, I'll make a better penis joke. Maybe even a boob one if I get in the mood."

"I thought you were telling crappy jokes to keep us *out* of the mood while we ate."

He closed his eyes and counted to ten. Nope, his cock wasn't listening. It wanted her. Now.

"Woman, you're one taunt away from me bending you over counter and fucking you hard."

He didn't hear her, but he scented her arousal. As soon as the sweet scent hit his nostrils, he knew tonight would be the night he had her beneath him.

Logan wouldn't mate her tonight though.

He couldn't.

Not fully.

There were two parts to mating—the wolf and the man. Tonight, when they made love, he'd come inside her, filling her up. That would start the mating process and bond the human part of themselves tentatively. Then, when it was time, they'd each mark the other with their fangs on the fleshy part where the shoulder met the neck.

That would connect their wolves and the mating bond would snap into place. Once mated, they'd connect on a soul level, gaining a new strength and warmth from a place he'd only dreamed about. He honestly couldn't wait but knew he would have to in order to ensure his Cailin was taken care of.

Even if in the process, it hurt them both.

He wouldn't complete the mating until he knew for a fact she was here for him and wouldn't regret it. He would give her the comfort she needed tonight and take the touches his own wolf needed. The touches he was sure her wolf craved as well. Then, if she still wanted him, he'd complete the mating the next time.

He wouldn't have her resenting him for mating with her so soon after the tragedy.

They were both worth so much more than that.

Once he pulled the steak off the grill and potatoes out of the oven, they ate at his table, sitting side by side. She leaned into him as they ate, and he pressed closer. She didn't cling—that wasn't her—but she did show what she wanted at least.

Or what she thought she wanted.

He hoped to God it was what they both craved.

They talked of nothing relevant, but what they both needed. He wanted to know everything about her, and his wolf required it just the same. Logan also wanted to ensure the man within knew and held her with the care she deserved.

He didn't want their mating to be because of fate.

Fuck the fates.

He wanted Cailin—mate or no.

After they cleaned up, they sat together on the couch in his living room. The air ripened with anticipation, cloying, heady.

He ran a hand through her hair and played with a strand, their gazes never leaving each other.

"What is it you want, Cailin?"

"You," she answered with no hesitation.

He tilted his head. "I'm demanding. I'm not a submissive wolf you can walk all over to get your way."

Cailin lifted a lip and bared fang. "Have you ever known me to be with a man I could walk over?"

Logan growled, snapping his teeth. "There will be no mention of other men while you are with me. They don't exist. It's only you and me."

Cailin raised her chin. "Deal, because I don't want to hear about the hordes of women you've had before."

Hordes? Ha. He could practically scent her insecurity and felt like an ass for bringing it up. "Like I said, just you and me. Can you handle me? All of me?"

Cailin grinned a grin so full of promise he about came in his pants. "Oh, I think so. But the real question, Logan Anderson, is can you handle all of me?"

He growled, low, the vibrations washing over both of them. "I don't want a woman who won't rake her nails down my back and make me bleed. I want you to bruise me while I grip your hips so hard as I'm pounding into you that you'll bear my mark for days. I want to fuck you hard against a wall then have you pin me right back, sucking my cock and showing me your strength. That's who I want. And Cailin Jamenson, that's who you are."

She groaned and closed her eyes. He reached out and cupped the back of her neck, pulling her closer.

"One thing, princess."

"What?"

"Tonight we can't mate."

She pulled back, her eyes wide, pained. "What? I'm good enough for a fuck, but not enough for the long term?" She tried to get up, and he pulled her onto his lap, holding her tight.

"I said tonight, Cailin. I don't want to think back on our mating day and think of this day." He wasn't lying, but it wasn't the full truth. He could have told her the full of it, but she'd say she was ready when he wasn't sure *either* of them was.

She let out a sigh. "I guess I understand that, but it doesn't make me feel any better."

He nipped at her ear, then licked the sting. She shuddered in his arms, and he groaned at the friction on his cock.

"I'll make you feel better," he promised.

She turned into him. "Oh really?"

"Really?"

Then he kissed her.

Hard.

She opened for him, groaning into his mouth. He grinned then wrapped her hair around his fist, moving her head so he could deepen the kiss. Cailin wiggled and moved so she was fully on his lap, straddling him. He groaned as his cock pressed against her heat. With a moan, she threw her head back, rocking on him, knocking his hand lose.

He moved both hands so they were on her hips, digging into her as he fought for control. His wolf wanted to flip her over so she was on her knees, claw off her pants, and fuck her hard from behind. He wanted to sink his fangs into her shoulder, marking her as his for all to see, the mark so deep it would never fade and they'd both ache for weeks.

Soon, he told his wolf, *soon*.

He pulled her against him, kissing her again, letting her sweet taste settle on his tongue. He couldn't wait to lick her all over and make sure his scent sank deep into her pores. There would be no doubt she was his—woman and wolf.

And who he belonged to.

She ground on his cock, and he had to stop her before he came too fast, wanting the pleasure to linger, and for fuck's sake, he needed to be in her. Keeping his gaze on hers, he pulled her top off and sucked in a breath.

"Fuck, baby, look at those tits. I'm so happy you didn't wear a bra."

She blushed all over, her nipples reddening as they tightened. "You like to talk dirty, don't you?"

He gave her a feral grin then licked her nipple, loving the way she pushed her ample breast into his face.

"You like it when I play with your tits?" She nodded. "Good, because I'm going to bite and lick them until you come. And maybe one time I'll come on top of them so they're dripping with my seed, covered and all mine."

"Jesus, Logan. I'm going to come just with your words."

He rolled her nipples between her fingers and licked his lips. "Come all you want, princess. I'm going to make you blow more than once tonight."

Logan reveled in her taste as he sucked her nipples into his mouth one by one. He bit, nibbled, and laved them, wanting them hard and sensitive. While his mouth was on one, he palmed the other, pinching and cupping.

"Damn, I love your tits."

Cailin chuckled, her eyes closed as she pressed into him. "Please, make me come, Logan."

"Anything, princess. Anything." He lifted his hips slightly so her clit hit his cock. She rotated her hips, grinding on him as he bit down hard on her nipple, pinching the other one with enough pressure that he'd leave a small bruise.

A mark they alone would know she wore.

"Logan!" she shouted as she broke apart in his arms. He couldn't wait to have her come on his tongue, his cock, anything.

"Fuck you're gorgeous when you come."

She met his gaze and dug her nails into his shoulders. He was sure he'd bear the mark later, and his wolf howled.

"More," she growled. "More. Fuck me hard, Logan."

He grinned and stood up with her in his arms. She immediately wrapped her legs around his waist, her lips going to his neck. He could feel the tension in her body and knew that came from wanting to mark him.

It hurt like hell that they wouldn't be doing that tonight, but it wasn't the right time. She'd kick his ass later, but it was for the best.

As soon as he got to his bedroom he set her on her feet and knelt before her. She grinned down at him and ran a hand through his hair.

"I think I like you at my feet."

Logan snorted, then pulled off her pants, his nostrils flaring at her scent. "Damn, baby, no underwear either? It's like you're already unwrapped and ready for me. And as for me at your feet on my knees? As long as I can taste this sweet pussy, I'm game. You'll just have to return the favor."

She sucked in a breath, her hand tightening in his hair. "Done, now eat me."

"As you wish, princess. Hold on to my shoulders so when your legs go weak you won't fall."

"Confident, are you?"

"Baby, I made you come, and I didn't even touch this sweet cunt. I can't wait to fuck you hard and have us both coming."

"Promises, promises."

"Wench."

"Brute."

"Mine."

Her eyes darkened. "Prove it." She put her hands on his shoulders, and he licked her clit.

She shuddered and moaned.

Good.

He spread her pussy, wanting to see all of her. Damn, he loved the look of every bit of this woman, and he was well on his way to loving her in truth. He speared her with his tongue then licked around her entrance before sucking and nibbling up to her clit. When she rocked her pussy into his face, he sucked the hood before licking her clit with quick swipes, knowing she was already on the edge.

Logan pulled back and licked his lips, almost coming at her taste. She whimpered, and he fucked her with two fingers, her delicious cunt tightening around him as she rocked.

"Almost there, Cailin."

She met his eyes, her pupils dilated, her mouth open. "Logan."

"Come for me, Cailin. Come on my hand. Show me how much you want it."

Their gazes never broke as he curled his fingers, rubbing over her G-spot, that little bundle of nerves swollen and ready. She came hard, her body bowing, her nails digging into his shoulders.

"I want to be inside you," he whispered as he stood up, holding her close to him.

"Let me taste you first," she murmured.

He groaned. "I won't last long that way."

She raised a brow, that seductive grin all too enticing. "Oh, poor baby. Can't handle too much? Maybe you should sit down so you don't go weak-kneed."

He lifted a lip, growling, before crushing his lips to hers. She pressed herself against him, kissing just as hard back. He nipped her lip then tugged her hair. "Suck me off then, princess."

She rolled her eyes. "Sure, make it your idea. Whatever."

He snorted and just about came at the sight of her on her knees, her wide eyes looking up at him.

"You'll have to take off your clothes you know," she teased.

He relinquished control of her hair and stripped quickly, his cock bobbing against his stomach he was so hard. When she took him in hand, her palm sliding up and down his length slowly, teasing, his eyes rolled to the back of his head.

"Sweet goddess."

"My name is Cailin, but you can call me goddess when you're coming down my throat."

Logan chuckled then brushed his knuckle along her cheek, the moment sweet yet so fucking hot. "Anything you want, princess."

"I want your cock in my mouth."

His wolf clawed at him, wanting more. "I'm all yours."

"Good."

She palmed his length, squeezing. *Holy shit.* When her tongue dashed out, licking the seam of his cock, he gripped her hair, trying to steady himself. She played with the head, sucking and licking, until she lowered her jaw and swallowed him, as much as she could.

He was too long for her to take him all, but fuck, he loved the way she felt around him. Wet, greedy, and all his.

She pulled back and let go of him with a slurp before sucking him down again. He let her set the pace, forcing his hips to stay still before he pumped into her mouth and spent himself. When his balls tightened he tugged on her hair, pulling her back.

"I wasn't done yet, Logan."

He reached down and lifted her into his arms, crushing his mouth to hers. "I want to come in your pussy, Cailin. I don't want the first time I come inside you to be down your throat. I'll do that soon."

She panted against him. "Show me."

"Turn around and grip the dresser, facing the mirror. I want to see your face while I fuck you, but I want to go from behind. That way I can go as deep as possible."

She grinned and did as she was told, wiggling her ass. "Let's see if you can top me."

He shook his head. "I'll only top you if you top me back. Push back against my cock, baby, fuck me as hard as I'm going to fuck you."

"Then do it."

He gripped her hips and entered her in one thrust. They both stilled, gasps escaping from their mouths but nothing else.

Holy. Fuck.

"You're so fucking tight, Cailin."

"Move, Logan. Please. I...I need you to move."

"Since you asked so nicely." He pulled out then pounded back in. Their gazes met in the mirror, and he grinned, loving the way her eyes darkened, her hair wild around her face. Her breasts swayed with each thrust, and he couldn't wait to suck on them again.

"I love your cunt, Cailin. I love the feel of it around me. I love the way you squeeze me when I'm in you. I love that you're going to milk my cock and take every ounce of me. You ready for more?"

"God, I love the way you talk. The way you fuck."

"Good."

He thrust into her a few more times, almost ready to go, but he didn't want to come in this position. Not this time. He pulled out, and they both whimpered.

"I was so close," she whined.

He turned her so she faced him and kissed her, nibbling on her lips. "I want to face you when I come. Okay?"

Tears filled her eyes, and he kissed her eyelids. "Please, Logan. I want it all."

He held back a curse, knowing what she wanted and knowing it wasn't the right time. He led her to the bed and placed her on her back. When he slid into her heat, their eyes on each other, their fingers tangled, he knew he'd lost himself to her.

While before it was hard, fast, and all them in between, this time he thrust into slowly, knowing they both rose at the same time, the crest barely a whisper away.

"Mine," he said, his voice so low he wasn't sure she could hear it.

"Yours, Logan. Yours, mine, forever."

He groaned and came as she did the same around him. His body shook, his heart thudding hard against his chest. This woman...this mate. Goddess, he'd never felt so spent, so...complete.

He stayed deep within her, their bodies sweat-slick, loose, and sated. When he pulled out, he kissed her cheeks, her eyelids, her lips then moved to the bathroom, getting out a warm towel. He made his way back to the bedroom and washed her slowly. Her lids lowered, but her gaze never left his as he cleaned her off, being oh-so-gentle on her delicate pussy.

He tossed the towel away then moved her so she was underneath the covers. He slid in behind her so they lay the way they had the night before. Their fingers tangled, and he inhaled her scent that mixed with his.

"Good night, my Cailin."

"Good night." He'd never felt so close to someone, so ready for that next step. While his wolf craved for more, he knew that waiting until after they were both ready for the complete mating was necessary.

That didn't stop him from wondering if he'd made a mistake forcing her hand.

He just hoped Cailin forgave him for the look he'd put on her face when she thought he wasn't looking.

She was worth more than a night of passion after a day of pain.

He'd prove that to her.

He hoped.

CHAPTER SEVEN

Cailin woke up, once again surrounded by
warmth. Her wolf whined and nudged her,
wanting more, wanting what should have been
theirs in the cool morning. While she should have
been snuggling closer, inhaling the dark and heady
scent that was all Logan, she couldn't. Not when her
heart was breaking at the lack of the bond.

It hadn't happened, no matter how hard her wolf
had begged and the woman inside had pleaded
however silently. Logan had rejected her in the
cruelest fashion.

They had given in to one temptation only to deny
both of them the ultimate of pleasures and
connections.

She never thought that after a night where she'd
never felt closer to a person in her life that she could
feel so...unwanted.

Though she'd felt so full the night before, Logan
inside her, over her, *part* of her, she hadn't known she
could feel so empty.

She wasn't supposed to miss something she'd never had to begin with, but, dear goddess, she craved it.

He'd broken her when she thought she'd already been fractured beyond repair.

Yet here she was, lying in his arms, his scent surrounding her as he slept.

Damn him.

Logan's large hand stroked her belly before moving higher, cupping her breast. She refused to push into his touch, not wanting to lower herself any more than she already had by giving in and sleeping with the man she'd stayed away from for months without mating him.

Logan rolled her nipple between his fingers, and she bit her lip so she couldn't call out, begging for more.

Ah, it seemed the wolf wasn't asleep.

Damn him anyway.

"Good morning," he mumbled against her ear, his sleep-heavy voice, deep and sexy as all get out.

She tried to say something back, but her voice caught in her too-tight throat. She blinked back the traitorous tears, cursing herself for being so weak when she'd tried to be so strong for so long.

He might have said the night before that they were waiting until they were both ready, but she'd seen the lie in his eyes. Oh, there was truth in those words, but that wasn't all of it. He was holding something back, holding *himself* back, and she'd been the one to take the brunt of the pain.

She couldn't even relish the morning after the best sex of her life because he'd make her feel like she was *nothing*. Who was he to do that?

Who?

"Cailin?"

This time his voice was more awake, and she could detect a hint of worry.

"Did I hurt you last night, princess? Was I too rough?"

Cailin closed her eyes, willing those damn tears away. She had to get out of his bed, out of his home. She needed to get back to her life, regroup, and find a way to heal the pain of all that had been lost and learn to live alone again.

He'd rejected her by being with her but not fully.

She couldn't take any more.

She wouldn't take any more.

Before she could rethink and change her mind, she wiggled from his hold—not an easy thing to do with the metal-like band of his arm tightening around her waist. She pulled as hard as she could and finally stood by the bed, searching for her clothes.

"Cailin, baby?"

"Don't call me that," she snapped. "Don't call me baby. Or princess. Or anything that means something to you when I clearly don't."

Logan's glowered then got up, towering over her, naked, sweaty, and so alpha her wolf wanted to bow her head in submission.

Fuck that.

"What the fuck, Cailin? You jump from my bed and shout these things that make no sense? What happened?"

"It's more like what didn't happen."

He blinked at her and tried to reach for her. She flinched, moving back.

The hurt on his face was almost her undoing, but she remained strong. She had to. He'd hurt her and damn him for making her feel bad about wanting to breathe again.

"Baby, what's wrong? Other than the obvious. Tell me."

She swallowed hard, fighting back tears. She would not cry in front of this man. Not anymore. He didn't deserve it. She didn't trust him.

"What's wrong? You pulled away, Logan. You don't want me? Fine." *Lie.* "But that doesn't mean you can just fuck me when your wolf gets horny. We only completed half the bond so we can part. Yeah, it'll hurt like hell, but we'll live. You should have worn a condom if you didn't want me. But you're an asshole, so I'm leaving."

She knew she was sounding hysterical at this point and not making any sense, but goddess, she just wanted to leave.

She wanted to run into her mom's arms and have her for comfort.

The shock of knowing that would never happen again slammed into her like a freight train, and she gasped, her eyes filling with tears.

She had to get out of there.

Now.

As soon as she turned, Logan grabbed her arm. "Seriously? Where the hell did this come from, Cailin? We were warm in bed after a fucking amazing night. Why are you running away?"

"Running away? Fuck you. Fuck you so hard. You denied our bond. Don't you get that?"

Logan's eyes glowed gold. "No. No, I didn't. Jesus, Cailin. We both talked about it. It wasn't the time. Wasn't the day."

She shook her head. "No, you talked about it. You declared. I shouldn't have even done it, and now I have to live with that. I'll own that. But fuck you, Logan Anderson, for taking all the control."

"Fuck. You know why I didn't bite you? Didn't mark you? Because fate fucks with us, Cailin. I didn't want to mate with you last night because we thought we had to. Because we were both in pain. I want to have the night where our souls connect be worth more than covering wounds. I want to actually love you and you love me. So I'm a fucking romantic. Sue me. I wanted us to actually have something more than bitterness and hiding before we were ready to connect our souls."

Her heart lurched, and she shook her head. The words were nice, and she knew he wasn't lying then, but they couldn't erase the hurt.

"We *will* mate, Cailin. I know we will. We just need the right time." His eyes pleaded, and she wanted to do nothing but throw her arms around his neck and never let go.

So of course she needed to leave. Needed to be the Cailin Jamenson with her outer shell and a heart so hidden no one knew it was there.

"No, Logan. Fuck you. You don't get to decide when we mate. *We* do. You don't get to declare it all and make the decisions. I told you I wouldn't be your beta, wouldn't submit. So no. I'm leaving. I don't know if I'm coming back, but right now looking at you makes my heart hurt and makes my wolf want you more than I should. I can't do that. I need to go."

"Cailin, princess, don't leave."

"You might have the strength of an Alpha, but you aren't *my* Alpha." The shock of pain at just who was her Alpha then hit her hard, and her knees buckled. Logan gripped her tighter, his hands almost bruising her skin.

"I know I'm not your Alpha, baby. I just..."

Cailin held up her hand, not able to take anymore. "I need space. I knew you were holding back, and I shouldn't have let it happen. I won't stand for it again. I'm not weak, yet you're making me feel it."

She pulled away, and this time he let her.

The loss broke her, her body shaking.

He'd let her.

By the time she made it to Maddox's house, tears flowed down her cheeks. She hadn't felt anyone around her so she knew others hadn't seen her break. Nor had she realized she'd been on her way to Maddox's.

The door opened before she made it down the walk, and he was striding toward her, his arms outstretched. Her knees buckled, and he had her in his arms and cradled to his chest, walking back to the house before she could take a breath.

Strong arms held her while smaller hands stroked her back. While she hadn't thought she had any tears left, she'd clearly been wrong. Her wolf howled, but the human part of her slowly grew numb, her tears staining Maddox's shirt. She could hear murmurs around her, but she didn't listen. She just knew she was safe for the moment in Maddox's arms.

Not only was he her brother, her blood, but as he was the Omega, her wolf calmed. His powers flared, and her wolf settled, the smaller bond she held as a Pack member to the Omega soothed her, her body relaxing in his hold.

"There now, ladybug butt," Maddox whispered. "Rest easy, I'm here."

The nickname from her childhood jolted her awake from whatever kind of semi-conscious state she was in, and she giggled.

Giggled.

"Stop calling me that, Mad," she whispered, not serious in the least.

"You'll always be my ladybug butt, Cailin. You're my little sister, not just my Packmate. Now tell me what happened." The last part was in a deep tone, ordering.

Her wolf bristled, not liking Maddox showing his dominance. If it wasn't for the fact that he was also the Omega, Cailin wasn't sure he'd even be able to force her wolf to act, but as it was, she was lower in the hierarchy.

Just one more thing to resent on a day—no, week—in which she wanted to run and hide.

"I don't want to talk about it."

"Cailin."

She looked up at Ellie's sharp tone. The quiet woman rarely spoke harshly, preferring to hide in the background. It only made sense considering how she'd grown up in the Central Pack under the thumbs of a sadistic ruling Alpha and his Heir—her father and brother.

"Tell us what happened." The other woman held out her hand, and Cailin took it instinctively. "We need to know if you're in danger. If any of us are. Maddox knows that you're in pain, and it's something even more than...than what happened to us on the field, but we need to know more."

For a moment Cailin wondered what all she'd missed if Ellie knew exactly what Maddox was thinking, but then she remembered that the two of them held a special type of mating bond where they could not only feel each other but also hear each other's thoughts if they so desired.

The pain arcing across her heart at the thought of never having that, or even a semblance of that, with Logan didn't surprise her.

Not when she knew it would more for a lifetime of hurt.

Cailin sighed, not wanting to share but knowing she needed to. It was so unlike her to burden others with her problems, but at some point, she didn't have a choice.

"I slept with Logan last night."

Maddox growled, low, deadly.

Perhaps blurting it out to her brother like that with no context wasn't the best idea.

Awkward.

"Did he hurt you?" he asked.

"Not the way you think," she said quickly while scrambling to her feet. "He didn't do anything I didn't ask for...he just didn't do *all* that I asked."

Maddox narrowed his eyes, and Ellie sat next to him, soothing her mate. "Explain," he ordered. "As you're my baby sister, my *precious* baby sister, you don't want to know what's running through my mind right now."

"I meant he didn't want to mate with me." Saying the words aloud was almost freeing. And even as she said them, she knew it was an overreaction.

Goddess, he'd said he'd wanted her and would mate with her in time, and yet what did she do? She ran away. She'd felt hurt because he'd made the decision for both of them without talking to her. In retrospect, he might have made the better choice for them both, but he'd made a mistake in not discussing it with her.

That made her angry more than hurt, and she clung to that. Anger she could work with. Hurt made her weak.

"Are you telling me he slept with you and didn't complete the bond? That he used you?" With each word, Maddox's voice grew harsher, and Cailin knew she'd made a mistake in telling him.

What had been a private thing now would involve not only her brother, but the rest of her family as well.

Damn it.

She hated her impulsiveness, her mistakes.

"Forget about it, Maddox. I'll deal with it." Which was what she should have done to begin with. Now she would have to deal with the ramifications.

Logan would have to deal with the ramifications.

"Forget about it?" Maddox stood, and Ellie stood with him, trying to pull him back. It wouldn't work though. Once a Jamenson male was on the rampage, there would be no stopping him. Not when it came to protecting family. Or at least what they thought of as protecting family.

"I need to talk about it with Logan."

Her brother narrowed his eyes then turned toward the door. Cailin gripped his arm, but he kept going, pulling away from her.

"Don't hurt him, Maddox."

Maddox growled and turned back. "I won't kill him."

Cailin huffed. "That's not what I said, but I'm glad you won't kill him. But I don't want you to hurt him."

"That I can't promise. He hurt you."

"But it was a misunderstanding." Or so she thought.

"No, you don't get to cover for him. His words and lack of actions hurt you, so he gets to deal with us. Deal with you when you're ready. And even if he hadn't done what he did, he would have to deal with all of us. You're our baby sister. He needs to know who he's messing with."

"I'm not your baby anything, Maddox!" Now her anger veered toward her brother, her wolf growling for the protection of the man who would be their mate.

And he *would* be their mate, damn it.

"Let me deal with this."

"Maddox!"

He stormed out of the house, no doubt on the way to get their brothers, and Cailin took off after him, only to be held back by Ellie.

Cailin turned on her heel and growled, immediately feeling like a heel for doing so to this woman who had been through so much. She needn't have worried though, as Ellie just raised her chin and took the brunt of Cailin's anger.

"Let him go. They were all going to come to blows eventually. They're your brothers. All of us Jamenson woman can kick their asses later for acting like brutes."

"It was my problem. I shouldn't have shared."

Ellie shrugged. "Maybe, but it would have come out eventually. Maddox felt your pain, and I had to hold him back from running after you as it was. I couldn't do it again. And these men need an outlet right now. They're all so lost. We all are." Ellie's eyes filled with tears, and Cailin gripped the other woman's hand.

"They won't hurt him. Not really. Logan wants you, and he's well on his way to loving you. You know this. Whatever he did, he did it for a reason, which was most likely a man's reason, which means he was an idiot." Ellie gave her a small smile, and Cailin snorted. "They're men. Sometimes you have to mold them and guide them the right way. Don't worry, honey. It will all work out. It might be fate that you're together or it could even be preordained, but it takes more than the moon goddess for a mating to work."

"I need to go find them," Cailin said, ignoring the mess in her head. She'd fucked up by coming here as she'd done, but so had Logan. That didn't mean Logan should have to bear the brunt of her brothers' anger. After all, they were still grieving as much as she was.

"Come sit and eat something, shower, and get dressed. I know you have a couple things here from when you stayed over to watch Charlotte. We all pretty much have a few things in each other's closets. You need to feel fresh and relaxed, and then you can work on what needs to be done."

Cailin sighed. "I suppose I do need a shower."

Ellie rolled her eyes. "Considering you have Logan's scent drenching you, yeah. I mean, sure, it works for what you need, but I was ready to hold back Maddox before he calmed you down since he scented Logan on you right away."

"Crap."

"Well, from the whisker burn on your neck, even though you want to kick Logan's butt right now, you seemed to have had a good night."

"I love you, Ellie."

"As you should."

Cailin followed the other woman into the kitchen and passed by Charlotte, Ellie and Maddox's daughter, taking her hand as she did so. The quiet little girl snuggled close, giving Cailin's wolf exactly what she needed to calm down before she took her next steps.

She just prayed her brothers didn't hurt Logan too bad.

****

Logan scented them before he heard them.
All of them.

It seemed the Jamenson brothers had held back long enough, and it was time to let them see what he was made of.

His wolf growled.

Good.

Because after that fight, he needed to release some tension before crawling back to Cailin. Oh, he'd crawl. There would be begging and pleading until she took him back. He'd been a fucking idiot to hold back, though she'd overreacted too.

Not the best way to start a mating.

Logan rolled his shoulders, rubbed his neck, and then opened his front door. He took a step outside, closing the door behind him, ready as he'd ever be to face the Jamenson brothers.

Kade was up first, his hands fisted at his side.

"I'm your Alpha, Logan." Kade's face and demeanor did not betray any emotion. Good. The wolf was learning. No weakness would be shown. Their Alpha was strong. Logan knew Kade was probably howling inside, ready to tear into flesh and kill anyone who had hurt his family, but on outside, Kade was smooth steel.

Alpha.

Right now, though, he was also an older brother.

Good.

Josh, Reed, Adam, Jasper, North, and Maddox stood behind Kade, similar expressions of overprotectiveness on their faces. It didn't surprise Logan in the slightest that Josh was part of the crew. Though he wasn't a blood brother, he *was* one of Reed's mates and the idea behind protecting the little sister of the bunch rang through clearly.

"Yes, you're my Alpha," Logan finally said. "But right now you're sure as fuck not representing one. That's fine. You're Cailin's older brother, but you don't get to try and intimidate me into doing whatever you think is appropriate in this situation. I know Edward stepped back in most cases when each of you mated, and I deserve the same respect."

A couple of them flinched at Logan's use of Edward's name, but none of them took a step to move away.

"Respect?" Adam barked. "You hurt our sister."

Logan held back the agony of having done so, not wanting to show the others he was in just as much pain as she was. "What goes on in our mating is between Cailin and myself."

"Fuck that," Reed said, surprising Logan. "She's our little sister, and you don't get to make her feel like shit."

Logan swallowed hard. "Is that what I did?"

Maddox came closer so he was nose to nose with Logan. "She came to me weeping, Logan. I know you denied the mating. You better tell us why, then you go to Cailin to do the same. You owe her that. You owe her more than that."

"You think you can come into our Pack, use Cailin, and get away with it?" Josh added. "You're wrong. So fucking wrong."

"I thought you were better than that," Adam put in.

Jasper let out a sigh, and Logan turned in the other man's direction. "Why? Why did you do that?"

"Yes, Logan," North said, "tell us."

Logan lifted a lip, baring fang. "I didn't deny the mating. I want her. And don't tell me what the fuck I'm thinking. She left because I didn't want to mate last night, the night of your parents' funeral." And because he'd held back, but that was between him and Cailin. "I want to love her, and I want that same emotion back when we're mating. I might sound like a pussy, but fuck you for thinking we both don't deserve that."

"You made her cry," Kade said back.

It was no use. These men needed the fight. Sure, they wanted to protect Cailin and take care of her problems for her—something Cailin would in no way appreciate—but they also needed to let out their own aggression.

Well, in that case, Logan could help them out.

"Bring it then," Logan said. "All of you. I'll take you all at once or one at a time. I don't give a fuck. You want to fight? I'm game."

The punch to his face didn't surprise him. The fact that it was Maddox who threw it did. Logan didn't fight back hard, knowing he deserved what he got. He'd hurt his mate, and he needed to bleed. There was no question. He wouldn't, however, show weakness.

Each of the brothers looked at each other then Adam nodded. Apparently he'd been the one to draw the shortest straw. Adam growled and Logan sighed, knowing he'd have to fight back to protect his wolf, but not too hard in order to protect Cailin. Neither one was putting much effort behind their hits, but each of them had blood on them nonetheless.

"Stop!"

Logan turned at Cailin's voice and therefore didn't duck in time, letting Adam's fist hit him square in the jaw. The man might have only one leg, but that didn't mean he couldn't punch like a fucking mountain man.

Fuck.

"Jesus, Adam! I said stop."

"I was in mid-swing."

Logan was kneeling on the ground by that time, trying to see past the stars and little birdies circling around his head. Cailin had her hands on his face, his wolf leaning into the touch.

"Baby, are you okay?"

Baby? Was that him? He blinked up into her pale green eyes and nodded. "I have a harder head that that."

"Don't I know it?" she mumbled then narrowed her eyes. "I can't believe you were all fighting like a bunch of fucking idiots and rednecks."

"We needed to fight," Reed said from behind him.

"We're men. It happens," Josh added in.

Cailin stood and put her fists on her hips. Logan could see the pain ravaging her features, but she didn't cry. He didn't think she would in front of them. And considering how much he'd fucked up, he wasn't sure she would in front of him either.

"Go home to your mates. They all know what you've been doing out here and will deal with the lot of you. For the record, I went to Maddox because I needed my Omega, not my brother. Shut up." She said that last part as North opened his mouth to speak. The man might be blind, but he still could hit really fucking hard. "Don't talk. I don't want to hear it. What happens with me and Logan from now on is between us. And, for that matter, what *doesn't* happen between us is only for us. No more interfering. No more waving your dicks around. There is enough to worry about without adding what Logan and I do or do not do."

Kade cupped her face as Logan leaned into her, needing her touch. "You're important, Cailin. You're our sister. We get to be overprotective. It's part of the job." Cailin opened her mouth to speak, and their Alpha shook his head. "But we'll let you be alone with him now."

"Let?" Cailin growled.

Jasper let out a breath. "Fine, not *let*. Like we could ever let you do anything. We're your brothers, so we're allowed to be idiots when it comes to you.

Now go fix whatever the fuck you did wrong, Logan. Then come to us as a couple or not. We just need you both. Got it?"

Logan nodded and stood, taking Cailin's hand in his. She didn't pull away, so he took it as the best sign he'd get.

The brothers touched her cheek, one by one, slowly walking away, bruised, bloody, and slightly worse for wear. No doubt they'd each go home to their mates and get their asses kicked once again for interfering in Cailin's life.

He squeezed Cailin's hand, but she didn't squeeze it back.

Didn't look at him.

Time for the groveling to begin.

CHAPTER EIGHT

Cailin used all of her strength not to fling herself onto Logan and never let him go. Damn wolf and mating urge. She was stronger than that. Or at least she pretended to be most days.

"Let's go inside and talk," Logan said.

She didn't look at him. Couldn't look at him. Not when her emotions were all over the place. Anger, fear, hurt, need, desire, and pure rage roared within her, pushing down the pain of her loss that she knew she'd never quite lose, only numb over time.

By the time they were in his living room, she was seated on the couch with her hands in her lap and he sitting on the coffee table in front of her, Cailin had started to sift through her emotions.

"I'm sorry I ran out without actually listening or talking this morning," Cailin started.

Logan's eyes widened, and she held back a snort. Yeah, she might have surprised him with that one, but she was far from done speaking.

"You don't have to apologize, princess." Logan's gruff voice washed over her, tingling in some places she'd rather not think about at the moment.

"You're right. I didn't have to, but I wanted to. I left and then ran to Maddox, not thinking about how he and the others would react. I brought our own problems out in public and ended up having to break up a fight. Don't even get me started on that."

The side of his mouth quirked up in a grin, and she held back a moan at how charming he looked. She was still in pain and didn't have time to moon over him.

He'd have to explain himself fully.

And grovel.

Yes, groveling would be good right now.

"I was so pissed off, Logan. I still am. You don't get to decide what's good for us, what works for us. Life-altering decisions, and mating is a big one, need to be made between us, not declared by you."

Logan sighed, running his hand up and down her thigh. Her wolf took comfort in the action while the woman did her best not to jump his bones. He wasn't in the clear yet. Far from it.

"You see that mating right away is out of the norm for some, right?"

Cailin narrowed her eyes. "Telling me what's right again, are you?"

Logan growled. "We spent a year tiptoeing around each other, Cailin. You held yourself back from me, and I did the same. Then the night that we bury your parents, *after* they die for us, you want to mate? Yes, I wanted to hold back. I didn't want to be your mistake. I'm sorry that I hurt you, but I was protecting both of us. Yeah, I went about it the wrong way, but I didn't want to end up with you resenting me for taking advantage of your pain. Can't you see that? I've loved your strength since I've met you, and I know that I'm well on the way to full-out loving you. But if we had mated when we both weren't thinking clearly? We would have ended up like Adam and Bay when they first started, crying, in pain, and not happy. I wanted more for us. I'm sorry."

Cailin blinked, startled by Logan's impassioned speech. "Logan..."

Logan stood quickly, pushing the table back. He was on his knees in front of her, his head in her lap, before she could finish her sentence...or even remember what she was about to say.

"I'm sorry for making you cry, baby. God, I'm so sorry. After all we've been through separately and together, I take what was supposed to be a night for us and ruin it being an asshole."

She ran her hand through his hair, the silky tendrils brushing over her skin, calming her wolf...and the human part of herself.

Finding every ounce of courage she possessed, she told him what she wanted. What she felt.

"I want you, Logan. I want to be your mate. I'm ready to take that plunge and find out what we could be with each other. Is it too soon? Maybe. But I'm tired of fighting fate. Fighting what I'm scared of. We have a hell of a war in front of us when it comes to the Centrals, and I'd rather you be by my side than away from me because we're too scared to take the next step."

Logan lifted his head and cupped her face. She leaned into his touch, the calluses on his hands grounding her in the present, rather than in the fear of the future or the pain of the past.

"We're a couple of idiots, but damn it, my wolf is ready for you. Is the man? Honestly I don't think anyone could be ready for the woman in front of me. And that's a good thing, princess."

Cailin grinned. She'd heard the latter a time or two. "And you think anyone could be ready for you?"

"I guess that's why we're mates."

Cailin's smile fell and she shook her head. "No, we're not mates yet. Not really, Logan."

His thumb brushed her lips. "Then let's get on that."

"Seriously? That's the line you're using? 'Let's get on that?'" She rolled her eyes, happy for the levity in a situation where she felt she was floundering.

Logan stood, lifting her up in the process. "I can do better." She wrapped her legs around his waist and rested her head on his. "Cailin Jamenson. Yours is the soul I want connected to mine, the soul I need. Your fierceness and strength have never and will never be diminished. I want to spend the rest of my long life with you and fight by your side. I want to fall in love with you in every way possible. I want to watch you grow round with our child. I want to see the way you smile and snark back until the day we are no longer of this earth. I will never hold you back, even when my wolf is begging me to protect you. I will find a way to protect you and have you protect me in the process. I want a partnership, a friendship, a relationship. I want it all."

Cailin swallowed, tears filling her eyes.

Logan licked his lips, and her gaze followed his tongue. "I want it all, Cailin. I want forever. I'm not easy, but I know you're sure as hell not easy."

She punched him hard, and Logan grinned.

"See? The abuse already."

"I'll show you how tough I am," she taunted.

His smile fell, and he looked serious. "I know how tough you are, princess. I've stood back because I knew you needed time. Once more, I held back last night because I thought you needed more. I was wrong. So fucking wrong. But you know what that means? I'm not holding back anymore. You're mine, Cailin Jamenson. I'm not letting you go."

"Good. Because I'm not letting you go either."

Logan bit her lip, and she shuddered, the slight sting feeling oh-so-good. "I won't give you a choice, princess. You want me? You've got me. I'm going to mark you tonight, make love to you, fuck you hard, and show you what it means to be with me. We can worry about the practical parts of what our mating will be and how we will need to learn each other later. Right now? Right now I need in you so bad I can barely think."

"Then be in me."

Goddess, please, be in me.

Logan grinned. "Since you asked so nicely." He wrapped her hair around his fist, tugging her head to the side. With a growl, he licked one long swipe over her neck and shoulder—right where he would soon mark her.

She groaned and dug her nails into his back, wanting more, *craving* more. Her wolf nudged at her, pushing her to go faster, harder.

"What are you grinning at, princess?" Logan asked, his eyes glowing gold with arousal.

Cailin leaned in and nipped at his chin. "My wolf wants it hard. Fast. And now. I was just thinking that the woman in me doesn't have a problem with that."

Her mate—oh goddess, that sounded good to say—grinned. "That I can work with, princess. That I can fucking work with."

Logan crushed his mouth to hers, burying his tongue against hers, and she moaned. He kissed her as though this was the last moment they would have together, as though he'd die without her there to quench his thirst.

"I need to taste you," he growled, low, filled with promise.

She arched into him, wrapping her legs and arms around him as he carried her to the dining room table.

"I'm going to taste every inch of that sweet cunt, let your juices run down my face, and then you're going to suck my cock and show me how talented that wicked tongue of yours is."

If there was an Olympics for dirty talk, Logan would win gold hands down. Hell, he'd win silver and bronze, too, for that matter.

Her panties were drenched from his intent and words alone.

And from the way his eyes lit up as he inhaled her arousal, she was sure he knew what he'd find when he stuck his hands down her pants.

Oh goddess, please let him stick his hands down my pants.

He stuck his hand down her pants.

Okay, so it was more of a gentle caress after he set her down on her feet. His eyes never left hers as he palmed her belly then moved lower, oh so lower, until he wiggled his fingers and slid them underneath the waistband of her jeans. She did her best not to let her eyes cross as he cupped her pussy over her panties in a possessive hold that made her want to howl in triumph.

"So wet for me, princess. I'm going to lick up every drop."

He slowly slid his hand back out then knelt before her.

"Got to tell you, Logan, I sure like the look of you on your knees at my feet," she breathed as he peeled off her pants and panties in one swoop.

"You've said that, princess. Your wish is my command...for now." He grinned at her then scrunched the bottom of her shirt in his hands.

"Let me help." She tugged off her shirt, undid her bra, and threw them both in a pile as quickly as she could. "Help me with your shirt. I want to look at all those muscles as you lick me."

Her soon-to-be mate gave her a rough chuckle then stripped off his shirt, the movement making each muscle in his arms stand out.

And he was hers. All hers.

Before she could say as much, he had his hands on her ass, pushing her up. She reached back to steady herself on the table and wiggled slightly so her bottom rested on the edge.

Then Logan went to town.

He licked around her clit then sucked on her lower lips, breathing hot air every so often against her. She squirmed at his touches, wanting more, but then he put his hand on her stomach, keeping her still.

She loved it when he did that.

Cailin let her head fall back as he sucked her pussy, spearing her with two, then three, fingers. He curled them at that perfect angle, pressing against that swelling bundle of nerves, and she knew she was done for.

With his name on her lips, she came, her body blushing, heating, and still craving his hard cock inside her.

She finally opened her eyes to watch him staring at her, hovering as he licked her juices off his lips. Holy hell, that was such a hot thing to see.

"My turn." With effort, since she'd just had one of the best orgasms of her life, she hopped off the table and knelt before him. "Turn a bit and grip the table. I want to suck you down."

He did as he was told then brushed his hand through her hair, a small smile on his face. "Got to say, Cailin, I like the look of you on your knees at my feet."

She grinned as she undid his pants, carefully sliding the zipper down. "See? Perfect for each other."

With his help, she got him out of his pants and had her hand on his cock before he could answer. The weight of him warmed her palm, and she slid up and down his length, getting to know every inch of him. When he panted harder, she licked the crown then around the head before taking her time to taste those inches she'd just studied. His salty flavor settled on her tongue, and she wanted more. She licked up and down his shaft then sucked on his balls, rolling them in her mouth one at a time. Her mate rolled his hips, and she knew she'd teased him long enough.

She sat back on her haunches, relaxed her jaw, and then swallowed him all the way to the root.

"Holy fuck, Cailin," Logan breathed.

Undaunted, she breathed through her nose, letting his cock slide down into her throat. Then she swallowed.

"Fuck!"

Her eyes watering, she let him slide out of her mouth and then sucked him down again, this time using one hand to cover the length that couldn't fit in her mouth. She bobbed her head, hollowing her cheeks, loving the control she had over him.

Oh yeah, this big bad-boy dominant wolf might have his hand wrapped in her hair, might be pushing her head so she took him deeper, but *she* was the one who set him on edge.

She was the one currently letting her free hand reach around to his ass so she could play with his hole. He shifted his stance to give her better access, and she grinned. Oh yeah, her bad boy was totally dirty.

As soon as she pulled back to lick her finger, she met his gaze. Damn it, she couldn't wait to mark him. To be marked by him.

Soon.

She sucked him down again, this time using her finger to breach his hole. Her mate sucked in a breath then relaxed as she found his prostate. She rubbed it softly, still sucking his cock, and let her body do what it knew best.

Taking care of her mate.

"I'm going to come, Cailin."

Good.

She didn't let him pull her away but, instead, pressed harder until she heard him shout and felt his cock stiffen in her mouth before come landed on her tongue and down her throat. She swallowed fast, taking as much as she could until she was sure he was spent.

At least for now.

"You shouldn't have done that, mate of mine," Logan said as he carried her to the bedroom, a very satisfied cat-in-cream expression on his face. "I wanted to come in that pretty pussy of yours."

"You're a werewolf with supernatural stamina. I think you can come more than once in a night."

He threw his head back and laughed before throwing her down on the bed. She bounced and glared.

"Hey!"

Logan dropped right next to her, putting his hands behind his head. "Giddy-up."

"Oh my God. Giddy-up? That's your line?"

"My cock was just down your throat. I think we're past lines."

"True," she said as she straddled him. Who knew sex could be so much fun?

He moved then, gripping her hips. "Ride me hard, and then I'll fuck you harder. Then we can mark each other and claim ourselves as mates for all eternity. You in?"

"In." She slid down his length slowly until he was fully seated within her, stretching her so much she thought he must have grown since the previous night. "Or should I say, you're in?"

Logan gave a strained chuckle. "I see how it's going to be. Bad dirty jokes until we're laughing so hard even as I'm inside you that we're both crying. I like it."

She grinned. "Me too."

Then she moved.

She rolled her hips, letting him stay within her fully as the base of his cock rubbed her clit. Taunting. Teasing. Then he gripped her hips harder, lifting her slightly so he could thrust in and out of her at a dizzying pace. She braced herself on his shoulders as they fucked each other, his cock slamming into her as if he couldn't go deep enough.

"Need. More."

At his growled words, she came again, surprising herself, then gasped as Logan switched positions. She found herself on her back, one leg over Logan's shoulder as he pistoned into her, sweat rolling down both of their bodies. She clutched at him, her nails digging deep, breaking skin. She didn't care. She just needed him inside her.

As soon as her body arched over that threshold again, she lowered her leg, baring her neck. She needed his fangs in her. Logan moved her head back and met her eyes. For a moment she thought he was changing his mind, and a fresh slash of pain cut into her heart, and then he kissed her.

So soft, a bare whisper of lips even as he thrust into her with all the strength of a dominant male.

"Mine," he growled low.

"Yours," she whispered back through tears.

She moved her head back into position, and he bit into her shoulder. She cried out as she came, her pussy tightening around his cock. A warm magic, like a sense of heat, electrifying anticipation, and home, slid through her, the beginning of a bond, as her wolf howled in triumph.

Logan pulled his fangs out then moved so his neck was in view. Without a second thought, she bit into the meaty part of his shoulder and claimed him as her own.

The mating bond snapped into place.

Warmth, earth, goddess, moon, and everything else that shattered her mind slid through the bond, arching into her as Logan came. She met his gaze, both of their eyes glowing gold, and knew she'd found her forever.

He rested his forehead on hers, his cock still buried deep, and sighed. Not a sigh of exhaustion, but one of happiness, joy, and everything she felt as well.

They'd done it. They'd mated. Happiness slid though her, and she smiled.

This was what she'd been waiting for and hadn't known it.

This.

CHAPTER NINE

Logan slid oh-so-gently into Cailin, her body warm around him as he slowly woke up. Her wet heat surrounded him, clutching at his cock as he pulled back out before slowly sliding back in. He moaned slightly, her cunt so fucking sweet that he could barely breathe for the warmth and sensation.

They were on their sides, the early morning light dancing on her pale skin. He nudged her hair off her neck, licking and sucking, his perfect breakfast treat. She tasted sweet all over with just the hint of salt from their energetic activities the night prior.

He cupped her breast, tweaking her nipple, and she moaned. Her nipple pebbled between his fingers, and he rolled it, loving the soft feel against his calluses. The bite and scruff marks dotting her skin showed his ownership of her body, her soul. The similar bites and bruises on his skin revealed the same of him to her.

They belonged to each other.

So. Fucking. Perfect.

"Good morning," he rasped out, his voice low, wanting. Damn it, he couldn't wait to feel her pussy tighten around him as she came. She was so beautiful when she peaked, when her eyes would widen, her breath catching. Just the thought of her lips parting in a sexy pout almost pushed him over the edge.

And she was *his*.

"God, Logan," she groaned and pressed her ass back into his groin, causing his dick to slide even deeper into her wet, greedy cunt. "What a way to wake up. Can we do this every morning?"

His wolf preened at the thought of her being in his arms every morning, and the man growled, wanting more. Wanting all of it. "Any time you want me inside you, princess, all you have to do is ask." He pumped again, this time pinching her nipple between his two fingers hard enough to elicit a shout from her. He loved the way she reacted to his touches. His pets. He thought about his words then stilled before picking up the pace as he made love to her. "Wait, you don't even have to ask sometimes. Just give me a look, and I'll be inside you so fast you won't even know what happened." Oh yeah. He might just make sure they were naked all the time when they were at home. It would make it easier for them to have sex any time they wanted.

That was the mating life.

And apparently the mating urge was riding him hard.

She laughed, a deep, raspy chuckle. "I hope I'll know what happened if your cock is in me."

He collared her throat and leaned down to lick the bite mark from the night before. They both shuddered, and he held back from coming. "You'll know, Cailin. You'll fucking know."

"Then fuck me."

He grinned at her order and did as he was told. After all, he was a reasonable dominant wolf. If his mate ordered him to fuck her, he'd do it.

Mate.

Goddess, he loved the sound of that word.

He lifted her leg and wrapped it around his upper thigh so he was filling her as deep as he could go. She pushed back at every thrust, fucking him as hard as he fucked her. This was why she was perfect for him.

Well, this and so much more.

He couldn't wait to find out all of it.

They rode each other, their gazes meeting each other's as he collared her throat. She could collar his next. He'd submit to her just as she to him. This was why she was his and he hers. As they both came, their bodies sweat-slicked and primed to start the day, he knew he wanted to do this every morning.

He just needed to make sure the Pack was around long enough to make a future filled with mornings with his mate happen.

At that sobering thought, he pulled out, turned her on her back, and kissed her softly. They nibbled and sucked at each other's lips. Lazily waking up until he was hard again, but knowing they needed to get up and start the day.

"Move in here with me," he whispered. They hadn't discussed it, not really. But they were mates now. He couldn't let her go.

"No," she whispered back.

Logan froze. "What?"

She arched her back, his dick getting hard again. He gripped her hip. "What, princess? You don't want to move in with me?"

She shook her head. "My place is bigger. We can keep this one for a bit until we're ready to move into the larger place. But I've been in mine longer than you've been in yours, and we'll have room to grow there."

She ducked her head and blushed, and Logan bent, licking her mating mark. They both shuddered. Damn he loved her blush. Her reactions.

And if he were honest with himself...

Her.

"Deal, princess." The thought of them growing as a family, as a mated couple made him want to howl, but they had other pressing matters to deal with first.

"Shower then food?" he asked, nibbling on her neck.

She moaned beneath him before raking her nails down his back. He grunted, but the pain felt so fucking good when it came from her.

"Get off me, big boy, if you want to eat. And by eat, I don't mean me. I need nourishment. You worked me hard." She winked, and Logan snorted.

"Big boy?" He quirked a brow, and she rolled her eyes.

"You call me princess. I needed a name for you." She grimaced as if she'd just thought about the connotations, and he kissed her brow. "I guess I can't call you that in front of everyone."

He thought about the beating he'd take if she did so in front of her brothers then winced. "Probably not."

"Yeah, that wouldn't end well. I'll think of something to call you that doesn't have to do with your cock."

"It's a good cock." If he did say so himself.

"Good? Please, Logan. It's all right."

Logan narrowed his eyes. "Want me to show you *exactly* how all right my cock is? Don't you remember riding it last night, calling my name and screaming because I filled you up so much you felt like you were ready to burst."

And there went his cock again, ready to go.

"Stop making me almost come at your words. We need to get going. As for your nickname, I'll think of something that won't elicit a reaction from my brothers." She patted his chest and grinned. "I'll take care of you, though, if my big bad brothers come at you."

He snorted then gave her another quick kiss before hopping off of her. "I'm sure you could. But I'd still refrain from using big boy in company. Not unless you want to make everyone jealous?" He gestured toward his still-hard cock, and Cailin wiggled her eyebrows.

"Dork." She licked her lips.

"Your dork." Damn, that sounded good coming off his tongue.

Her eyes darkened as her hand went to the very deep mating mark on her neck. "Yes, all yours. Now let's shower so we can start our day." Her eyes clouded this time, and he could feel the sadness over the bond. He was still getting used to that, feeling what she felt if only a fragment, a whisper.

When she stood in front of him, he slapped her ass, earning a rake of nails down his chest—not too much of a punishment as his wolf begged for more to add to the numerous marks already on his body—and pulled on his pants. If they took a shower together, they'd never get anything done, and they needed to stop by Kade's. The elders were meeting with the new Alpha to discuss Caym and the evacuation of the Pack.

Things were rolling; he'd been spending so much time recently worrying about Cailin and himself, it was time to focus on the Pack.

The mating bond flared, and he knew Cailin felt the same way.

He'd have to get used to that. Cailin knew what he was feeling as well. Though they didn't have the connection Maddox and Ellie did, where they could hear each other's thoughts, he knew their bond was strong. It would last through a war and so much more.

It had to.

He had to believe.

He started the coffee and got a slab bacon and a carton of eggs. Maybe he'd make some toast to go with the protein, but whatever. Not the most romantic breakfast, but he was damn hungry, and he knew he'd worked Cailin enough that she'd be hungry too.

The satisfied smirk he knew lay on his face made his wolf preen once again. His wolf might have had the taint of darkness that came from the moon goddess, but right then, it was practically a tamed puppy.

Cailin did that.

He'd just taken the bacon off the grill when he scented her ice, temptation, and roses over the smell of breakfast. He faced her and grinned after turning off the stove. Last thing he needed was to burn down his kitchen or have grease splatter over his bare back because he couldn't keep his gaze off his fucking beautiful mate.

"All clean?" he asked. He traced her body with his eyes, wanting to take in every bit of her. He'd been holding back for so long, not wanting to crowd her, that he felt as though he could finally be himself around her.

"Yep and you're all dirty. Just how I like you." Her eyes widened, and she smiled. "Oh my God, coffee. Give me." She held out her hands, and he filled a mug, handing it over as he grinned at her bouncing.

Too bad she'd put on a bra with her jeans and top. At least she was barefoot so he could see her feet. Since when did he have a foot fetish?

He cleared his throat, determined to get through the day—at least the next hour—without jumping her. "Creamer and sugar are on the island." The kitchen island where he'd enjoy eating her out one day soon. Maybe after their meeting. "I know how sweet and creamy you like your coffee."

"Don't knock my sugar addiction."

He held up his hand. "I wouldn't dream of it."

She opened her mouth to say something, but just as she did so, the atmosphere in the room...changed. Sharp tingles broke out over his arms and leg and his ears began to ring. Logan clutched his head, the pressure in the room becoming unbearable. The mug slipped through her fingers, crashing on the floor, but he couldn't hear it.

He held out his hand, reaching for her and she did the same. He had no idea what was going on, but they needed to get out of there. Fast. A gust of wind blew through the house even though the doors and windows were all locked tight. Cailin's hair whipped around, hitting him in the face and he pushed it out of the way, trying to see a way out of whatever the hell was going on.

Her fingers brushed his, and he leaned, clasping her hand and pulling hard. She hit his chest, and he looked down into her eyes. Yes, there was that same fear he held, but the anger and determination radiating in her body made him stronger.

"What is it?" she screamed over the roaring wind.

He held her closer, his limbs heavy. He couldn't move from the spot, but at the same time he hoped he stayed there and not get blown away. If they weren't careful, Logan knew this might be the end.

Whatever *this* was.

"I don't know!" he shouted back. "Just hold on to me."

"Not letting you go," she mouthed.

His wolf knocked against his skin, begging to get out and fight, but there wasn't anything solid to fight. Just a nothingness and roaring wind.

But was it wind?

It didn't knock anything off the counters or walls. It just rammed into them, pushing them closer together until he felt as though his bones would break if something didn't change soon.

This had to be the fucking demon.

He clutched Cailin to him even as he tried to find a way out. Cailin's eyes were on her surroundings, her body trying to move, trying to pull him with her. They were protecting each other even when there wasn't a way out.

That was why she was his mate.

A darkness surrounded them, as if a void of magic had opened up and swallowed them whole. Dark clouds pummeled them and bright spurts of light arched over the clouds, creating a storm of hell he'd never seen before. He screamed as what felt like hot pokers stabbed across his skin. He tried to cover Cailin's body with his own, but whatever magic attacked them seemed to run through him and hit her anyway. She arched into him, her body shaking and her face pale as the magic cascaded then slammed back into them.

Blood trailed from her nose and he knew that he must have the same on his face. Whatever pressure pressed into them was slowly killing them. If they didn't make it through the other end of the vortex—or whatever the fuck this was—soon, they'd die.

He couldn't lose her just when he'd finally found her.

Just when he thought they'd never get out of the tunnel of wind and pain, they slammed into the ground. He'd rolled in the air, taking the brunt of the pain, but Cailin had still hit as well.

They were both on their bare feet, bleeding and ready to fight in the next breath. Cailin pressed her back into his, covering him.

They were fighters then.

Pack.

His wolf growled, trying to take over again, that dark magic in his blood ready to fight any threat. Again, he pushed it away. Cailin's safety was priority.

"Where are we?" Cailin asked. He knew she was looking around the room just as he was.

They were in a cement room with no doors. No windows. He had no idea how they'd gotten there. Not really. And he had no idea how to get his mate out of there. His wolf rebelled, growling, clawing. It wanted out. It wanted blood. The darkness that seeped into his blood and his soul, threatened to overcome him, but he held it back. He'd let it out to defend his mate and himself against the demon, but not in front of his mate.

Not alone.

He didn't trust himself enough.

He reached back and squeezed her hand. She clutched it tightly before letting go. They would both need their hands to fight.

If that was what this was to be.

Logan inhaled deep, scenting Centrals and cursing. "Central land. Or at least we're near some of the bastards."

"I've got that much. Fuck. I didn't know Caym could do that. Bring us here."

123

He could sense the rising fear in her words, but then she pushed it away. This was his mate—strong and fierce. They could succumb to their fear later.

Right then they needed to find out exactly where they were and devise a plan to get the fuck out of there.

"I don't see an exit, do you?" she breathed.

The air in the room shifted, and Logan growled. Ready.

Caym appeared in front of them as if sliding through smoke. "Welcome." The demon smiled, all sharp teeth and evil temptation.

Cailin growled near him, low, deadly. But she didn't move. Neither did he. This was the man, the demon, who'd killed her parents. They hadn't yet finished grieving, yet here the damn thing was.

And yet they were all ready to fight again.

Though the elders of the Redwood Pack were trying to find a way to take down Caym, they hadn't succeeded yet leaving Logan and Cailin shit out of luck.

He'd just have to pray Caym was merely toying with them. Showing them his power before letting them go.

At least that's what he hoped.

"Fuck you," he spat. The demon could kill them in an instant—even as they pleaded. There was no use playing nice.

Not anymore.

"Tut tut, little wolf." Caym licked his lips, his gaze on Cailin. "Don't anger me too much, or I'll have to see how tasty your sweet mate is. Oh yes, love the markings. You bit her hard, did you? Like the taste of her blood in your mouth? The power that comes from tearing into her flesh as you pound into her? Maybe you're a little more demon than I thought."

Logan growled, not letting the demon bait him into attacking first. Not when there wasn't an exit.

"Now, you're probably wondering why you're here. That's easy. You need to die."

Caym smiled, and Logan gripped Cailin's arm. She didn't move, but he could feel the pain through the bond. She was ready to add more scars to Caym's face like Lexi had done or even remove the bastard's head altogether.

But without the magic of the moon goddess—more light than he possessed—they wouldn't stand a chance.

And they all knew it.

"I've already tried to kill the two of you before, and we know how that ended up. Don't we?"

Logan growled again as a wave of fresh pain slammed into the bond. Cailin was holding on by a thread and he wasn't doing much better.

"You two are such hard wolves to kill, what with people dying for you left and right."

Why was Caym focused so much on him and Cailin? That would be something he'd think about once they were safe.

If they ever were safe again.

He needed to get Cailin out of there, or he wouldn't be responsible for what his wolf did. He wasn't strong enough to save her in this room—maybe in any room—and the failure plaguing him enraged his wolf even more.

"Watching the mighty Alpha of the Redwood Pack fall for the little brat was mighty satisfying. Even if that wasn't my intended purpose. Killing his mate? Oh, that was a two-for-one deal."

Cailin whimpered, and Logan cursed. He knew she had to be kicking herself for showing that weakness, but at this point, there was no denying it.

They *were* weaker than the demon.

Fuck it all.

"Funny how dear old Patricia died *before* you mated." Caym tilted his head. "Makes you wonder if you two only mated to make sure her death meant something. Or whatever other sentimental babbling bullshit you need to sprout. Do you two even *like* each other? Or is all the sex just guilt? Something to think about."

"Fuck off, Caym. You're reaching here for words to hurt us." Sure, they were working, but he'd be damned if he'd let Cailin think he didn't want her. He'd already done that once trying to protect her. He wouldn't let the demon do it to her again.

Caym's smile vanished, and he snarled. "Watch your tone, wolf of darkness. You might think your secrets are yours alone, but you can't hide them from me."

He felt Cailin's curiosity along the bond, but she'd have to stay curious a bit longer. He'd explain everything to her once they got of there.

If they got out of there.

"Now, where was I?" Caym asked then snapped his fingers. "Ah yes." He opened his hand, and a long whip covered in razor blades and crushed glass appeared in his hand.

Holy fuck, how much power did this demon have now that he was the Alpha of the Central Pack with their life forces connected to him?

Logan had a feeling he was about to find out.

"Ready?" Caym grinned.

Logan turned, flinging himself over Cailin as they hit the ground. The first flare of the whip dug into his skin, flaying his back.

Cailin screamed under him, and he ground his teeth, blood seeping down his back, soaking their sides.

"We'll get out of here," he whispered through clenched teeth.

"Logan," she breathed.

The next sting of the whip cut into his shoulder near the mating mark, and he howled.

They had to get out of there.

Soon.

Or all would be lost.

He wasn't strong enough to protect his mate, and now she would know that.

She would see his weakness.

The next slash cut deeper, and he met her gaze.

He'd protect her. Not matter what.

He had to.

CHAPTER TEN

Cailin clutched at Logan, holding back her screams at the pain on his face. Damn him for taking the brunt of the pain, for protecting her. Her wolf howled, clawing at her. Their mate was in pain, and the only way to stop it was to take the pain herself.

She'd do that in a heartbeat, but Logan wouldn't be budged.

He was stronger than her, even as he bled.

Her Logan.

Her poor, sweet, Logan.

"Oh look, little princess, another wolf is bleeding for you," Caym taunted as he cracked the whip again. Each time it hit Logan's skin, her mate flinched but didn't let his gaze leave hers. Blood seeped into her clothes, and a tear slid down her cheek.

"Your parents died for you, and now you're letting your mate do it too? No wonder you're nothing in the Pack. You're weak. Useless. Unwanted. People die for you, but you're not worth it, and you know it. You'll die soon. Alone. Unworthy. Never remembered because the people who would care are already dead because of your selfishness."

Each word slapped at her, but it was nothing compared to the pain Logan must be feeling. The pain she felt through the bond alone made her want to weep—or claw the fucking demon's face off.

Yes, the latter would help.

She could cry later when she and Logan were safe and warm. Because they would be. They wouldn't end like this, damn it.

"Fuck you, Caym," Logan grunted.

She cupped his cheek and licked her lips. "Let me take some, Logan. Move."

"Never, mate of mine. Never."

She shook her head. "You don't have a choice, love." Love. Yes. That's what she felt. But she'd tell him properly when he wasn't bleeding on her. Bleeding *for* her.

With one last look, she kissed him softly then pushed.

Hard.

Cailin rolled on top of him then screamed as the lash of the whip cut through her shirt and into her skin, marking her back, left shoulder to right hip. She would be marked for life, but she didn't care. Logan didn't deserve to take all the pain.

She could bear it for him.

Logan gripped her hips and tried to move her. "Cailin! Don't you dare."

"You don't get to bleed for me alone, Logan."

Caym laughed behind them. "So sweet. Fighting over who shall take my whip. That makes it a little more fun for me in some respects, but don't worry. I have enough pain for each of you."

It felt like hands clutched at her, but she knew it was Caym's magic. The force threw her into the wall, and she grunted. Logan reached for her, but he couldn't touch her. The magic threw him into the opposite wall, and she blinked, her head aching from the impact.

Chains slid out from the wall and locked Logan into place, the pressure so tight she could see them digging into his skin. One chain wrapped around his neck, forcing his gaze in one place.

Hers.

Oh, God.

What did Caym have planned?

She tried to move, but invisible hands held her back. Caym took the few steps needed so he was in her line of sight, the whip in his hand, a menacing grin on his face.

"It's always the same with you mates," the demon drawled. "I hurt you, you bleed. But you don't feel nearly the amount of pain I need until I hurt someone you love. It happened with every single one of you, and now I suppose you and your fucking precious dark wolf are the same. You didn't scream until I hurt Logan. So, now, in order to make sure Logan feels what I want him to, what I need him to, I'll make you bleed, dear princess. I'll make you bleed while he watches, helpless to do anything knowing that he wasn't strong enough to protect you. Yes, I do believe that will be perfect."

Cailin swallowed the bile in her throat.

Yes, the pain would be excruciating, but goddess, she didn't want Logan to see this. Not when he couldn't do anything but watch.

This demon needed to die.

Now.

But she wasn't strong enough.

No one was.

Caym grinned then flicked his wrist. The tail of the whip barely touched her skin, but goddess, it hurt. The blades dug into her skin and tugged along the wounds before the demon drew the whip back for another strike.

She held back her tears, her screams.

She'd do that for Logan.

Forcing herself to stay as calm as possible, she met Logan's gaze. His eyes glowed gold, his wolf fully at the surface. He growled, his need for her to be safe so powerful over the bond. If she hadn't been held up by magic, she surely would have fallen to her knees under the weight of it.

Caym hit her again, this time the side of the whip marking her chest. The glass shards cut into her skin, and she held back another scream. Blood seeped from her wounds, dripping down to the floor.

Goddess, make it be over.

Soon.

She couldn't bear to have Logan watch it.

Caym hit her again. Then again. Each time the numbness surrounding her gained strength, but not enough that she couldn't feel the whip. No, she felt every strike, but the ongoing torture of it burned to a sweet numbness that she knew was all Logan.

Oh yes, her mate was taking her pain along the bond.

She didn't know how she could do it, but she'd get on him later for helping her when he needed to worry for himself.

Then she'd learn to take his pain as well.

Logan screamed from his side of the room. Blood seeped from his wrists and ankles where manacles and chains bound him to the wall. She tried to speak, tell him she'd be okay and to close his eyes, but she couldn't get her throat to work over the pain.

Or the numbness.

The damn wolf was taking her pain, and she hated it. He wasn't a Healer or an Omega who had been trained to dampen some of it so it didn't hurt as much. He was her damn mate, and he didn't deserve what he was doing to himself.

Caym hit her again then stepped back. She opened her one good eye, the other swollen from the edge of the whip. If she lived through this, she'd end up with a scar—or four.

Not that she cared. She just needed to get her mind off of what was happening...what *could* be happening.

"It was always you two, you know," Caym whispered, and her wolf perked up.

"What?" she rasped out, her tongue thick.

"It was always the fucking princess and her bastard mate."

She had no idea what he was talking about, but she'd keep that information for later. And there would be a later. She couldn't die like this.

She couldn't die with Logan watching and without being able to touch him one more time.

They hadn't even had a full day with the mating bond, and now Caym had ruined it all.

She'd be damned if she'd let the demon take Logan from her.

She'd just lost her parents.

She couldn't lose anymore.

"It's always the last," Caym murmured as he set the whip down, the echoing sound sharp against the stone walls.

Thank God.

"Always the useless."

Killing this demon would make her day, her week, her life.

"I've always wanted to try this," he whispered.

That couldn't be good.

She met Logan's gaze, mouthing her words. "Okay?"

He tried to nod, winced, then mouthed. "Yes. Be safe."

Tears filled her eyes, but she blinked them back. She had a feeling neither of them would ever be safe again. Maybe they never had been. Maybe safety had always been an illusion and she'd wasted too much time running from her fate and her feelings. Now she could lose it all before she'd even grasped it fully.

Regrets meant nothing, only actions. She had to remember that. Though being bound and bleeding didn't allow for much action. If only there was a way to escape.

If only...

Caym grinned then snapped his fingers. All at once, the walls melted away, forcing Logan and Cailin to their knees. She slammed into the ground, pain radiating through her legs. At least she was alive to feel pain. That was something.

Magic pushed her down to the ground. She forced her head up to glance at Logan, who struggled with the same force pushing him. Goddess, she just wanted to touch him.

Then gut the fucking demon.

"Stupid wolves," the demon sneered. "There were never any walls. Never any ways to escape because everything was an illusion. *My* illusion. You've always been my puppets now you'll die in a way that will make the others remember. There is only death for the Redwoods. I watched the life drain out of the pathetic Alpha and his mate's eyes. I'll now watch the two of you beg for your lives then die. There will be no rescue. No survival. You'll die like you've always been fated to."

"Fuck you," she grunted.

"You've always been so insolent," Caym said, his voice bored now.

Cailin tried to lift her hand, reaching for Logan, or a rock to smash the demon's head in. Right then, she and her wolf didn't know which she wanted more, and she had a feeling Logan wouldn't begrudge her for choosing death and maiming over him.

Caym strode over to them until he stood between her and Logan. He blocked her view of her mate, and she growled, only to suck in a sharp breath as the magic pressed down on her harder. Caym knelt in front of her then trailed a finger down her cheek. She flinched, and he slapped her.

Hard.

"Bitch. But don't worry. Flinch all you want. I'm going to chain you both to the trees you love and break down the dam holding back the lake. Not only will you drown next to your precious, precious mate, I'll destroy the border to the neutral zone, killing the forest you love. All in a day's work, and then my plans can continue. Without you two in my path, I'm unstoppable."

So many things ran through her head at once. Drowning? Goddess, that was one of the ways she *really* didn't want to go out if she had to die. Destroy the forest? Her Pack would survive this, but the forest was part of her soul, just like her wolf. That's why she *was* a werewolf. And why were she and Logan so important? It didn't make any sense.

She had to live so she could figure it out.

Then kill the demon.

Magic slammed into her, forcing her back into a tree. Logan rocked into the tree beside her. They were close enough that she could feel the heat from him, but she couldn't touch him, couldn't lean in and promise everything would be okay.

Because it wouldn't be.

Caym appeared before them then grinned.

Evil bastard.

He tilted his head, and chains dug into her skin, tying her to the tree. She gulped and fought against them. Each tug bruised, each pull burned and cut.

Caym reached out, brushing a lock of hair behind her ear, and she held back the bile rising in her throat. Only Logan got to do that. Only Logan got to touch her, love her.

No, this wasn't love from the demon. She knew that. This was something so dark, so endless, she didn't know if they could live through it. As her body worked itself against the chains, she tried to think of another way out of it, but she couldn't.

She would die there, a breath away from the mate she'd finally had a chance with, and no one would hear her scream.

No one but the mate who would die by her side.

"Goodbye, princess," Caym sneered before blinking away.

She hated the word from his lips. That was Logan's name for her. Logan's alone.

"Logan," she whispered. Her voice hurt, and goddess, she didn't know what to say.

"Don't give up, Cailin," he grunted. He still had cuts and bruises all over his body, and she knew he was still bleeding, just as she was.

She struggled against her bonds. If she could just get her right hand from the twisted position Caym had placed her in, she could maybe move a little better.

"I won't. Damn it. I wish I could at least touch you." Her wolf clawed at her, wanting their mate. "I think if I could just do that, my wolf wouldn't be freaking out so much."

She turned her head, facing Logan, who struggled against his chains the same way she did. Blood had seeped into his jeans, and his bare chest looked somewhat clean. She knew it was his back that had been hurt the most. His back that was currently pressed up against the hard, rough bark of the tree as he tried to free himself.

"I think I can get my arm free if I keep going, princess. Don't give up."

Cailin curled a lip. "I won't give up. I'm stronger than that." Though she wasn't quite sure if that was exactly true anymore.

"I know, baby. I'm just saying that to needle you. The angrier you are, the stronger you are, the harder you fight."

"You're such a brute, but I'll take it all." She cried out as she twisted her wrist too hard, the bone snapping. "Oh fuck." Her vision went blurry for a moment, and she had to take deep breaths.

Logan growled. "What did you break?"

"My wrist," she groaned. "Fuck. I can't move it. He chained me too fucking good."

The sound of roaring started to fill her ears, and the hairs on her arms rose. Animals screeched around them, running away. Birds above them flew in the opposite direction from the roar, and Cailin met Logan's gaze again, the worry in them just as potent as her own.

"He broke the damn," he whispered.

"I can't move, Logan." She heard the panic in her voice, but he didn't comment on it.

"I'm almost there, Cailin. Don't give up. You got me?" If only she could reach him. "Don't give up, princess. I'll get you. I promise."

The intensity in his eyes grew with each word, so thick she could almost reach out and touch it.

That was if she could move.

They each struggled against their bonds in a futile hope they could move. The pain of not being able to touch him became unbearable, almost as much as the pain in her body from the bruises and cuts.

"Get out, Cailin. You got me? We won't have much time." The roaring increased, and she knew the water was coming.

Fast.

"The water will hit us hard. If we're lucky, it will break the trees, and then we can get out. Use all your strength to get free and break the surface. I'll find you. I promise." Her wolf begged for him, and she nodded. "I'll find you."

"Not if I find you first."

He cracked a grin even in the dissolute situation, and she knew she loved him.

"Logan, I—"

Before she could profess her love, the water slammed into the tree. She hit her head against the bark, her vision going hazy. The water rushed around her, covering her head. She couldn't see Logan anymore.

She couldn't see anything.

Think, Cailin.

Go slow.

You can do this.

She swore the words were spoken in her mother's voice, and that calmed her enough to think about what she had to do next. The tree broke under her feet, and she hit the ground, still attached. The rush of water pulled her against the dirt and rocks, cutting her more.

Some of the chains loosened, and she wiggled free except for her broken wrist. The damn chain held her down, the pain excruciating. She couldn't breathe, and she couldn't see beyond making out shapes. Every time she tried to move, blinding pain shot through her making her want to vomit.

She bore down, ignoring the agony, and pulled. She felt another bone pop, but she didn't care. She'd live without that hand if she had to.

She just had to live.

Her head went hazy as she pulled. She was running out of oxygen. Fast. She couldn't make out where Logan had gone. Couldn't bear to think it.

Her limbs became heavy, but she couldn't give up. Not without knowing if Logan had made it. She pulled one more time, the pain nauseating, but she couldn't move.

Oh goddess, this was it.

Damn it. This *couldn't* be it.

Strong arms wrapped around her waist, and she leaned into them.

Logan.

Her head bowed, and her body was dying even though she couldn't give up. He bent over her, pulled at her chains at the angle she hadn't been able to get, and broke her free. She used her last remaining energy to kick up. Logan pulled her with him.

As they broke the surface of the water, she took a deep breath. Choking on water and the burn of new oxygen.

"Hold on to me," Logan shouted over the water.

She wrapped her arms around his neck, careful of her wrist, and took in their surroundings. The fucking demon had broken the damn. Water rushed around them, breaking trees and rocks in its path. They'd been directly in the center of it all, and if they hadn't been wolves, they'd have died right away.

If it hadn't been for Logan, *she'd* have died.

"We need to get to a safe place," she yelled. "Once we get to land, we can wait for the water to pass, and then we can swim to safety."

"I'm looking."

She stayed wrapped around him, swimming with him because she couldn't let him go. She had the energy to swim alone, but she'd be damned if she'd let go of his touch.

"There!" he shouted. "There's land over there that the water isn't rising up against. It's not going to get any deeper, so we can rest."

He faced that direction, and they swam as hard as they could.

She looked over her shoulder and screamed. "Logan!"

He looked over his shoulder and pivoted, protecting her. A log slammed into him, and he cursed before dropping his head to her neck.

"Logan! Damn it. No." She could feel his breath, and her wolf calmed slightly. He was just knocked out. Thank God. With her remaining strength, she swam, forcing Logan to float beside her. He'd gotten hurt because of her, damn bastard, but if the log had hit both of them, she would have been knocked out too.

Damn him.

Finally, sweet finally, she made it to land. It must have once been a large hill, but now it looked like an island in a new lake. She pulled Logan to the dry soil and threw her body next to his. It hurt like hell, but she didn't have the energy to do anything better.

She'd worry about heat, comfort, and getting home in a moment.

They were alive.

They would be safe.

She leaned up on her unbroken arm and brushed Logan's hair from his face. He fluttered his eyelashes, coming to slightly.

"Cailin?" he rasped.

Oh goddess, she loved his voice.

Loved him.

"You're safe," she whispered.

"I'm with you. Of course I am."

Damn the wolf knew the right words.

Once they got home they'd worry about the demon and his words. She and Logan were important, and there had to be a reason.

Maybe they could end them. Maybe they were the key.

They had to find out because this was the end. The Redwoods couldn't go on like this.

They needed peace.

They needed a dead demon.

CHAPTER ELEVEN

Logan crushed Cailin to him as gently as he could, their clothes finally dry from the sun, but their bodies far from healed. Their bodies shook, the adrenaline from trying to survive wearing off rapidly. He inhaled that scent that was all Cailin, his wolf finally calming now that his mate was relatively safe.

As safe as they could be in the middle of a flood in enemy territory.

When she pulled back, she patted his arms, chest, and hips, as if making sure he was real. He ran his hands up and down her body, doing the same. He took in each wound, each bruise. Caym would pay for all of it. He'd said it before, as had countless others before him, but it didn't make the oath any less real.

"We need to get out of here." They weren't safe. Far from it. Caym could come back at any moment to check to see if his plan had worked. Logan didn't know why the demon hadn't just killed them outright, but he had a feeling it had to do with Caym's sense of power and immortality. The demon didn't think he could die and wanted Logan and Cailin to perish in the worst way possible.

Cailin sat up, bringing Logan with her. He winced, his back burning. He knew it was ripped to shreds, much like Cailin's. His wolf powered forward, clawing at him, wanting to kill for what had happened to his mate, but Logan took control. He needed that strength to get home and heal.

Then they'd find a way to kill a demon.

"Can you swim?" he asked as he looked down at her wrist. He bit back a curse and gently took up her arm, cradling it to her body. "How bad is it?"

"Bad," she breathed. "I'm not gonna lie and tell you it's rainbows and unicorns. I need Hannah. You too. Then we'll be better off."

Logan nodded, knowing their Healer would help. Hopefully the Redwoods were on the search for them. He didn't know how long they'd been gone. Not that long, honestly, but he was pretty sure the others would have noticed their absence. And for all he knew, they'd felt the vortex within Logan's home as well.

"Let's go home," he whispered, brushing his lips to hers. He had to pull back quickly, not wanting to take her then and now so they could remind each other who they were and *what* they were. That would come later.

This was hardly the time.

They stood, leaning on each other more than they should have, but he didn't care. They *only* had each other here, and in the future, well, he didn't know what they'd have other than themselves.

"We're going to have to swim a bit to the next dry area," he explained. "The rushing water seems to have died down a bit, or at least receding, but I don't want us letting go of each other."

Cailin squeezed his hip. "I wasn't planning on letting you go. Ever."

He kissed the top of her head. "This is going to suck."

She snorted. "Pretty much. Let's go."

The water might have felt cool on a heated body any other day, but right then, the stinging up and down his legs, and eventually his back, hurt like a motherfucker. The current wasn't strong. The water had finally found its equilibrium. Sticks and branches brushed them, sometimes scratching at their skin, but they were able to avoid the bigger pieces that would hurt so much more. They kept their hands on each other, relying on one another when they got tired, and eventually made their way to the other side of the newly created lake.

Out of breath, in pain, and ready to be wrapped around his mate, Logan pulled Cailin to the bank and collapsed on the dirt and mud. Cailin ran her hand up and down his back, careful of the bleeding wounds.

"Almost there," she whispered, the pain in her voice so immense Logan paused.

"Yes, princess. Almost there."

He sat up, aching in every bone from the movement. When his gaze landed on this side of the lake, he cursed, his wolf howling. "Jesus, baby. What the fuck did Caym do?" He turned so he could see her face.

A single tear streaked through the dirt and grime, her eyes blank. "He ruined it. He ruined it all. All those trees...the life here? It's gone." Her voice broke, and he pulled her closer, damn the cuts and bruises. "He's not just killing us, he's killing everything we stand for...and we're useless. So fucking useless."

Logan was at a loss, unsure what to say. He'd never felt so out his depth, out of place. "We'll find a way."

"We've been saying that for years," she snapped then closed her eyes. "I'm sorry."

"Don't be, princess." He cupped her cheek. "We're tired, hurt, sore, and pissed the hell off. Let's get home, and we'll take the next step. We won't give up, Cailin. We won't back down."

She nodded, and they stood, grimacing with each movement. "I need a hot shower," she whispered.

"I'll take one with you."

She snorted, just what he wanted. "Only you could think about sex at a time like this."

He grinned. "I was just saying I'd get wet with you. You're the one that made it dirty."

"Thank you."

He held her unbroken hand and kept moving. "Anything, Cailin. You know that. Anything."

They made their way, barefoot, bleeding, and silent. Every once in a while, he'd risk a glance at Cailin, making sure she was still here. He felt her gaze on him and knew she was doing the same.

About four miles into their journey, he scented a wolf that made him almost fall to his knees in gratitude.

"Hannah," Cailin whispered, sheer relief flowing through their mating bond.

"Thank God."

He tugged her hand and picked up the pace, determined to make it to Hannah and the others as quickly as possible. Cailin needed to be Healed.

Now.

"Cailin!" Josh yelled from the tree line.

Logan let out a breath at the sight of Noah, their Pack doctor, Hannah, Josh, and Reed. They were saved.

Though, in reality, they'd already saved each other.

"Oh God, you're okay," Hannah said as she came up to them. Then she got a good look at them. "No, no you're not okay." Tears filled her eyes then she raised her chin, now the Healer at the surface.

Reed came up to Cailin's side, his face calm. "Let me help you to the car. We're parked pretty close since there's a road near us. Hannah could feel you guys so we followed her. Can I pick you up, Cai?" He said it to Cailin, but Reed also met Logan's eyes.

They all knew Logan's wolf was darker than the rest and, right now, highly on edge. He nodded, knowing that it wasn't his decision in the end.

"Please," she whispered, and Logan was lost.

God, she'd broken him. She'd willingly go into her brother's arms and show weakness because she was in pain. That hadn't been the Cailin he'd first met and being newly mated it was hard for both of them to go to others for help, but they needed it.

"Can Josh take Logan?" she whispered as Reed settled her against his chest.

Logan raised a brow at the partial-demon, now his brother-in-law. Ah, he understood now. Cailin would only give in if Logan was taken care of. Oddly enough, her thoughts let him give in.

"I'll lean on you," he said. "It seems I'm losing a bit of blood." Now that he thought about it, he became lightheaded. "Okay, maybe it was more than a bit." The last of the adrenaline wearing off, and he fell into Josh's side. Josh, stronger than a wolf because of the demon blood running through him, picked Logan up. Because of his size, it was an awkward hold, but Josh didn't even seem out of breath as they made their way to the car.

Noah held Hannah's elbow under the watchful eyes of her mates as they made their way over the rocks and trees to where they'd parked the SUV. The only reason Logan was able to remain conscious was because he needed to keep an eye on Cailin. He knew that she was awake for the same reason. They were too dominant, too new in their mating to let anyone else take care of them without the other near.

After carefully getting them into the back two seats of the SUV, Reed started the engine and headed back toward the den.

"Where are we?" Logan asked, realizing he had no idea where they were. They'd known instinctively to go a certain direction because of their wolves, but he hadn't known how far he and Cailin would have had to trek on their own.

Josh, who sat in the passenger seat, looked around at them. "Twenty miles from the den on the neutral land." His eyes clouded over. "At least what *was* land. You'll have to tell us what the fuck Caym did."

Twenty miles? Fuck. He and Cailin might not have made it then. Not with all their wounds.

Magic pulsed against him, and he looked over to see Hannah Healing Cailin. Her palms hovered over Cailin's wrist and her cuts and bruises. His wolf calmed even more at the sight. Their mate would be okay.

Noah sat on the edge of the seat Logan lay on, cleaning out his wounds. It was a testament to how much pain he was already in that he hadn't felt the other wolf doing that.

"Most of the ones on your front are superficial," Noah explained, his focus on his work. The man had gone to medical school and was still young, Cailin's age in fact. He'd taken over North's job when the Jamenson brother had been blinded in the attack with Caym.

Logan didn't have much to do with Noah most days considering the wolf had once dated Cailin. In fact, he was pretty sure the little bastard had taken her virginity. His wolf growled, but he kept it inside. Noah looked up, his eyes carefully downcast. Noah might have been a dominant wolf in his own right, but he had nothing near Logan's power.

"Hannah is going to Heal your back so we have you in fighting shape," Noah went on. "If you're done peeing all over the seat to mark your territory, I can change seats with Hannah to take care of Cailin."

Logan growled at the wolf's choice of words.

"Logan, stop it," Cailin snapped. "I'm yours. You're mine. Get over it. Noah's my best friend. Remember that. This isn't the time. In fact, it will never be the time. We're moving on. Got it?"

Logan pulled his gaze from the smirking wolf and looked at Cailin. He took a deep breath, letting her scent wash over him. "I'm good. My wolf is a little too close to the surface right now, and I'm not thinking clearly when it comes to you."

Cailin nodded, reaching over the seat to cup his cheek. "I know. I'm the same way. I just don't have an ex in the car with me. We're good. Now let Noah and Hannah switch places so she can Heal your back. I need you in one piece. Okay?"

Logan nodded and turned on his side, letting Hannah move into position. Warmth spread over his back, and he let out a sigh. It didn't hurt but felt odd to have his skin knit together as his wounds closed.

"You're not overdoing it, right?" he asked the Healer.

"I'm good," she responded, her voice a melodic charm as she worked. "I'm in the zone, and other than Cailin's wrist, nothing needs too much of my attention since your wolves will heal the rest of it. They already are. Plus I have my men here to pull me back."

"Damn straight," Reed and Josh said at the same time.

Logan grinned, his gaze still on Cailin. His eyelids became heavy as he Healed, Cailin's doing the same.

"Sleep," he whispered, and his mate nodded. He let his eyes close and knew he'd be safe with his family, his Pack, around them. Safe as they could be in a world such as it was.

By the time they'd told Kade and the rest of the Jamensons what had happened, four hours had passed, and all Logan wanted to do was crawl into bed with his mate and mark her again. And they both *still* needed showers.

They walked into her home—no, he supposed it was *their* home now—and immediately started stripping.

"I need to get clean," she whispered.

"I'll help," he said as he led her to the bathroom. He turned on the shower to get the water warm and turned back to his mate. "Princess?"

She licked her lips. "I was so scared, Logan." Her voice broke, and he crushed her body to his.

"I know, Cailin. I was so fucking scared too. We're safe. We're here together."

She nodded against him, her arms tightening around his waist. "Make love to me?"

Logan pulled back, cupping her face. "What did I say about asking, love?"

"Just do it."

He smiled then and pulled her into the shower. He let the spray hit him hard in the back first before letting it touch her.

She raised her face into the spray, the dirt, grime, and God knew what else washing off her as she leaned into him. Logan leaned as well, knowing they both needed each other in more ways than one.

After he poured some of her floral-scented shampoo into his hand, he washed her hair slowly. She moaned as he massaged her scalp, wanting to make sure she was as relaxed as possible.

"That feels so good," his mate mumbled. "But I need you in me. Remind me we're here. Please."

He rinsed her off then kissed her neck before picking her up by the waist and setting her on the shower ledge that was a perfect width for her ass. She let out a little gasp of surprise, and he picked up the loofah and put a little soap on top after he'd wet it. With sure concentration, he slowly and methodically ran the loofah over her shoulders and down her arms, ending with her fingertips. With their gazes connected, he set the loofah aside and held her hand as he washed the palm and each of her fingers.

Then he washed her other hand before going back to her chest. Licking his lips, he washed between her breasts before lifting them one at a time, making sure he cleaned every inch. Her breath quickened as he took care to clean her nipples very thoroughly. They hardened into tight buds beneath the bubbles, and he fought the urge to lick them clean—soap and all. Call him a lunatic. He gave in somewhat and cupped her breasts, molding and squeezing.

"I've said it before, but I'll say it again, I love your tits, Cailin."

She let out a laugh. "I love you touching my tits."

Reaching behind him, he grabbed the shower nozzle and rinsed her off. His throat worked as he watched the line of soap run down her body to between her spread legs.

"Not done yet," he said, his voice gruff.

"Logan..." she whispered, begged.

He put the shower head back then washed up and down her legs, using his hands instead of a loofah so he could massage as he went. Cailin let her head fall back to the shower wall as she closed her eyes, letting him take care of her.

That above all else spoke of the depth of emotion, the depth of trust forming between them.

Bond or no bond.

He ran his hands up and down her thighs, each movement bringing him closer to her cunt, already wet and ready for him in a way that had nothing to do with the water running down her body.

She let out a little gasp as he teased her opening with his finger then met his eyes. With a grin, he breached her with two fingers, curling them so he could rub against her G-spot. Her mouth parted as her pupils dilated, and her eyes glowed gold. He worked in and out of her, his other hand on her throat, collaring her.

"I'm letting you do this," she whispered with a smile.

He grinned back, still fucking her with his fingers oh-so-slowly. "I know." That's why he did it, why it was worth even doing in the first place.

When she clamped down on him, her back arching in that sweet surrender of release, he moved his hand then thrust into her to the root, leaving them both gasping for air.

He moved his hand from her throat, bringing both hands to her hips so he could pump into her without knocking each other out in the shower. The feel of her hands on his back, her nails digging in as she fought for control made his wolf howl and the man inside to take her even harder.

So he did.

Their gazes never leaving each other, he pumped into her tight channel, the cooling water from the shower having no effect on the heat spiraling between the two of them. He slammed into her with all his strength and she lifted her hips to meet him thrust for thrust. The fact that they looked at only each other as even their breathing synchronized, made it more intimate than pure hardness against a wall.

Soft and hard, that was his Cailin.

That was their mating.

The scent of blood filled the air as she broke the skin on his back, her nails digging harder. He smiled a feral smile and slammed home once more, coming hard within her as she squeezed his cock, milking him during her release.

"Logan!"

He captured her mouth with his, fucking her with his tongue as they both came down from their bliss before resting his forehead on hers, out of breath.

He'd die for her, bleed for her, ache for her. She was his.

He just hoped it would be for longer than this moment.

CHAPTER TWELVE

I t was now a month since her parents had died and she'd been tortured at the hands of the demon, yet Cailin could still hear the screams in her dreams.

Sometimes she was still awake when she heard the screams.

"Cailin?"

She blinked, clearing her thoughts at the sound of Mel's voice. The Jamenson women were scouring through old texts the elders had given them, looking for a way to defeat the demons. The children had all been evacuated from the Pack, along with many of their other Pack members.

The loss of innocence, the lack of laughter and giggles made Cailin want to weep.

She cleared her throat. "Sorry, were you talking to me?"

Mel tilted her head, the Alpha female taking note of all of Cailin's tics. "I was just asking if you were done with the book; you haven't moved past page two. What's wrong, honey?"

Mel was only two years older than Cailin and hadn't spent the majority of her life within the den and living among wolves, but right then, with the power running through her veins, Mel seemed so much wiser.

"I'm just inside my head," Cailin said honestly. "No worries," she lied. "Here, take this one." She handed Mel the book underneath the one she'd been trying to read. "I'll actually work on this one now that I'm awake."

Mel took the book, set it down, and then pulled Cailin into her arms. Mel had been standoffish, afraid of touching others because she hadn't been used to it. Times had changed, and now she was just as tactile and loving as the rest of them—if not more so.

Hannah blew out a breath then fluffed her curls. The woman's hair would not be tamed, not matter how much she tried. Cailin had a feeling it was just one more thing Reed and Josh loved about her.

"So, I need chocolate," their Healer said, closing the book she had with an audible thump.

"Did someone say chocolate?" Ellie asked, closing her book as well. She smiled then, the darkness that had been in her eyes for so long finally fading away to a shadow. Maddox and Charlotte were so good for her.

"I brought molded chocolate, actually," Willow said with a smile. Jasper's mate stood up and went to a basket near the door. "I've been toying with chocolates for the bakery." A sad smile reached her face. "Well, at least I had been. Now with everyone gone..." She shrugged. "It hadn't seemed prudent. But Jasper and I were home alone without Brie and I..." Tears filled her eyes, and she shook her head. "Help me eat this so I don't eat it all on my own."

Bay stood up and helped Willow with the basket. "I could use a handful or four of chocolate. Without Micah at the house, I swear Adam is a nervous wreck."

Lexi raised a brow, taking a piece of chocolate from the basket. "Just Adam?"

Bay blew a raspberry at her. "Okay fine. We're all nervous wrecks. Hence the chocolate."

Cailin took a milk chocolate molded in the shape of a wolf's head and bit down. Flavors burst on her tongue, and she practically had an orgasm right there. "Oh God, Willow. Make these. Please. I'll pay you. Lay prostrate at your feet. Just tell me what you need." She gobbled up the rest of her piece quickly then reached for another.

In a world of war, pain, and loss, sometimes chocolate made things just a little bit better when hope was lost.

Cailin bit into her next piece, this time a paw print, and leaned against the armchair. Bay and Ellie had both taken the seat, cuddling into one another on the large piece of furniture. Willow leaned on Mel's legs from the floor next to the couch while Hannah and Lexi sat next to Mel.

Everyone ate silently, the nirvana that was Willow's chocolate too decadent for words. She'd be a hit when the Pack could reconnect and use the bakery again.

That thought cooled her quickly.

What if they never came back?

"What is it, Cailin?" Ellie asked. "I'm not the Omega, but Maddox told me that you're feeling something way off." She tapped the side of her head and winced. "Sorry for acting like a Peeping Tom, or whatever, but we're all worried. Not just about you, but everyone."

Cailin finished the last of her chocolate, licking her fingers to make sure she got every last morsel. It was, after all, the best chocolate in the history of chocolate. And if she kept thinking about it, she'd be able to ignore the looks and worries of others for a few more moments.

She let out a sigh. Not even chocolate could fix this. "What if they can't come back?"

Willow choked on a sob and shook her head, and the other women—all mothers now—closed their eyes, petting each other. Bay's hand came down on Cailin's shoulder, and both of them let out a breath.

"There has to be a way," Cailin continued. "You know? Absolute evil might be absolute, but that doesn't mean it's unbreakable. It just means it's pure."

"And that's what Caym is," Mel added. "He's tortured us, killed us, and taken so much of what we hold dear. But we're still here. Never forget that. We're not backing down, even if that seems like the best thing to do."

"She's right," Bay added. "Caym might be my father..." She winced, and Ellie rubbed her shoulder. "He might be my father, might have my blood, but he's nothing to me. Nothing. There was a way to get him to this plane. There will be a way to get him out."

Ellie let out a breath. "The Centrals killed my cousin to bring him here, and Caym killed my twin to stay. We know death brings him here."

"Maybe life will send him back," Cailin breathed.

Hannah sat up, a frown on her face. "That would be a balance, a symmetry, that the Fates would like. But how would that work?"

Cailin closed her eyes, willing a magical plan to pop into her brain where everything would become pretty and perfect. So not going to happen. Not in the world she lived in. Not in the world Caym lived in.

"So we need life," Cailin whispered. "Or something like it. Or maybe we're going down the wrong track. I mean there have been births since Caym showed up after all."

Lexi moved so she sat next to Cailin, leaning in. "Maybe not the right birth. It's a track. One we haven't really looked at. Well, Emeline might have, but she hasn't told us yet. That elder is so quiet I never know what she's going to say when she *does* speak."

Bay let out a small laugh. "She's cagey because that's how she's had to live for hundreds of years. She's getting better. And she's honestly working on Caym and North."

Lexi winced. "She's working on the spell that caused North's blindness, but my mate won't let her work too hard. He'd rather take out the demon than get his sight back."

"That's my brother for you," Cailin said.

Lexi gave a sad smile. "Yes. That's my mate. And as for *my* brother, you're making him happy, Cailin. I don't know if I've said that. I love that we're sisters in two bonds."

Cailin leaned into Lexi, her wolf rubbing along her skin, liking the other woman's new wolf. Lexi had been a latent wolf, stuck in her human skin and not able to shift, until recently. Things had changed so much since everyone started mating, and Cailin wouldn't change the outcomes. People had found their other halves, their bonds. They'd had children and found even more to adopt into their families. The good didn't outweigh the bad, not yet. But it was a start.

Mel rolled her shoulders then let out a breath. "Okay, we have more books to look at. The men are all at Jasper and Willow's with more books. I say we work for another hour then head to them. At some point we all need to cuddle." The Alpha female blushed. "Or whatever."

Cailin closed her eyes and groaned. "Please don't tell me any details. It sucks that all my girlfriends are mated to my brothers. The images in my brain right now require more than bleach. Maybe a blow torch."

Lexi giggled. "Just don't talk about *your* mating, and we're golden."

Hannah laughed, her eyes dancing. "You mean you don't want her to talk about Logan's penis?"

Lexi made fake gagging sounds, leaning into Cailin. "Stop it. Please. For the love of the goddess. Stop it."

"It's a nice penis," Cailin said deadpan, and the women broke out into laughter.

"Nice? That's it?" Ellie asked with a smile.

"I'm not listening," Lexi said as she plugged her ears.

"Well, it's nicer than nice. Like oh-my-god-let-me-bow-down-to-you-and-stare-in-utter-amazement nice." Cailin batted her eyelashes at Lexi, who growled.

"I'm a freaking wolf so that means I can *still hear you* when I cover my ears," the other woman mumbled. "Maybe I'll start talking about North's penis."

"Oh God, please don't," Cailin shouted.

"I hear Lexi likes North's penis so much she does *exactly* what she's told," Willow teased.

Lexi blushed then shrugged. "What can I say? North knows exactly what he likes and tells me what to do. It's hot."

Cailin closed her eyes and prayed to the moon goddess for this conversation to end. "I'm sorry I brought it up."

Mel raised a brow. "Brought what *up,* honey?"

The women laughed again, the last of their tension easing away. "Okay, I'm done," Cailin said, finally catching her breath. "Let's get another look at those books." She moved to stand, only to blink, becoming lightheaded. "Whoa."

Hannah was at her side in an instant, her hands hovering over Cailin's body.

"I'm fine," Cailin said, more to herself than the women in the room. "Just got up too fast."

Hannah cupped her face, her eyes full of light. "Maybe, but, honey, that's not all."

"What?" Cailin asked, worry filling her quickly.

"You're pregnant," Hannah said simply.

Cailin blinked. "Uh, say what?" Pregnant? No way. She'd just mated with Logan a month ago. And before that, she hadn't had sex in a year. Or maybe more. When had she and Noah broken up anyway?

"Cailin, look at me," Hannah said.

"What?"

"You're pregnant, honey. You and Logan are going to have a baby."

Cailin swallowed hard then smiled. "A baby?"

Hannah nodded. "Yes, sweetie. Now do you want us to take you to Logan now? I don't think we'll be doing any more research tonight, and your mate is bound to feel something off in the bond if you keep looking so dazed."

"A baby."

The girls took their turns hugging and kissing her, showing how happy they were with the new arrival.

A baby.

She put her hand on her flat stomach and smiled. She was going to be a mom. Logan, a dad. Even surrounded by war, the loss, the pain, they'd made something special.

She needed Logan.

Now.

"I need Logan."

Hannah laughed. "Yes, honey. We know. Go to him. He's right across the bend. Can you make it on your own?"

Cailin nodded then stood up. "I'm good. I'm *really* good." Scared as hell, but she'd worry about that as soon as she told Logan.

A baby.

Goddess, a baby.

****

"Sorry we beat you up."

Logan snorted at Jasper's words and closed the old text. There wasn't anything about a demon or binding spell in there anyway. "We're good. I beat up North when he mated Lexi, so we're even."

North raised a brow, his clouded eyes on Logan even if he couldn't see. "Really? That's how you remember it?"

"Just telling them the truth."

"You're so full of it," North barked with a laugh. "Whatever helps you sleep at night."

North laughed again, and Logan let out a sigh. At least they could all laugh at the little things. Right then, looking at book after book that told them nothing wasn't helping.

Logan sat on the floor, surrounded by books and Jamensons. While he was connected on some levels through his mating with Cailin, he still didn't feel as much a part of them as he should have. Each of them had been through years of connections and were all brothers.

All except for Josh, of course, but the man was one of Reed's mates so he already had his place. Josh had already had his place outside of the mating as well.

Logan, again, felt like the odd man out.

Which made him crazy because he shouldn't have felt that way. He'd been helping protect the Pack with Adam's Enforcer duties and Edward before the attack and his mating of Cailin. He'd already started cementing his role in the den before everything had gone to shit, yet he still felt out of place.

His wolf needed something more, something to counteract the extra magic in his veins due to the moon goddess.

Yet he had no idea what it was and how he was going to fix it.

It might just be something he'd have to get over as time moved on.

At least he had Cailin. She was worth everything.

"What's wrong?" Maddox asked, his eyes as probing as ever. The Omega had done his best not to push when it came to Logan, but sometimes there was only so much a man could do.

Logan understood that, but it didn't mean he wanted to deal with it right then.

Jasper, who sat by Reed and Josh, tilted his head. "You've been off for a while, man. I know it doesn't have to do with Cailin because when you're with her you're the most relaxed we've ever seen you."

"It's true," North added. "I might not be able to see it, but my wolf and I can feel it."

"We've each been through so much shit I'm pretty sure we can help," Adam put in.

Logan wasn't sure the man was even conscious of the fact that he rubbed his prosthetic leg while he said it. Logan couldn't even bear to think about the pain the other man must have been in when Caym had ripped the limb from him. He held back a shudder.

Adam was stronger than most when it came to pain, and Logan respected him for it, but that didn't mean he wanted to talk about his feelings.

Especially when Logan wasn't even sure what his feelings were at the moment. He couldn't put it to words himself, so how was he supposed to explain it to others?

Logan blinked and looked up as Kade got up from his chair and made his way to Logan's side. The Alpha sat down next to him, his shoulders back but heavy, as if the weight of the world rested upon them.

In reality, that was the case.

If the Redwoods lost, they would die, and the demon's focus would move from their den and onto the world at large.

Humans weren't safe.

They never had been.

"You're lost," Kade announced from beside him, his voice low, deceptively casual.

Logan blinked. "Lost?" Was that what he'd been feeling? Yes, but not really. He'd found Cailin, cementing himself to her. He shouldn't have needed anything else.

"Lost," Kade repeated. "You're mated to our sister, yes. You have that bond. But what about everything else? You aren't just Cailin's mate, same as she isn't merely yours. You're both individuals who have purpose. Cailin's found hers by helping Jasper."

Jasper let out a sigh. "I don't know what I would have done without her. Now that the Pack is evacuated, my role is really to help those who remained behind. Meaning us."

"You, though, you don't have a place," Kade said, and Logan winced.

"That's how I used to feel," Reed said. "I'm one of the only ones without a power in my family."

"You're not alone there," North added in. "But we found what we needed to do within the Pack to help out. It soothed us and our wolves within."

"I don't have the power from the moon goddess, but Edward appointed me as one of his enforcers," Josh said softly.

They paused for a moment, remembering the Alpha whose life had been cut short. The father that had been ripped from them far too early.

"That brings up something I need to discuss with all of you," Kade said at last. "Some of the men who were my father's enforcers won't be working for me. They're older than I am, watched me grow from a pup. Even though they will bow down to my wolf to acknowledge my dominance, I can't ask them to bow for the man."

Adam cursed. "You know they will, Kade. They'd put their lives on the line for you. They've done so in the past."

Kade nodded. "That's true. But they're in pain from losing their Alpha as well. I know in my heart and through the bonds that not all of them want to continue. I'm okay with that. I want to bring in new enforcers anyway. Men that are mine. Not just my father's."

"That makes sense, Kade," Maddox added. "It doesn't make you any less of an Alpha to want to make your own circle. It's what's been done in the past, and frankly, what must be done now."

"I'm with you, Kade," Josh said, his tone not letting in any argument. "I fought for your father, I stand by my mates' sides, and I will fight for you."

Kade quirked a grin. "I would expect no less from you, Josh. Plus, you didn't watch me as a pup. I can use that."

Adam rubbed his jaw. "Until you and Mel have more children, or until the goddess moves our powers around, I'm your Enforcer."

Jasper nodded. "Yes. As the Enforcer, you protect the Pack. That won't change. But as enforcers, we need men to protect the Alpha." He grinned. "Not that Kade can't protect himself, but you know us wolves. All claws and teeth. We need the extra."

Kade turned to Logan and narrowed his eyes. "That brings me to you, Logan."

Logan raised a brow. "Me?"

"Yes, you. You're fucking strong. Loyal to those you protect. And you're one hell of a wolf. I could use you as an enforcer. What do you say?"

Something warmed within him, and he nodded before thinking it through. Yes. Yes, *this* was what he'd been missing. A purpose for himself, for his wolf.

"Good," Kade said then cut his palm with a knife he pulled from the sheath. "I vow to be your Alpha. To protect and rule in the goddess's grace."

Logan cut his palm, the stinging gone in an instant under the intensity of his Alpha's gaze. "I vow to protect the Alpha as an enforcer. To protect under your rule in the goddess's grace."

They put their hands together, cut to cut, and another bond snapped into place. Not the same as a mating bond, nor the same as Pack member to Alpha. This one was of pure loyalty, pure dedication.

He was an enforcer.

He had a place.

And it felt fucking amazing.

Logan grinned as Josh did the same with Kade, another small bond sliding into place with the partial demon. Each of the enforcers would have to be in place soon, and Kade would have a job to do in order to find who fit, but Logan knew it would come.

He couldn't wait to tell Cailin.

Speaking of...

The scent of ice, temptation, and roses...and something else he couldn't quiet put his finger on filled his nose, and he was on his feet before he could think.

"What's wrong, princess?" he asked as she flew into his arms. He wrapped his arms around her and tugged her close. He could feel the others surrounding him, but he ignored them, needing Cailin alone.

She pulled back, tears in her eyes. "I...I'm pregnant," she blurted out.

Staggered, Logan took two steps back, Cailin still in his arms. "Pregnant?"

She smiled then. Full-out. Goddess, she'd never looked so beautiful. "We're having a baby."

He smiled back, his wolf howling, practically thrusting his chest out so all others could see how manly and virile they were. Oh yes, like Logan was all alone in making this baby and the fact that this came so soon after their mating would be the shining example of how potent his seed was.

"A baby." He lowered his head, so he could whisper the next part in her ear—though they were wolves and everyone could probably hear it anyway. "You are going to look so fucking gorgeous pregnant. I cannot wait."

Cailin laughed before crushing her mouth to his. He kissed her back. Hard. Eventually the women came into the house, and he felt hands on his back, congratulating him, but they could keep.

Right then he had his mate in his arms, their baby in her womb. That's all that mattered for the moment.

He'd die to protect them. He just hoped it wouldn't come to that.

He had something worth fighting for.

CHAPTER THIRTEEN

I t was so quiet.

Too quiet.

The moon goddess hunt was upon them, and Logan hadn't known it could be this quiet, not during a Redwood Pack hunt. Sure, he'd had quieter when he'd been on the run with Parker and Lexi, but this was different. Back then, until Parker could shift, Logan hunted alone, letting the moon goddess replenish and rejoice in his wolf in all the magical ways possible so he could burn off the excess adrenaline, and then he'd come back to their hideout. Lexi hadn't been able to shift then, and he'd known the hunts always hurt her.

When Parker became old enough to shift, they'd taken slower hunts, teaching the pup how to protect himself in a world that was far too big for a little boy.

Now, though, the quiet seemed to be magnified by the lack of wolves and the lack of something crucial and inherent to the den itself.

It couldn't be one with so much of the Pack missing.

Only the Jamensons and the select few that had remained behind were ready for the hunt. Those were the strongest of the strong—minus the soldiers who had gone with the evacuees to provide protection. All wolves could fight, but not all of them could fight to the death. The submissive wolves should never have to. Hence the reason they'd been evacuated.

Now the remaining wolves were ready for the hunt, ready for the moon goddess to shine upon them and remind them why they were wolves. Remind them what they were fighting for in the first place.

Everyone knew the final battle was coming. They could taste it on their tongues like a potent drug, ready to take its final victim.

Cailin leaned into his side, and he held back a smile. He'd been doing enough of that since the night before when she'd come into his arms, telling him about the baby. He was so freaking happy about it.

And so freaking scared.

Not about being a parent. No, he'd helped raise Parker after all. He'd had some practice, and he knew Cailin had with all of her nephews and nieces. It wasn't about that at all. Sure, he had the normal fears any soon-to-be parent would, but that wasn't all.

They were in the middle of a war he wasn't sure they could win. Not with the resources they had and not when they couldn't find the resources they so desperately needed.

And now he was going to be a father. He and Cailin were bringing an innocent baby into the mix. It took all within him not to package her up and send her away with the other wolves who'd been taken away.

She wouldn't have anything to do with that though. Not that he'd asked her. No, he valued his neck more than that. He couldn't let her out of his sight, not right then. Not with his wolf on edge. In fact, his wolf was so on edge he didn't think that even this moon hunt would help.

The only way to ensure her safety was to be by her side at all times. Much to her annoyance. He couldn't send her away, and even if he could, he'd be forced to go with her or his wolf would never relent.

However, for some reason, his wolf *knew* they had to be here for the final battle. It wasn't that he thought he was important, far from it, but he knew he was part of something far greater than anything he could have ever hoped for.

He was now an enforcer for the Alpha. He'd protect not only Cailin with every fiber of his being, but Kade as well. They were his two main goals, and his wolf prided itself on that.

Logan had a purpose.

He just had to live up to it.

He also had to tell Cailin about the darkness and extra power from the moon goddess. He should have done it ages ago and surely should have before they mated, but he'd been scared. He was dominant enough to admit that. Logan couldn't lose her. Not when he'd just found her in his heart and he in hers.

"Hey? What's wrong?" Cailin asked, tugging his hand.

He squeezed hers back and lowered his head. "I have something to tell you before we start the hunt. Okay?"

She furrowed her brows but nodded. "Okay, big boy," she whispered.

Logan closed his eyes, fighting off the smile. He heard snickering around him, so he had a feeling her brothers had heard.

"What did we say about that nickname?" he grumbled.

His eyes shot open as Cailin pinched his ass. "What?" She laughed. "You still haven't helped me come up with a new name, so I'm going with that. Plus, I wanted to see you smile." She tugged on his arm. "We have a few minutes before we all strip and shift for the hunt, so we can talk over here."

She led him to a group of trees close enough that they could hear if anyone shouted, but far enough away that he could talk with her privately.

"What is it?"

"You know that I'm a stronger wolf than others, right?"

She nodded, a frown on her face. "Of course. I've always known that. Your wolf is closer to the surface than most. But you have great control, Logan. If you're worried about hurting me or something, don't be. I trust you."

He let out a sigh, her words filling him with hope, but he needed to tell her everything before she could truly trust him.

"That's part of it. The other part is...damn it. Okay, remember when Lexi told us she heard the moon goddess when she was fighting Caym?"

Cailin nodded. "Of course. That's why she was able to scar him in the first place. I can't believe the moon goddess actually had the power to help then though."

"That's because Lexi's an Anderson."

She tilted her head. "What? What does that mean?"

Logan licked his lips. "The Andersons are said to have come from the direct line of the first hunter. The hunter the moon goddess made into the wolf to teach him about the souls of others less than him."

Cailin's eyes widened, and she took a step back. "You...you're saying you're of the original line of wolves?" she breathed.

"That's the legend anyway. I'm not sure if that's true, but we've always had extra...gifts in each generation."

"Is that why Lexi was latent? That doesn't make sense."

Logan shook his head. "No, that was a genetic defect. That has nothing to do with the moon goddess. She found her wolf eventually because she had North to help her, as well as the bite of two Alphas." He shuddered at the memory of Edward and Gideon ripping into his sister's flesh so Lexi could find her wolf and live without pain.

"So what does that mean? What gifts?" Cailin rubbed his arm, and he leaned into her touch. Needing her more than she knew.

"Some of us are stronger than other wolves. Others have special powers that I'm not sure of, but I know they're in the legends of my family. As for me? I'm closer to the moon goddess. While Lexi got the light. I got the darkness. I'm stronger than others because my wolf hunts and knows dark to dark. That's how I found North in the forest that one time. That's how I've been able to hide my family for so long. I was able to track when someone out to get us was getting closer. I'm not pure, Cailin. I have control because it was forced upon me at an early age, but I'm not a good wolf."

"Bullshit."

He blinked, meeting her gaze. "Excuse me?"

"Bullshit. You're a good wolf, baby. You're a fucking amazing wolf. You don't use your powers for evil or whatever a comic book villain would say. You protected your family. You've protected your Pack.

And you protect me. So what if you have a wolf closer to the surface? You've only used it to protect those you love. You're an asset. You're not like Corbin and the rest. Stop making yourself feel like less because you're not like others. I love you for who you are, Logan, not what you think you're missing."

He smiled softly then. "You love me?"

His mate blinked, covering her mouth with her hand. "Uh..."

"You said it. You can't take it back."

She lowered her hand, licking her lips. "I was waiting to say it in a more romantic setting. Not in the middle of the forest with my brothers lurking about."

"I love you too, princess. And the fact that you're taking me, all that I am? Makes me love you even more."

He crushed his mouth to hers, collaring her throat in the process. She moaned beneath him, her nails digging into his ass.

"Glad we got that settled, big boy," she whispered when they pulled apart.

"What did I say about that name?"

Her hand brushed against his cock before squeezing. Hard. "What can I say? You're a big boy. Now, if you're done being emo, we need to go hunt. Then you can show me just how much of a big boy you are."

His already hardening cock filled even more, and he cursed. "Do realize how hard it is to shift and hunt with a hard-on?"

She grinned. "Then we better get to it." She cupped his face, her expression becoming serious. "I'm not making light of what you told me. I'm just saying it doesn't matter to me the way you were afraid it would. I'm taking all of you, Logan. You're mine, and I'm not letting you go. If you ever feel that your wolf is becoming too much, then you tell me. Tell your Alpha. That's what a Pack is for. We won't let you falter, the same way you won't let me stumble. We're a team, Logan. Never forget that."

He brushed his lips to hers once more, a weight lifting off his shoulders.

"You two ready to hunt?" Kade called from behind them.

"Ready as ever," Logan whispered.

"We're on our way!" Cailin yelled out then gripped his hand. "Come on, I need to feel the ground beneath four paws, and then, when our wolves are spent, you can fuck me hard into the ground so we remember we're wolves and not human."

He groaned and walked beside her. "Stop turning me on, woman."

She fluttered her eyelashes. "Like I can help it."

He lowered his head and nipped at the fading mate mark. "I'll have to mark you again, princess. Show you who's boss."

She shuddered in his hold. "Fine, but then I get to mark you as well."

"Deal."

"If you're done molesting my sister, we're ready to shift," Kade said dryly.

"Don't tell me you're not going to get all up on Mel when we're done with the hunt, brother mine."

"She's got a point, honey," Mel teased.

Kade closed his eyes, and Logan had a feeling the man was praying for patience. "If we're done..." He rolled his shoulders and opened his eyes, looking every bit the Alpha he'd been groomed to be.

"We're here to hunt as a Pack," the Alpha began. "We're not full yet, we're not complete, but that doesn't mean we're not Pack."

The others, including Logan, howled.

"We will hunt as one. We will live as one. We will fight as one. We are the Redwoods. We do not fail!"

Logan howled louder, Cailin's tone blending into his in perfect harmony. Everyone began to strip, tossing their clothes to the side. It wasn't sexual. It was freeing. It was wolf.

He went down on all fours beside Cailin, letting his wolf come to the surface. It brushed along his skin, ready to come forth. He tugged on the bond he held with his wolf and shifted, bones breaking, tendons snapping. His body altered, his face elongating, fur sprouting.

Soon he stood on four paws rather than kneeling as a human. He threw his head back and howled, the others joining him as they shifted. As it was, he was third in line when it came to shifting, Kade and North the only two faster than him.

Once Cailin shifted into her beautiful pure-white wolf form, he took off, ready to burn off the adrenaline in his veins.

His paws pounded into the ground as he ran beside Kade. The others followed them, their wolves on the prowl. He vaulted over a fallen log, loving the feel of the wind in his fur, the soil between his toes.

This was why he loved being a wolf. The freedom to enjoy the forest in a way humans never could.

Animals scattered around them, and others darted after them. Some needed to hunt in truth that night, but right then, all he needed was to protect his Alpha until it was time to take Cailin off in their own private corner and mark her as his.

Again.

After an hour of running, Kade looked over his shoulder and nodded before turning to nip at Mel's heals. He chased her to a secluded area, no doubt about to mate with her just as Logan was planning on with Cailin.

He turned on his heel, facing Cailin's white form. Goddess, he loved the color of her fur, the feel of her wolf beside his. He rubbed his body along hers, and she stood still. The woman might be his equal, but his wolf powered over hers—something they both loved and craved.

He opened his jaw wide and gently bit her neck, not breaking skin. Her wolf shuddered under his, and he growled softly, needing.

He pulled back then nudged her toward a nearby clearing. She padded away, and he followed, taking in their surroundings and his mate.

Once they were there, they each shifted, leaving two very naked, very sweaty humans in their place.

Cailin bared her neck, and Logan howled, almost coming at the sight.

He growled, and they were on each other in an instant. Teeth, mouths, and bodies, pressing and grinding as if they couldn't get enough of each other.

Honestly, he knew he'd *never* get enough of her. Ever.

He backed her up to the nearest tree, lifted her legs, and thrust into her. They both stilled for a moment, catching their breaths.

"Your cunt is so fucking wet, Cailin."

His mate gripped his shoulders then rocked her hips, taking more of him in. "Of course I am, Logan. You're mine. Now fuck me. Now." She winked. "Please."

"Far be it from me to leave you wanting." He pulled out slowly, her tight pussy gripping him hard, then slid back in. They both panted as he kept pushing deep inside then pulling back out. He gripped her hips hard and pummeled into her, his mate pushing right back, taking and giving as much as he was.

"Damn it," Cailin cursed, "the bark is digging into my back."

He pulled out quickly, took them both to the ground, and got her onto all fours facing away from him in the next instant.

"I'm sorry, princess," he said as he ran his hands up and down her back. They hadn't broken the skin, but there were scratches nonetheless.

"It's okay, just get back inside me, Logan. I need to come." She wiggled her ass so he slapped her cheek. Hard. "Jesus!" she panted, tilting her butt back for more.

"I see we're going to have to have more fun with this in the future," he teased as he gripped his cock, placing it at her entrance.

"Only if I get to spank you too."

Logan paused then nodded, forgetting she couldn't see him. "Anything you want, Cailin. As long as I get to do it to you too." He slid into her wet heat, and they both groaned.

"I like the sound of that," she gasped, her fingers digging into the soil beneath her.

Logan lifted so he was on one knee then thrust into her over and over again, his balls tightening. He didn't want to come, not then. He wanted to see her blush first, feel her clamp around his dick once or twice before he came.

She always made such beautiful little noises when she came.

Cailin arched her back, taking him deeper. Needing more, he lowered himself then picked her up so her back lay against his chest. He angled his dick, rotating his hips upward so he could fuck her and still keep touching her in as many places as possible. With one hand on her hip, he gripped her chin with the other, forcing her gaze over her shoulder.

He took her mouth in a passionate kiss, fucking her with his tongue, mimicking the movement of his dick within her pussy. When he pulled back, they were both out of breath and on the edge.

"Play with your tits then your cunt," he ordered, a low growl that vibrated through both of them. "I want to have you come on my cock, and then you can ride me in the moonlight."

"Dirty, dirty, man. I love it."

He kept his hand on her chin and throat as she pinched her nipples. Each movement made her pussy clench around his dick, and he had to suck in a breath so she could come first. When her hand slid down her belly to roll over her clit, Logan just about lost it.

"Are you wet?" he asked.

"God, Logan. You're inside me, of *course* I'm wet. Please, please, harder. I'm going to come."

He rolled his hips at the same time that she flicked her finger over her clit, and he watched as her eyes darkened.

"Logan." A bare whisper, but so filled with awe and need that he could barely breathe.

She was still coming down from the aftershocks as he pulled out of her and lay on his back. He pulled her on top of him, and she slid down his length, riding him hard. He knew he wouldn't last long like this, but damn, he wanted to see her face, have her be in control as he came inside her.

Cailin arched her back, keeping her gaze on his as she palmed her breasts. He cupped her hands, tangling his fingers with hers as he thrust up one last time, balls rising, coming hard. She slammed down on his dick and smiled, her body slack as she fell on top of him. He ran a hand down her back so he cupped her ass, his fingers spreading her so he could fill her up as much as possible.

"We have to do that again," he whispered, close to falling asleep.

"We will. Don't worry. We will."

He couldn't wait.

CHAPTER FOURTEEN

Cailin paced the floor, tugging at her hair. Frustration colored her thoughts having become a common occurrence in her everyday life. Her family stood in Kade and Mel's living room, books scattered around them, the sense of failure lying heavy in the air.

They'd spent the past four days building up their defenses and strengthening their wards. Two of the Pack members that had stayed behind were witches, mates of wolves in the Pack, and they had done their best to put as much of their energy as they could into the wards. It didn't mean they could keep the demon out—it seemed almost nothing could—but it did mean they could keep out the other Packs and humans.

It wasn't that the Redwoods were afraid other Packs would take advantage, but it was always a possibility. Wolves were secretive creatures, always living in the shadows even when they tried to blend with the humans. Each Pack lived on its own and had its hierarchy and rules. They usually left each other alone—the Centrals being the overwhelming exception to the rule.

The Redwoods couldn't be too careful. Especially with the humans. They had been fighting, killing, and at war with the Centrals for so long, it was sometimes easy to forget that they were also in hiding. The wards protected the wolves as a whole from the watching eyes of the humans.

With the growing surveillance and interest in the supernatural, they were lucky as it was that they hadn't been found out. Cailin didn't want to think about what would happen if their existence was ever made public.

She held back a shudder.

The end of the war was coming; they all felt it deep in their bones. They needed to ensure their secret was safe from the watching eyes of the people who didn't understand, who never could understand.

When her family and the others who had stayed behind, around forty members or so, weren't working on the wards and other defenses with Adam, they were looking for a way to take down a demon.

That was what made her feel useless.

Defeated.

They'd been looking for years.

Years.

Ever since Caym had first shown up on the Central land and had first attacked them along with Hector and Corbin, her family had been looking for a way.

And they'd still come up short.

It didn't make any sense. Somehow, the demon had moved between planes and had come to the human realm, escaping from hell. That meant he could be sent back. There had to be a way. Her family had found other ways to hurt the demon over time, but it had never been enough.

When Hannah, Josh, and Reed bonded, they'd formed the trinity bond, a special bond between the three of them that had held enough power to hinder the demon somewhat. Caym couldn't call forth other demons to the human realm to help him defeat the Redwoods, which thwarted his other plans.

That had been one point in the Redwood's favor, but there hadn't been that much more. Over time, each of her brothers and their mates had defeated one aspect of the Central's regime—Josh killing Hector, North killing Corbin, the others making a mockery of the most gruesome of each of the Central's plans—but now they were at the end of it all.

Cailin had to do *something,* or she wouldn't be able to face herself in the mirror in the morning. Everyone else had been a part of taking down a piece of the Centrals, yet Cailin had always been in the background. She should be fated to help with this.

Only she didn't know what *this* was.

Strong arms wrapped around her middle, stalling her movements, and she stiffened. She didn't want to be comforted right then. She wanted to finish working up to a good mad and then stomp off and find a way to kill a demon. Logan buried his head in her neck and nipped along the mating mark.

Her knees buckled, but he held her up. Only the fact that her brothers and their mates were in the room held her back from moaning.

Logan knew *exactly* what to do to calm her.

The bastard.

"Stop looking like you've done something wrong, princess," Logan whispered, his words so low Cailin wasn't sure her family, even with their keen wolf hearing, would be able to hear them.

Good.

She liked having him to herself even in a room full of people.

Logan's palm rested on her belly, on the baby in her womb, and her wolf melted. He would make such a good father. If only Cailin was sure that they'd all live long enough to see that come to fruition.

"Stop worrying," he barked softly. Only Logan could bark softly at her—a reprimand coated in gentleness.

"I can't help it." She turned in his arms, resting her head on his chest. His arms came around her, caging her into his hold, and she sighed. If only it were this easy to feel better, to ensure that they had a future.

If only...

She'd been thinking that a lot lately.

Tears filled her eyes, and she cursed. "Stupid hormones."

"I think I cried like every hour when I was pregnant with Brie," Willow said from the couch.

Her words reminded Cailin she wasn't alone with her mate, but in a room full of her family and their watching eyes. She pulled back, wiping her face, and lifted her chin.

"I'm fine," she lied.

Logan raised a brow, but let her go. "We're all a bit tired," he excused.

She bit back a retort. She didn't want to fight. Not when he was just trying to help. It didn't matter that it made her feel weak when she couldn't hold herself together. That was her problem, her insecurity.

She'd been doing so much better at it, but clearly not well enough.

Cailin rolled her shoulders, determined to get this demon off her land and back in hell where he belonged. He deserved to roast on the spit of hell's flame for all eternity. To have Caym die in their realm wouldn't be enough for her. That'd be too quick, too easy.

Her wolf growled, liking this side of her.

Good.

After picking up one of the books she'd scoured before, sure she might have missed something, she sat down on the floor. Logan picked up one for himself then took his seat right beside her. The heat radiating off of him steadied not only her wolf but the woman within. From the way his shoulders lowered after his nostrils flared, inhaling her scent, she knew her presence did the same to his wolf.

That's why they were mates.

They calmed each other as equals.

The soft knock at the door brought Cailin's head up, her hackles rising. It seemed she'd always be on edge from here on out. From the stances of the others in the room, she was not alone in that respect. She inhaled, scenting the elder Emeline on the other side, and calmed. Logan ran a hand down her back, soothing her even more.

The man's hands were a work of art and pleasure.

Jasper opened the door as he'd been the closest of them, letting Emeline in. The elder, who looked to be in her twenties though she had to be around five hundred years old, drifted into the room, her eyes wide, slightly...off.

Emeline had lost her mate, no, her potential mate, as the woman hadn't had the chance to fully bond with him, over a hundred years ago. The act would have broken some—it had broken her brother Adam in fact before he'd met Bay—but hadn't broken Emeline fully. Instead, she'd taken refuge within the elder circle, effectively cutting herself off from the others and the world.

She was just now becoming one of theirs again and was putting all of her effort into saving the Pack.

As it was, it had been Emeline who had found the ways to take down the demon and the Centrals in the small ways they had.

And from the way the woman clutched the book in her arms to her chest and the manic way she breathed, Cailin had a feeling she might have something more.

Oh sweet goddess, she prayed that was the case.

"What is it, Emeline?" Kade asked, his voice reflecting his new role as Alpha rather than the brother she'd known. Kade had slowly been shifting toward someone of authority, someone her wolf would protect with her life.

Though the change meant that her father was really gone, she couldn't help but be proud of her brother.

She shook her head. There would be time to reflect over what had happened later. Now she needed to focus on Emeline and what could be something far greater for the Pack.

Emeline blinked at the sound of Kade's voice, bringing her back to the present. Or at least that's what Cailin thought the other woman was doing. The elder was an enigma for sure, but was slowly becoming their friend.

"I think I found something," she said at last, her voice holding that airy quality that reminded Cailin of fairies and memories.

They all started talking at once, the noise almost deafening. Cailin couldn't blame them, as she'd been one of the ones to speak—Logan as well—but she knew this wasn't helping. They just couldn't hold back. Not anymore.

She winced at the sharp sound of Kade's whistle. Everyone quieted, sheepish expressions on their faces.

"Take a seat, Emeline," Kade said. "Tell us what you've found."

"Do you need something to eat? Drink?" Willow asked then glared at Cailin.

Apparently Cailin growled at Willow's interruption.

Oops.

"Like I was saying, Emeline, do you need anything? You look like you haven't slept in far too long, darling. Tell us what we can do for you."

Emeline opened her mouth to speak but stopped as the door opened again. Growls from her family cut off as Noah walked into the living room, a covered plate in one hand, a mug in the other.

"I have food and hot cocoa for Emeline," her ex and now best friend announced as he set it on the coffee table. He then gently pushed Emeline down into a chair by her shoulders and took the book from her hand. She reached for it, but he shook his head.

The sight of this twenty-something wolf and doctor caring for Emeline with such a firm hand made Cailin want to smile.

There might be hope for everyone yet.

"Eat and drink, woman," Noah said softly. "I was on my way to your place with food because I know you don't take care of yourself like you should. I'm your doctor. It's my job to take care of you."

Cailin held back a snort and met Logan's eyes.

Yes, her doctor. Sure. That's why Noah was caring so much.

She'd let her friend have his privacy.

For now.

Emeline narrowed her eyes at the younger wolf. "What I have to say is very important."

Noah nodded. "Then say it while you eat. I made finger foods so you can snack at least. You wouldn't have eaten it if you had to stop and use a fork." He grinned, and Emeline blinked at him.

Interesting.

Noah took the cover off of the plate and gestured. "Eat and talk."

Emeline bit her lip, looking between Cailin's brothers.

"You need to take care of yourself, Emeline," Kade admonished. "I'm sorry for not keeping a better eye on your welfare."

The elder took a bite of a stuffed mushroom and swallowed before she began. "As I was saying when I walked in here, I think I found something. I don't know if it will work, but it's better than anything else we've had in the past."

"What did you find?" Cailin asked, unable to hold herself back.

"I was thinking on what you all told me before. How Caym was brought forth through death, so maybe life would be the one way end him for good."

"Life?" Kade asked. "You want us to create life?"

Cailin froze, Logan doing the same beside her. Her hand slowly went to her belly, to the newly created life resting peacefully in her womb.

The elder met her gaze and nodded, forcing the air out of Cailin's chest.

"No, no." She shook her head, her wolf raging. "I'm not sacrificing my baby. I...I can't." Tears slid down her cheeks. "I can't. Not for the Pack. I'm sorry. No."

Logan growled beside her, his arms going around her side, crushing her to him. "Never."

Her brothers and their mates started talking all at once, their voices rising at each passing moment.

From what she could tell, they were on her side, lashing out at Emeline.

At first, the elder shrank into herself, looking like the Jamensons had collectively kicked a puppy. Then Noah put his hand on her shoulder, and she raised her chin.

"Shut up. All of you."

At the sound of the usually soft-spoken Emeline giving them an order, they all quieted—even their Alpha.

"That is not what I meant. If you would actually let me finish, or in this case *start*, you wouldn't be so quick to judge." She let out a shuddering breath. "To think you'd believe I'd actually so willingly give up an innocent...I don't think I like your opinion of me."

"I know I don't like it," Noah growled, surprising Cailin at his strength.

Kade let out a breath. "We're sorry. We're all a little on edge...and the thought of hurting our sister? Yeah, we handled that badly. Tell us."

Emeline gave the Alpha a small nod. "Cailin and Logan have created new life. As far as I know, they are the only ones having a child of the royal blood." The others nodded, letting her know that they weren't expecting any children in the near future. "It isn't just the fact that you have a baby, Cailin. It's much more than that. You are the sole Redwood Princess. The sole daughter of seven children. Your blood is important. Logan is the sole son of the royal line that dates as far back as the original wolf. He is the Anderson wolf. Parker is as well, but because he hasn't reached majority yet, he is not the wolf in question."

Her brothers looked confused, but they didn't say anything right away. They knew Emeline had a stronger connection to the moon goddess than most and some of the Pack thought the woman could hear the goddess herself. There might be many Andersons out there, but if Emeline spoke of the connection, it was truth.

"I don't understand," Reed put in.

"The Andersons come from the line of the original wolf. They come from a great heritage, even if they don't live up to that station in life now."

Everyone looked toward Lexi and Logan but didn't say anything. They would discuss that later. They had to.

"What of our blood? What does our baby have to do with it?" Logan asked, voicing Cailin's thoughts.

Emeline nodded. "You need to show the demon life. Not death. To send him back to hell, you must create a binding with your blood. An actual blood sacrifice that is something as small as a prick of a finger as we collect the blood together. Very archaic, but very useful. The blood of the dark wolf of the moon goddess and the princess of the strongest of the Pack. Together, your blood sacrifice will open the portal, and the glory and wonder of the life within your womb will send him back to hell."

Emeline let out a breath.

"It's a little more complicated than that, and there's a spell that must be woven. It will take some time and most of my strength, but I can do it. I know I can. But I can't do it alone."

She met Cailin's gaze, and Cailin sucked in a breath.

It seemed her prayers had been answered.

She'd be the one to send the demon back.

Fate had spoken.

Only now, she wasn't sure she had the strength.

****

"It's always been us, hasn't it?" Logan asked later when they were back at their place. The meeting had ended soon after Emeline's announcement. Not much more needed to be said until the idea of what they had to do settled in.

He wasn't sure it would ever be truly settled.

It didn't make any sense to him, but he'd do whatever it took to protect Cailin and their unborn child. He might be the enforcer of the Alpha, but right then, he was a mate first.

Something that brought everything into focus.

"I think so," Cailin whispered then raised her chin. "Can we talk about it in the morning? We're doing everything then anyway. I need...I need tonight just to be about us and not the future or goddess knows what else. Please? I need you, Logan. I need you inside of me."

He couldn't deny her, not even for their own peace of mind.

Logan nodded then cupped her face, brushing his lips against hers. She relaxed against him, giving him control. That alone told him how scared she was.

Slowly, he backed her to the wall, her wolf brushing against his along the bond.

"Mine," he whispered.

"Yours."

He cupped her pussy though her jeans and patted her. "Soft or hard?"

"Both. Everything. Just love me, Logan."

He kissed her softly then undid the button of her jeans, sliding her zipper down so he could reach her better. He took both of her wrists in one hand, pinning them to the wall in a grip she could easily get out of if she wanted to.

She didn't break his hold.

With his other hand, he moved to trace a design on her throat and shoulder, teasing, tempting. She arched her back, and he ran his hand down her front, between her breasts, over her belly.

When his fingers slid under her underwear, she let out a little gasp. He spread her slowly then circled her clit with his middle finger. Her lower lip trembled as he twisted his wrist so he could use the heel of his hand to grind on her clit as he speared her with his fingers. Logan went slow, soft, relearning every curve of her so he'd never forget.

As he picked up the pace, her breathing became shallow, her cheeks going pink.

"Come for me, Cailin. Just to take the edge off. I'll make you feel good, baby. Come for me."

Her head hit the wall softly as she came, her eyelids going half-mast.

When she came down, he pulled back, licking his fingers. Her sweet taste burst on his tongue. He groaned, wanting more, and Cailin groaned with him.

"That was so hot," she whispered.

"You taste like honey, princess."

"I want to see what you taste like," she said as she stripped off her clothes then knelt at his feet.

He pulled his shirt off over his head then spread his fingers through her hair so he could cup her chin, forcing her gaze upward.

"You know what I taste like. Not that I don't want your mouth wrapped around my dick, but I want tonight to be about you."

Cailin went to work on his pants, pulling them down over his ass. He helped her take them off fully then stood naked before her, his cock pressed against her cheek. She wrapped her hand around him and smiled.

"I want you. Tonight will be about us. Not just me. And you know what makes me feel good? What makes me wet? Having you on my tongue and down my throat so I make you all wet with my mouth before you make love to me. That's what I want."

He swallowed hard and pulled on her hair, loving the way she let out a little gasp. Just a little pain, not much, but what they both needed.

"Then show me what you want, Cailin." He gripped the base of his dick with his free hand and lowered his shaft to her lips. "Suck me."

He closed his eyes as she sucked the crown of his cock, using the flat of her tongue to tease him. Goddess, he had to see her on her knees in front of him.

When he opened his eyes, he just about came at the sight of her hollowing her cheeks, sliding back from his dick and letting him go with a pop. He still kept his hand on the base, helping her guide him in, and his other hand tangled in her hair, keeping her hair back so he could see her eyes.

He loved those eyes.

She swallowed him then worked back, licking and teasing as she went down on him. Just as his balls tightened and he knew he was about to come, he tugged on her hair and pulled out of her mouth.

"I want to be in you when I come," he growled.

"Then be in me," she said simply.

He had her in his arms and on the way to the bedroom in the next breath. Licking his lips, he laid her down on the edge of the mattress then knelt before her, putting her legs over his shoulders.

"Logan, I thought you were going to make love to me. Not that your dark head doesn't look amazing between my legs."

He lifted the side of his mouth in a grin. "I *am* making love to you, princess. Before I sink into this gorgeous cunt of yours, I'm going to taste you. I want you on my tongue tonight. That little taste I got from my fingers being tight within your pussy wasn't enough."

It might never be enough.

Logan spread her lips, taking a good look at her. When he lowered his head, Cailin let out a soft moan, her hand going right to his head. He grinned then blew cool air against her. He flicked her clit with his tongue, exciting another moan out of her. When she started to squirm, he sucked, nibbled, and licked up and down her pussy, putting his hands on her butt so he could get even more access. He toyed with her back hole before sucking on her cunt, her juices running down his chin. As soon as he felt her on the precipice of another orgasm, he pulled up, moved her to the center of the bed, and slid inside her.

They both groaned, and he started thrusting slowly, flexing his hips. They clasped hands, their gazes on each other as they slowly made love. They'd had it fast, hard, and heady. Tonight, they just needed each other, just needed to remember *why* they were about to potentially sacrifice everything they had gained.

With one last gentle push of his hips, they both came, their mating bond flaring. Cailin gasped, tears running down her cheeks, and he kissed them away, wanting nothing more than to take her pain, her worry.

"I love you, Cailin Anderson." The mating bond had made her his, just as he was hers. The legalities would be changed later. The actual mating ceremony and even a marriage ceremony performed by the Alpha weren't necessary for each mating. It was something that could be done later—much later in some cases—if the pair wanted it. Logan wasn't even sure Cailin would want one for a long time considering her father wouldn't be performing the ceremony.

"Love you too, Logan Anderson."

Hovering over her as they were still joined, he forced himself to let go of the rage, the worry, the anger over the unknown and what was to come.

He and Cailin would make it work. They'd persevere.

They had to.

CHAPTER FIFTEEN

C ailin blinked at the unknown clearing, trying to settle herself. She wasn't on Redwood land. Wasn't near her den. No, her Pack and family were far away from what they'd known and hovered near the enemy.

Waiting.

The wind brushed through Cailin's hair, and she turned her face up, needing the connection with the forest and everything moon goddess and wolf more than ever before. Brute strength would be needed soon in the coming battle; she could feel it deep inside. First, though, they needed to use cunning and magic so old that not even Emeline had known of it without searching among the tomes.

The crowd gathered on the neutral ground, their enemy in their sights, as if from a long distance. The witches had used the remainder of their wards to protect their small group of fighters from the watching eyes of the Centrals, though they all knew it wouldn't last for long.

Just long enough to do what must be done.

She rolled her shoulders then moved from foot to foot, stretching. She had no idea what would happen after they performed the ritual, but she knew it wouldn't be good. In her worn jeans and tank, she felt ready to fight, even though she knew Logan wanted her to stand on the sidelines.

If any other case, he would have wanted her to fight alongside him, but with her being pregnant, she had a feeling he wanted to wrap her up in cotton and never let the world touch her.

That wouldn't be happening though. Not with her connection to what had to happen next.

Her wolf took the idea of fate relying on her as their due, something that made Cailin feel as though she was part of something greater than herself.

Once she and Logan woke after making love, they'd known it was time to end what had been plaguing them for far too long. Today would be the day they killed Caym.

There was no other option.

Endless battles, torture, tears, and loss culminated in the moment she and Logan would combine their blood as Emeline chanted the words of a long forgotten race of wolves and opened the door to the hells where the fire burned so bright and hot that not even the demon Caym wanted to go back.

Logan came to her side and did not speak, but his thoughts were evident on his face. He wanted to protect her but didn't know if he could.

She went to her tiptoes and cupped her cheek. "We will win." She didn't quite believe it, not yet, but she'd tell him that until they both could say the words and know them as truths.

Logan leaned into her touch and closed his eyes. "I won't risk you, Cailin," he growled.

"As I won't risk you. That's why we'll be together. We're not alone either, Logan. Look around. We're gathered for a battle, and we're not backing down. No matter what."

Her mate looked up and then over her shoulder. She followed his gaze and took in the sight of what would happen only once—what had never happened before.

Forty of the strongest Redwood Pack wolves alongside twenty of the strongest Talons.

It seemed the final battle in this war was on the horizon.

They would put all of their blood and lives into this to send Caym back to hell. That was the only outcome they could accept. The only outcome they could live with.

They'd fought the demon and his wolves before and had lost only because of Caym himself. This time, though, they had the magic they had long since searched for. They could break through the dark wards. They could defeat the demon.

That was, of course, if the magic actually worked.

Cailin swallowed hard.

The magic *had* to work.

Their plan was simple.

Use the magic Emeline had found and do the bloodletting of Cailin and Logan. That would start the process that would open the portal to hell. Emeline was sure that the magic would not only open the portal but also alert the demons of Caym's presence.

Cailin just prayed that the other demons stayed on their line between the realms.

They *really* didn't need more demons on their lands.

Then, when the wards were down due to Caym's attack, they would be able to fight.

"Are you sure this is going to work?" Gideon, the Talon Alpha, asked Kade for the third time.

Her brother closed his eyes, and she knew he was begging for patience. It wasn't that Gideon was annoying or even non-trusting. It was that the man was asking the same question they were all thinking.

Everything rode on this spell, and they'd never used it before.

Talk about pressure.

"We're here, Gideon," Ryder, Gideon's brother and Heir to the Talon Pack, said. "That alone means we're trusting them. Let's just get on with it."

It had surprised Cailin that so many of the Talons had come to fight. Not only had the Alpha and Heir come, but Gideon had brought one of his other brothers, Walker, who was also the Healer, and one of the Brentwood cousins, Mitchell, the Beta of the Pack. That made four high-ranking and powerful wolves ready to fight with the Redwoods.

They had promised before they'd be on the Redwood's side, Gideon and Mitchell even fighting alongside them before, but this show of force solidified something much deeper within the Packs.

She'd never known of two Packs to work so closely before. Wolves were so secretive, so reclusive, she wasn't sure this had ever happened.

Grateful didn't even begin to cover her feelings.

The Talons had brought their enforcers and other members of the Pack to help fight if Caym decided to push the battle closer. The other members of the Talons and their hierarchy had been forced or elected to stay behind and protect their Pack.

It made sense, as the Redwoods had done the same, even going so far as to evacuate to their hidden sanctuaries.

On the outside, everything seemed as though it was spiraling out of control, but Cailin knew differently. All paths and trials had been coming to this point, this time in space and existence. The final battle was here. She just knew it.

They would either win and defeat the demon or die trying.

There would be no in-between.

They had long since passed that barrier, that option.

"What is our next step?" Gideon asked Kade, letting his earlier question pass after Ryder's comment.

Cailin gripped Logan's hand, needing an anchor.

Kade met her eyes, searching, and she gave him a nod. She was ready. As ready as she'd ever be.

"Logan and Cailin will perform the ritual with Emeline. We will move and station our wolves around the wards and will fight when the time comes. Caym was so worried about Cailin and Logan before that we believe they need to be the ones to kill him. That doesn't mean we will let them go at the demon on their own." Kade met Gideon's gaze. "I want us both near them at all times. Two Alphas against the Central Alpha. Caym might have let most of his stronger wolves die during our war, but I wouldn't believe that is all he has. He's incredibly cunning. We will all need to be on our guard. I don't know what's up his sleeve, but together we can kill the Centrals that get in our way. With our magic against his, we should be able to finally send Caym back to where he came from."

The others around them, her family, her Pack, the Talons, murmured in agreement, the tension and anticipation in the air so thick she could taste it.

"Send him back to hell?" Walker, the Talon Healer, asked, his head tilted. "Is that your desire? Not to kill him, but to send him away?"

Emeline, the sole elder in their presence, moved to stand beside Kade. There was a power about her today that Cailin hadn't seen before. Almost as if the moon goddess herself surrounded the elder.

Interesting.

"We can try for both," Emeline answered once Kade gave her a nod. "While sending his corpse back to the hell realm so no part of him remains with us, we might only be able to lock him back within the demons. We don't know, but that doesn't mean we aren't going to try to make him pay for every sin, every death, every pain."

Cailin raised her head and howled at her elder's words, the others joining her. The Talons howled as well, their harmony sweet, poignant.

"We'll stand beside you," Gideon promised.

"As we will you," Kade vowed.

The Alphas shook hands, and a sense of power washed over her, tickling her skin, shocking down her back.

Emeline came to stand before Logan and Cailin. "Are you ready?"

Cailin looked to Logan, searching his gaze for any sense of worry. Her mate merely nodded then lowered his head, brushing his lips to hers.

"Together, Cailin. Always."

She nodded as well then followed Emeline to a stone bowl that someone, most likely Noah or Hannah, had set up on a pillar.

"Go to your positions," Adam called out, a sense of urgency in his tone.

This was it. All of it. Everything had come to this.

"We don't know how long this will take or what Caym will plan," Kade added. "Stay safe and stand beside your partner. We will not fail. We are Redwoods!"

"And we are Talons, allies, friends, fighters," Gideon called out.

Howls went up, and then they dispersed. She watched her family leave to take their places, mates with mates, friends with friends. Cailin swallowed the ball of emotion in her throat, promising herself that this would not be the last time she'd see them.

They would *not* lose.

They'd already lost too much.

Kade and Mel stood on one side of the pillar while Gideon and Mitchell stood on the other, surrounding Emeline, Noah, Cailin and Logan. Cailin had a feeling that only Emeline didn't know why Noah was there beyond his abilities as a doctor, but that was a problem for another time.

They'd deal with it all in the future because there would *be* a future to deal with.

Logan squeezed her fingers then placed their clasped hands over her belly. "For her or him. I'm not letting you go without a fight, princess. I love you too much for that."

Cailin blinked back tears but raised her chin, ready to take back her life from the depths of despair and loss.

"For her or him, Logan. I love you too."

Emeline looked between them, the sense of loss so potent within her eyes Cailin had to hold back a sob. The elder had lost even more than Cailin had over her life, but here she was, ready to fight. Cailin would do the same.

"I'm going to cut your palms and then bind your hands together with rope," the elder began. Emeline took a deep breath then licked her lips. "The spell calls for a binding of strength and memory." She held out a fraying piece of rope, so worn and used Cailin knew that this must have been something precious to the bearer. "This was the rope that held together my letters from my mate. I kept every single one he ever wrote to me before he died. We will use this to hold the two of you together in peace, ritual, and sacrifice."

Pain marred Emeline's features, and Noah put a hand on her hip, steadying her. The woman's eyes widened at the touch, and then she nodded, leaning into Noah's hold.

"Ready?" Emeline breathed.

"Yes," Cailin and Logan answered at the same time. "Always."

"Once I make the cut, the spell should work. Expect Caym to retaliate because we are cutting off his powers in some way in order to do this. I'll be chanting, weaving the spell, so I won't be of much use once I begin."

"I'll protect you," Noah vowed. "Keep your mind on the spell and what you need to do. I'll take care of the rest."

Emeline nodded, not turning to meet Noah's gaze, and Cailin was grateful for that. She wasn't sure she could handle the new emotions from either of the two people in front of her along with everything raging inside her own body.

"Hold out your hands," Emeline ordered.

With one last look at Logan, Cailin held out her palm, wincing as Emeline worked the blade with two quick, efficient strokes.

"Palms together," the elder ordered then began to chant in a language Cailin couldn't understand but knew it held power and meaning.

She started to become lightheaded, a warm sensation floating through her as Emeline bound their hands, the blood from her and her mate filling the small stone bowl.

All at once, it felt as if a hot poker sliced against her ribs, her lungs. She called out, not able to hold back. Logan yelled with her, something weighty, substantial slamming into her from the inside out.

Cailin met Logan's gaze as the demon screamed.

The fact that they could hear Caym not only in their heads but from the den itself didn't surprise her.

Not anymore.

Caym knew.

The mountain that the Centrals resided near roared.

Then all went black.

****

Logan woke to screaming, his nostrils burning from smoke. He tried to open his eyes, only to close them right away because of the blinding light. His head throbbed, the staccato drumming on his eardrums making him want to vomit.

He took a deep breath then cracked open his eyes, letting the light in slowly. As soon as he could keep his eyes open without the feeling of a hammer on his temples, he rolled over, reaching for Cailin.

"Cailin," he croaked out, his throat filled with what had to be dirt or ground rocks.

He pulled on his hand, wondering what was caught on it and cursed.

Fuck.

Cailin.

They were bound together with that damn rope. He blinked, getting the dirt out of his eyes, then looked down at his mate, unconscious, bleeding, and bound to him.

"Baby, wake up," he pleaded, his wolf on alert.

Whatever magic they had done, it had taken down the fucking mountain.

He couldn't sense any enemies around him, but he knew he was slower than normal from whatever had knocked him out. He needed to take care of Cailin then find his Alpha.

Then they could figure out their next step.

He had no idea if the magic worked and if this was the expected outcome.

Although he would have thought Emeline would have mentioned the explosion part if she'd known.

Logan leaned over his mate, brushing the hair from her face. He got a good look at the wound on her hairline and let out a breath. It didn't look deep, not at all. Head wounds just bled a whole hell of a lot.

He could hear others around him, moving, calling out, and from their scents, he knew they were Pack, not Central, but he needed to get Cailin up and safe.

With a growl, he let his claws out on his free hand and tore through the binding. He hoped he didn't fuck up the spell, but damn it, he needed both hands to protect his mate. As soon as he was free, he framed her face then went down her body with his hands, checking for wounds. Other than a few cuts and bruises, she didn't appear to have any broken bones.

Thank the moon goddess.

Her eyes fluttered, and he let out a breath. "Open those green eyes for me, princess. There you go. Wake up, Cailin."

"Logan?" She coughed, and he cupped her cheek, helping her turn so she could find her breath.

"I'm here. We've got to get up. Can you move?"

She nodded then winced. "Other than the headache, I'm okay." She let out a breath. "You heard him in your head, too, didn't you?"

He sighed. "Yes. Damn it. It didn't make the portal show up, nor did Caym go away it seemed. He knows we did something. What we did is anyone's guess."

"Help me up."

Once they were both standing, he crushed her body to his, needing to make sure she was real. He inhaled her scent, calming his wolf somewhat, but not fully. He needed the rage, the extra power that his wolf held, in order to defeat what was coming.

They all knew it.

"Cailin!"

They turned at the sound of Kade's voice then moved toward him and his mate. The Alpha looked like he'd seen better days, but he and Mel were in one piece.

"Did you find everyone?" Cailin asked, worry in her tone.

Logan gripped her hand, trying to steady her. His mate was strong, so strong that sometimes others forgot she could break. He wouldn't let that happen though. Not while he had breath in his lungs.

"Working on it," Kade said. "Find the others then get to Emeline. We need to figure out what the fuck happened."

Logan nodded then took Cailin's hand, leading her away.

"We need to find them," she whispered.

"We will," he promised.

He heard someone call out then ran to them, pulling Cailin with him. As soon as they reached the rock that had pinned Reed to the ground, Cailin was already pushing at the damn thing.

Hannah and Josh were there as well, using their strength—which wasn't much in Hannah's case—to push as well.

"I'd use my magic to move it, but I don't have enough control not to hurt Reed at the same time," Hannah said. She looked on the verge of tears, but was holding them back. Probably not to scare her mate.

Reed grinned from the ground, even though it looked more like a grimace. "Don't worry, darling. Josh is all He-Man right now, and we have Logan and Cailin too. I'll be out in a jiffy."

"Then I'll Heal you."

"Then you'll Heal me."

Josh gave Logan a look that said it all. If they didn't move the boulder soon, Reed would end up like Adam and lose his leg.

Damn it.

They stood on one side and pressed their hands on the rock, bracing themselves. "On the count of three," Logan said. "One...two...three!"

They pushed, shoved, and growled, using every ounce of their werewolf and demonic strength to push the bounder off of Reed.

Reed grunted, clearly holding back a scream.

Just when Logan was sure they wouldn't be able to move it, the boulder shifted, and Reed was able to pull himself out. Hannah was on her knees immediately, her hands over Reed's broken leg.

"Just Heal the bone, baby," Reed said through clenched teeth. "Save your strength for others. I have a feeling we're going to need it."

"Pull through the bond if you need more energy," Josh put in.

The Healer nodded, hard at work.

"We're going to find others. Meet you at the center with Kade," Logan said, meeting Josh's eyes.

"Deal," the other man said.

Luckily, the others were either all unharmed or relatively so. They gathered back at the center area where they'd performed the magic.

Emeline leaned heavily on Noah, her body looking as though she'd used more magic than she should have. Her hair stuck to her pale, damp face and her limps shook, though she looked like she was trying to appear brave and well. Whole.

"What the fuck happened?" Logan snapped, ignoring Cailin's pull on his arm.

"The wards are down," Emeline whispered weakly. "The demon knows we're here and we're up to something. That explosion was the final dark magic snapping."

"He's on his way then," Kade said grimly.

"And he's pissed."

Logan turned at Cailin's words and followed her gaze.

Wolves. So many wolves.

All of them in wolf form, their stronger forms, but that meant they wouldn't be able to move like a human and take on more than one at a time.

All of them looking as if someone had pushed adrenaline into their system.

They moved as a unit toward the Redwoods and the Talons with Caym prowling behind them.

The battle was on.

Logan just prayed the spell had worked somewhat, even if they hadn't transported him away, and they could kill Caym.

If not, all would be lost.

CHAPTER SIXTEEN

Cailin sucked in a breath as Caym held up his hands. Each Central wolf stopped where they were, their chests heaving. The Centrals froze without even *seeing* Caym move.

Shit.

"You've surprised me, Redwoods," Caym called out, his voice rising.

The demon's usual chiseled features and cool demeanor seemed to show wear and tear with the slight lines on the corner of his eyes and mouth. His hair moved in the wind, rather than being plastered to his head in that iced way he'd used to have it. Caym was on edge. That had to mean something was working, that the spell had done its job. She just prayed they could kill him or at least have the portal that should have opened pull him back in. All Cailin knew was that they'd hurt Caym. That was more than anything they'd done before.

And from the haggard way he looked now, they'd weakened him either through the spell, through his use of power to get here so quickly with his hyped-up wolves, or a combination of both. According to

Maddox and Ellie, Caym had looked weakened only once before, when he'd used all his power to bring back Corbin. Corbin, apparently, had to have died at the proper time for the demon. Then again, when they were fighting in the Redwood Pack circle, Lexi had scarred the demon with her claws.

Each battle might not have been huge in their eyes when it came to victory, but there were seven Jamenson siblings and only one demon.

They were wearing on him.

They had to be.

"Surprises don't matter in the end, however," Caym continued. "You might have taken down the wards, but you'll never be able to take me. I'm stronger than all of you. I've cut you, burned you, taken your children. I've killed the Alpha and his mate. I've made you bleed, made you scream, I've taken your hope. You have nothing. While I...I have everything." He held out his arms, that sinister smile on his face. "What do you have to fight for, Redwoods?"

"Everything," Cailin whispered.

Caym's gaze went straight to hers, and she raised her chin. Logan growled softly beside her, and she knew it took everything within her mate not to step in front of her, blocking her from the demon's focus.

"Ah, yes, the little princess and her pet," Caym sneered. "It's too bad you and your little wolf made it through the flood. The forest around the new lake didn't fare so well. Neither did the twelve humans who died in its wake."

Cailin's heart lurched in her chest, her eyes widening. She felt Logan's confusion over the bond but didn't dare remove her gaze from Caym.

Humans had died? Why hadn't they known about it?

"I see you didn't know, *princess*," Caym said on a laugh. "Stupid weak humans. Once I finish with you and the Talons that are hiding behind you with their tails tucked between their legs, I'll be taking care of the humans next. Nothing can stop me, Redwoods. Nothing will. I'm the powerful one here, and the era of the wolves is over. You'll bow before me, beg before me, and die before me."

"We took down your wards. We'll take down you as well," Cailin called back.

Caym lifted a lip and snarled. "A party trick. As for real magic? Look at the wolves in front of you. They're infused with my own power. They're stronger than you, faster than you, and will die for me, but not before you do. That, my dear princess, is real magic."

Cailin sucked in a breath, a quick burst of sadness washing over her at the thought of the poor wolves that had sold their souls for more power. No, that wasn't quite right. Not everyone had asked to be part of what the Central's Alpha had done. Some were innocents. Innocents with no hope now that their blood mixed with whatever the demon had done.

They had been a lost cause before. Now the danger in front of them looked insurmountable.

Logan leaned into her, his gaze on the scene in front of them. "If he's used so much of his power for those wolves, he might have hurt himself in the process," he whispered.

She nodded, agreeing with him. "He looks it, Logan. We're going to win this. We *have* to."

"He's going for broke here, and he made a mistake," Kade whispered on the other side of her. "We're going to take on the wolves like we'd planned. Mel and I will be with you and Logan as you go for Caym. Gideon and Mitchell as well. We can do this."

"I think the mistake in our past encounters, Redwoods, was that I went too easy on all of you," Caym taunted. "That won't be happening today. Attack!"

The wolves moved then, fangs bared, hackles raised. They came as one, their bodies moving at a rapid pace, their muscles straining at the excess energy pounding through their bodies. The sound was deafening. Howls, growls, and the pads of paws on the earth.

They were coming.

"Do as we planned!" Kade yelled, his claws out, ready to fight. "We're stronger. We're Redwoods. Take down the demon, win the war!"

The wolves howled, and Kade gave Mel one last hard kiss before they all went to their positions. The Redwoods growled, claws bared, ready to fight. Their muscles bunched with their own strength, not straining from the overabundance of magic like the Centrals were with Caym's energy running through them. Logan kissed Cailin hard as well, giving her a wink, then started toward Caym. She let her wolf come to the surface, her claws out, ready to fight.

She'd stay in human form, much like the rest of her family, so they could get closer to the demon. If they took the time to shift to wolves and back, they'd end up on the wrong side of a claw. Plus they fought in human forms with their claws partially shifted usually. It gave them a better chance at moving faster and a greater range of motion. Like their previous battles, the stronger wolves within the Redwood Pack were fighting that day. That meant each of them could partially shift. All of her family and dominants had been teaching the others the skill over time in preparation for this moment.

Walker and Ryder were the first to make it to the Centrals. They jumped as a unit, pouncing on those of the enemy directly in front of them. Four of the wolves in question attacked back, their teeth tearing into skin, growling and snapping their jaws. Walker punched one in the throat while Ryder broke another's neck. Together, the Talon pair killed the others, moving onto another set of wolves. They both ended up bloody and breathing heavily, but they hadn't lost.

These wolves seemed stronger than anything Cailin had ever faced, but that didn't mean she'd give up.

A wolf jumped out from behind a bush, teeth ready to clamp down on her arm. She ducked, rolled, and then turned back, knowing Logan would protect her instinctively. The wolf had turned back on a dime, ready to kill. Cailin growled back, then raked her claws down its side. She could feel Logan behind her, hear him fighting another wolf. The wolf in front of her twisted so he could bite again, but she moved out of the way quickly, Logan doing the same. Tired of fighting this wolf when she needed to get to Caym as quick as possible, she ducked, pushing her claws, hands, and arm through the wolf's side.

It whined, and she bit back a curse. No matter how evil the magic running through her enemy was at this point, she didn't want it to be in pain. Not when this was all Caym's, Corbin's, and Hector's doing.

She quickly ended its life by piercing its heart, then pulled her blood-soaked hand back. With a sigh, she turned back to Logan who had just finished snapping the neck of his opponent.

Two down. So many more to go.

Logan gave her a nod after doing a quick check over her body. She didn't blame him because she'd done the same, checking for wounds he might have missed with the excess adrenaline running through his veins.

Willow and Jasper fought another set of wolves around thirty feet from them. It was six on two, and despite the fact that Willow hadn't been born within the den and had only just learned to fight, the odds were still in the Redwoods' favor.

A wolf pounced on Willow, knocking her to the ground. Cailin pivoted on her leg, trying to make it to Willow's side in time to help, but Jasper was faster.

Actually, *Willow* was faster.

Her sister-in-law rolled out from under the wolf in one swift move, jumped on its back and snapped its neck before Cailin could blink.

Damn.

Jasper disposed of two more wolves, then wrestled another, Willow helping at his side.

Another wolf bared its teeth in front of Cailin and she ducked as it tried to jump on top of her. She rolled forward then turned back on one foot, kicking out. Her foot connected with the wolf's flank and it went to the ground. She snapped its neck before it could bite her.

Cailin looked over her shoulder as Adam shouted out. Adam and Bay were on the other side of Willow and Jasper, fighting as a unit. Even though Adam only had one leg, no one would have been able to tell from the way he was fighting. Wolves jumped on him and Bay, but the Centrals weren't as strong as Cailin's family. Not when her family was fighting the way they were.

Or maybe they were, but her family was fighting with a spirit more resilient than anything else they could face. With that and the luck of the moon goddess, the Redwoods could win.

It could really happen this time.

Reed, Healed from his bout with the boulder, fought another set of wolves alongside Josh. They circled Hannah who wasn't as skilled in hand-to-hand combat. Josh had at least six blades and guns strapped to him since he, too, couldn't shift his hands into wolf claws. Hannah disposed of each wolf that tried to get near her mates when their attention was on another wolf by lifting the ground the opponent stood on and flinging them away. Sometimes the witch would bury the wolf if she got the right angle.

One did not mess with a Redwood witch.

Maddox and Ellie were on the other side of Cailin and Logan, her sister-in-law looking as determined as she'd ever seen her. This Pack had once been her people, her *family*. Then they'd turned on her. Though, in all reality, they'd turned on her long ago, being too weak to protect her from the taint and evil within.

The mated pair, their moves so in sync Cailin knew they were talking to one another through their unique mating bond, killed and took down the wolves quickly with efficient strokes.

Even with the Talons helping, the Redwoods were outnumbered four to one since Caym seemed to be using the last of his Pack to win this battle. Each Central wolf was stronger than they had been before, but they weren't fighting as a team, rather, they fought with the vicious intent of death at all costs. They were just cannon fodder in the scheme of things, even if they were stronger than that.

North and Lexi were off to the side, Lexi in front of North, directing her mate where to go. It physically hurt Cailin to watch her brother fight because she knew that, despite his heightened werewolf senses, he was still blind in a battle that could take him out instantly. However, he and Lexi had taken that into account. Lexi would fight and take down the wolf initially, letting North end its life as soon as Lexi yelled out orders. If he'd been fighting with anyone else, Cailin wasn't sure he'd be able to do it, but he did.

And did it damn well.

She and Logan took down two more wolves, their chests heaving, sweat slicking their bodies.

"Damn it, we're not even close to Caym," she called out.

Logan reached around, squeezing her hip. "We're closer than we were before. Have faith. We're getting there. And with the two Alphas pummeling their way through the crowd, we're going to be there before you know it."

"Such optimism."

He cracked a grin, though she knew it was forced. "Anything for you, princess. Now duck."

She did so quickly, and he took care of a Central that tried to pounce on her. She was getting too damn tired for this, and she couldn't afford to be sloppy.

"Thanks, big boy."

"Love you too, muffin."

She snorted, using the humor when she wasn't sure she if she could find it in herself to move a few more yards, taking down another wolf.

Mel and Kade fought ahead of them, their skills even sharper than they had been just a few weeks ago when they'd battled as a pair. The bond that came from being Alpha helped them, but it was the inner strength of who'd they'd been beforehand that made them who they were now.

Gideon and Mitchell clawed their way toward Caym as well, the Talon's fierce battlemates. Cailin was glad they were on the Redwoods' side.

Cailin and Logan killed countless other wolves, each slice, each rake of claws digging that much deeper into her heart. She was weary, heavy with the guilt of what they were doing, even if it was for the greater good. If there had been any other way to go about this, she knew her brothers and her Pack would have done so. The Centrals, though, had left them with no choice.

Logan broke the neck of one more wolf then froze, forcing Cailin to do the same.

Caym stood in front of them, the cuffs of his pants bloody, weary, but a fucking smile on his face.

"I see you've come to me," the demon drawled. "Good."

He held out his hands, magic sparking from his palms.

Fuck.

****

Logan threw himself over Cailin as the first scent of magic flittered into the air. His wolf pounded against his skin, wanting to gut whoever had dared try to hurt their mate. He let his wolf come forward, this time not pushing back the darkness. His wolf growled, strong, ready to defeat anything in their path.

Instead of the normal adrenaline coursing through his system, and the pain and agony that came from fighting it, a sense of peace washed over him. He looked through his wolf's eyes, though he was still in human form, and knew that whatever came, he would be ready.

He would be with his wolf and not fight it.

The more he fought, the worse it would be.

He'd already accepted it.

Just as Cailin had accepted him.

He braced himself over his mate, prepared to take whatever Caym lashed out...only nothing came.

He looked down at Cailin, who glared up at him.

"You need to protect yourself as well," she whispered.

He kissed her nose then looked over his shoulder.

Caym had both hands in front of him, his gaze on his palms and not the battle raging around him.

Logan quickly sprang up to his feet, pulling Cailin with him. "Lost something?" Logan growled.

Caym's head shot up, and he glared. "What the fuck did you do?"

Holy shit. It might have worked. They hadn't taken all the magic from the demon. Logan could still smell it, the burnt amber and sense of something far greater than himself, and from the sparks coming from Caym's palms, there was still something left.

But they'd taken out some of it.

"You're nothing without your powers," Logan said, careful to keep Cailin behind him, if only somewhat. There was no way he'd be able to hold back his mate fully. He had a feeling the only reason she even let him move her somewhat was because of the baby growing in her womb.

"But I'm not out yet." Caym screamed, the air around them seeming to lose oxygen.

Logan pulled Cailin to his side as the wolves dropped to the ground around them. A force field—or some kind of ward—pushed Logan and Cailin back a few feet, and they staggered to remain upright.

Caym twisted and bent at odd angles, but not breaking as magic and energy swirled around him, entering his body in swift strokes. From the way Caym screamed, Logan hoped it felt like sharp knives cutting into his flesh one by one.

Sharp knives the demon seemed to enjoy. To relish.

"He's pulling the power from them!" Emeline yelled as she ran to their side, Noah on her tail. The other man looked worse for wear, but Emeline didn't have a new scratch on her. Good for him.

The other Redwoods and Talons came to their side, trying to push through the ward, but it was no use.

Caym had killed his own wolves to regain his power and hadn't thought twice about it.

The Redwoods would have to wait until he brought down his own wards to kill him and then be faster than the demon himself. He looked over his shoulder and counted wolves, his breath leaving him for a moment in relief.

They hadn't lost a single one.

All of the Redwoods and Talons were accounted for and ready to fight.

One demon against an army.

They would win.

They had to.

Caym screamed again, this time flinging everyone to the ground. Everyone, that was, except Josh and Bay—the only two who shared his blood. They both fought to remain on their feet then charged at Caym.

Bay and Adam attacked, using their blades and claws. Caym laughed then went wide-eyed as Josh's blade sank into his belly. The wards were down around the demon, at least somewhat.

Yes!

Logan pulled Cailin to her feet, and he covered her belly, making sure baby Anderson was still there, then ran toward their target. Caym, bleeding and obviously in pain, swung out, knocking Bay in the face. Adam roared behind Cailin and ran to his mate, trusting the others to take care of the demon.

"Cailin! Logan! I need you," Emeline called out, and Logan stopped, turning toward the elder.

"What is it?" he asked, eager to take care of Caym once and for all.

"We won't be able to kill him, not like this. He'll just come back. He's that strong. We're going to have to open that portal and send him back to hell."

Logan cursed. "We tried that, remember? It didn't work."

Emeline shook her head. "No, we tried part of it. Remember the next part? Proof of life. The others will take Caym down, you and Logan must bind your blood one more time, but Caym *must* know you're pregnant. Then it will work. The moon goddess says so."

Logan narrowed his eyes. "The moon goddess is talking to you now?"

A faraway look came over the elder's eyes once more. "I hear things on the wind. I've always done so, but this time, when Caym screamed and killed his flock, I heard her. Please trust me. I want him gone as much as you do."

"Come on," Cailin yelled over the roars and growls of her people. "Emeline is right. We don't have much time. No matter what we do to the demon he just keeps coming back; we have to try everything."

Logan met her gaze, clasping her hand. "I'm not going to lose you. Not now. Not ever. You got me, princess?"

She nodded, licking her lips. She squeezed his hand back, and he tried to ignore the screams and growls around them.

Caym fought the others. His attention elsewhere, not on Logan and Cailin. He bled, shouted, and almost died. But it wouldn't be enough. It would never be enough without this next step.

Caym just would not die.

No matter what they did.

They'd killed all the wolves with Caym's help.

They'd killed the other Centrals' Alphas.

But it wasn't enough.

Not with Caym alone, powerful, and refusing to give up.

They'd have to fight fire with fire. Use magic that didn't have an outcome set in stone. The moon goddess might have said it would have worked, but Logan wasn't sure he had the faith that was required to believe. Not anymore.

If they couldn't kill the demon, then having him in an eternity of hell would have to do.

Kade called out in pain as Caym shocked Mel with magic, throwing her to the ground. Adam stabbed the demon through the heart, but then was flung to the ground as Caym healed right before Cailin's eyes. He'd taken the life forces of countless wolves to do what he was doing now, and there didn't seem to be an end in sight.

Each Redwood and Talon took their turn wounding Caym, but it wasn't enough. Caym fought back, but he wasn't as strong now as he once was. The others bled from their wounds inflicted by the demon, and Logan knew if he and Cailin didn't do this now, it would be too late.

"Josh! I need a blade," Logan called out.

Josh, bloody, bruised, and fading fast, threw one to them, not even looking. Logan caught it at the hilt and grinned.

"That man is crazy, but a hell of a good shot," Logan said, trying to make her laugh. She wouldn't laugh though. Not when her family was dying because they weren't strong enough. He knew that, but he tried anyway.

Logan sliced across his palm then did the same to her. He held back the wince at the pain on her face then slammed his hand to hers.

"This is for Mom and Dad," she whispered, and Logan cupped her face with his free hand. "Oh, Caym!" she called out, facing Logan, never letting her gaze leave his.

"Yes, princess?" the bastard called out even as he fought off what sounded like Maddox and Ellie.

"You're death, the epitome of everything we've feared. Yet you couldn't stop life."

Caym growled as Emeline began to chant again. Unlike last time, the magic swirled around them, blowing her hair into almost a vortex of energy and electricity.

"You couldn't stop us," Logan yelled over the roaring wind. "We're having a baby. That's life. You're nothing, Caym. Nothing."

Logan kissed his mate then, hard, their hands still clasped as the magic around them burst forth. Spirals of color and light shot around them, the vortex similar to the one that had taken the two of them to the demon before, now rushed around them, cementing them to each other. She kissed him back, and he relished in her taste, her *life*, as things exploded around them in shards of magic, pain, and shouts.

When he ripped his mouth from hers, he turned to face where Caym stood, his body shaking, blood pouring from the numerous wounds her family had inflicted.

The Pack gathered around him and Cailin, keeping away from Caym. There was something coming for him, and they all knew it, could scent it in the air, taste it on their tongues.

A portal opened behind Caym, and Logan held back a grunt, expecting the demon to be pulled into it, or even have more than just him standing there, but that wasn't what happened. No, instead, three men walked out of the portal, their eyes narrowed.

That wasn't the right way to describe them. They weren't men. No, they were demons. They had to be. And way fucking more scary than Caym had ever hoped to be. Logan shuddered, praying to the moon goddess that those three demons, and whoever else might be like them in the depths of hell, never pulled their attention from Caym and onto the Redwoods. He didn't think they'd survive that.

The demons didn't walk either. No, they stalked toward their prey like the three predators they were.

Caym.

"Tut tut, little brother," one of the demons whispered. Though Logan only thought he whispered it. His voice carried on the wind, surrounding them, almost brushing against him like spindly fingers. He tugged Cailin closer.

"You shouldn't have left the hells for the wolves," another demon said, his voice like crushed velvet. "You know better than to go above your station."

The third demon trailed his fingers up and down Caym's injuries. "It seems these wolves got the best of you, dear brother. They killed you. Oh yes, they did. The only reason you're still breathing is because Father wishes it."

Caym opened his mouth to speak, only to gurgle on blood as Jasper had split the bastard's throat.

"Don't bother speaking," the first demon said. "We will take you back home with us and take care of you."

From the way he said that, Logan wanted *nothing* to do with that kind of care.

"Yes, and then we'll show you what happens to little demons who break the rules." The second demon smiled, and Logan fought the urge to flee with Cailin in his arms.

"You've made a mess up here that we won't be cleaning up," the third demon said. "No, the lesser wolves and humans will have to do that themselves, but Father isn't pleased. He'll take that punishment out on you. And you know how much Father loves his punishments."

"Yes, a thousand years in the flames while nailed to the wall should be a good start."

"Then we'll freeze you to an ice block, and every time you move, you'll lose your skin, only to have it grow back."

"Oh yes, this will be fun. So. Much. Fun."

The three demons picked Caym up and began walking toward the portal without a look back. Caym screamed, gurgled, and kicked, but it was no use.

As the portal began to close, Logan let out a breath, only to suck it back in as the first demon looked over his shoulder and winked.

Winked.

Oh shit. He did *not* want to know what that was about.

The portal closed with a whoosh, and Cailin fell into Logan's arms.

"Cailin?" He pulled her closer so he could face her. What was wrong? Did the demons or the spell do something to her and the baby?

"We did it," she whispered.

He grinned then, full-out. Shouts and laughs sounded all around him, but all he could look at was his mate, his love.

"We did it, princess. We did it."

He brought his lips to hers, taking hers in a soft kiss, knowing there would be more later. Much more. They had an entire future together, ripe in the making.

He couldn't wait.

He'd found his mate, his fate, and his future.

What more did a wolf need?

CHAPTER SEVENTEEN

Cailin sank into Logan, ignoring everyone around them as she tasted every inch of his mouth, letting his taste settle on her tongue. She couldn't get enough of him and had to remind herself they weren't alone.

But goddess...

He'd almost *died*.

They all had almost died.

Logan pulled back, running his hand over her back. "We're safe, princess. Holy crap, we're safe."

Happy tears filled her eyes, and she kissed his chin, squeezing him hard. "Oh my God. It's over."

"Did you see those demons?" Adam asked from her side, and she turned to find her family, Pack, and Talons standing in groups, looks of awe and disbelief on their faces.

Cailin sank into Logan's arms, needing to rest but not ready to leave her family yet.

"I did," Kade answered. "We all did. I honestly don't think they'll be back for us though. At least not in our lifetimes."

Considering how long their lifetimes actually were, that was some proclamation. Not that Cailin disagreed with her brother in the slightest.

"So Caym isn't really dead?" Reed asked, leaning heavily into Josh. Hannah had her hands over her mate, Healing a wound on his side. Despite the fact that Hannah looked as if she'd Healed a little bit of almost every Pack member, she didn't *really* look worse for wear. The witch's power had grown immensely since they'd first met.

"No, I don't think so," Mel answered, her arms around Kade's waist. Her brother currently had his hand on Mel's back, rubbing small circles as if he couldn't get enough of her, as if he was ensuring she was still there.

That they *all* were still there.

"I think if he hadn't used the last of his powers to siphon into himself, we would have killed him," Willow added, her head on Jasper's chest.

Jasper had his arms around his mate and a large cut on his face, but it looked to be healing. "He sacrificed his wolves to give himself more power. We always knew he was a fucking bastard, but to do that? Crazy."

"We each got a few wounds in," Maddox said, his voice low, his arms around Ellie.

"I've never seen anything take that many death blows and still survive," Lexi murmured, leaning into North.

"And yet that wasn't enough to outlast the portal."

Logan's words made her want to hide under a rock, even with all they'd won that day. "Those demons...crap, you guys. They were worse than Caym, weren't they?" she asked, already knowing the answer.

"I think so," Gideon answered. "Jesus, I hope to God we don't ever have to deal with one of those in our Pack or in *any* of our Packs."

They all nodded at the Talon Alpha, she knew they were weary to the bone, yet still not really letting it sink in that it was over. It's how she felt.

"Goddess," Cailin breathed. "It's *over*."

Tears spilled down her cheeks, the actions and ramifications of what had just occurred washing over her. Logan leaned down and brushed a kiss over her head as the others murmured to each other, the same wonderment over their faces.

"What are we going to do with the bodies?" Ellie asked, her voice raw. "I...I know these aren't my people, not anymore. But they used to be."

Maddox brought her closer, whispering into her ear, and she relaxed somewhat.

"We'll bury them," Kade said, not surprising Cailin at all. Her brother was a good man. "They'll get their own graves, and we'll mourn the wolves they would have been under different circumstances."

"Thank you," Bay whispered. "We'll mark the ones we know at least." She opened her arms, gesturing to the vast field of bodies, blood, and torment. "There's too many for one day, but we can work on it."

"We'll help," Ryder put in. "We'll put them to rest as we put the battle, the war, to rest."

"I'll head back to the den and get the equipment," Adam put in.

"I need to contact the rest of the enforcers, let them know it's safe to bring everyone back," Kade added. "Let them know they can bring our children back."

Mel gave a watery smile. "Okay, we have that down. Let's get to work." She looked over the field where they stood, and Cailin knew that none of them wanted to do this bloody work, but they all had to.

It took hours, but with the help of the Talons and every Redwood available, they buried each and every body they found. They marked the graves of the wolves that Ellie knew on sight—the pain on the woman's face would haunt Cailin for years to come—and put a prayer on the ones they couldn't mark.

Once they were done, they were even dirtier and weary than they had been before, but this time was different. Now, instead of going home to pick up the pieces and pray for peace...now they had it.

She could go home with Logan and think of a future with the child in her womb without the worry of a war.

Cailin honestly didn't know if she ever thought that would happen, not with the way things had turned over the past few years.

The absence of threats, the idea of peace and tranquility, made her life seem stark.

Barren.

What was she going to do now?

Logan cupped her cheek, bringing her out of her thoughts. "Whatever you're thinking about, stop it."

"I'm stressing over the lack of stress. I think I need a nap."

Her mate leaned down and kissed her softly. "You need more than a nap, princess. And we have to rebuild the Pack and learn to grow with this new life of ours. Nothing is completely restful, completely over, but we're well on our way. Just put one foot in front of the other and know that you're never alone."

"I love you, Logan."

"Love you too, princess. Now let's get back to the den, sink into the bath, then sleep." He grinned. "And when I wake you up in the middle of the night by sinking my cock into that pretty cunt of yours, you'll remember exactly who you belong to...and who belongs to you."

"Sounds like a plan."

They made their way back to the group, their bodies ready to crash.

"If you ever need anything, *anything*, you come to us," Kade said. "I know you're rebuilding your Pack, and we're in our own tough shape, but we can't let another century go by with our two Packs side by side and not doing anything about it."

Gideon shook Kade's hand and nodded. "We'll talk more. We're not going to let this line of communication fall."

"Yeah, you can't get rid of us," Walker joked, and Cailin smiled.

"What about the Central land?" Ellie asked the question on everyone's mind.

Kade met Gideon's gaze, and the two Alphas seemed to have their own conversation in that look. "We'll let it become neutral land for now," her brother answered. "We still have a lot of rebuilding and cleaning up to do. Once we do that together, we can talk about what to do with what's left of the Central den. For now, between both of our wards, we can hide everything from the humans."

"Yes, we'll help with that," Gideon said. "I don't know if there are any Centrals left considering what Caym did with the Pack bonds at the end."

Cailin held back a shudder at the memory.

"When, and if, we find them, we will deal with them. Together."

At Kade's words, a new treaty between the Redwoods and Talons was formed, solidified over blood, pain, and loss. Cailin knew that wasn't the last time they'd hear from their neighbors. Not by a long shot.

Cailin rested her head on Logan's shoulders as Kade danced Mel around the living room, their children following them in a line of giggles and shouts. Happiness spread through her even at the bittersweet moment of having a family dinner at the new Alpha's home, rather than the home where she'd grown up.

It had been four weeks since the final battle where Caym had lost it all and her family had come out on top for once. Four weeks of cleanup, grief, and coming home.

Four weeks of peace.

Finn, Gina, and Mark each took turns jumping on Kade's back as he dipped Mel in their dance. The playful family fell to the floor in a heap of limbs, Kade taking the brunt. Cailin wasn't worried for their safety considering the group of them was laughing too hard to be truly hurt.

Jasper had Brie on his shoulders, doing a dance to the music Kade had put on for the family as Willow tried to get their daughter to stay still enough for a photo, a total lost cause for that little girl. Even Brie's pigtails were askew as she wiggled on Jasper's shoulders, pumping her fists to the beat.

Hannah stood between Josh and Reed, shaking her hips to the music, making her babies laugh. Josh held Kaylee in his arms, the big tough man looking adorable holding a child covered in pink. Reed had Conner in his arms and couldn't stop laughing as his son kept reaching out to play with Hannah's hair. The love of messing with the witch's tousled curls seemed to be a guy thing in their family.

Adam had Micah in his arms, the little boy resting his head on her brother's shoulders. Both of Bay's men were getting over man colds—as much of a cold as a wolf could get considering their immune systems. Bay leaned against her mate, a drink in her hand as she smiled at the dancing families.

Maddox sat on one of the couches, Ellie in his lap, as they had eyes only for each other, their hands on each other's faces as they communicated through their bond. Charlotte came up and knelt beside them on the couch, a smile on her little face. Cailin gave a happy sigh at the sight. It had been too long since that little girl had truly been joyous. Maddox grinned down at his daughter then pulled her close, providing the perfect photo op for Willow and her camera.

North and Parker were playing chess in the corner with Lexi helping North by telling him what moves their son made. Her brother really seemed to be getting used to his blindness—not that he was giving up. Far from it. Cailin had a feeling between her brother, Noah, and Emeline, they'd find a way to cure him.

There was always hope.

"Ready to eat?" Logan asked, his breath on her neck. She'd been feeling poorly for the past couple of weeks thanks to morning sickness, and it had been a bear to actually keep food down.

Right then though, she was famished. "I'm starving."

"Good. You need to keep your strength up." From the knowing gleam in his eyes, she knew *exactly* what he meant by that. Dirty, dirty wolf.

"Did someone say food?" Adam asked. He, too, hadn't been hungry until recently.

"Dinner's ready, just on the warmers," Mel added. "Come on all. I'm starving too."

Everyone went to the dining room table that had just been put in that morning. Cailin traced her fingers on the familiar table and sighed. At least she didn't cry this time.

No one spoke as they each sat down, getting the children set up in their chairs, but plates remained empty.

Kade cleared his throat. "I know we're eating here from now on, but it felt right to move Mom and Dad's table in here. It fit all of us before and...and, well, I didn't want to say goodbye to it."

Cailin smiled, a sense of peace washing over her. She'd never fully get over the loss of her parents, but now it wasn't a full-time ache every time she heard their names or anything about them.

"They would have wanted that, Kade," Cailin said. "Same as you making their home into the enforcer's den. That way the single men who are just becoming part of your crew can learn to work together. I don't think any of us could ever live there, you know? What you're doing is working ."

Everyone agreed, and after a moment of silence for what had been lost, they began filling their plates and started eating.

"I forgot to tell you," Kade said after they'd all been eating for a few minutes. "Mel and I were talking to Emeline about Finn and his new Heir powers, and she found a few things that might interest us."

Jasper perked up. "Really? What is it?"

"Usually, as you know, powers are given over after the Alpha is ready to move on. But since...but since it happened the way it did, we had to change quickly. Since Finn is so young, it changed how things will probably work out. Our next son or daughter will become the Beta when they reach a certain age, and then the other powers will show up either in our family or at least within our Pack around that time too. It will be a little weird since we'll have two generations of powers in one Pack, but it will work out."

"Meaning when it's time, I won't be the Omega anymore, but have the memories to help whoever becomes the next one," Maddox said.

Kade nodded. "That could happen in twenty years or a hundred. Sometimes Packs even skip a generation or two in changeovers since we're all so long-lived."

"The Talons are doing something like that right now too, right?" Cailin asked.

Kade frowned but nodded. "Something like that."

He didn't elaborate, but Cailin didn't pressure him. Some things said between Alphas needed to remain between Alphas.

"So we'll move on eventually," Adam said. "Things will change, but no matter what, we'll be a family."

Logan squeezed her hand. "No matter what."

Cailin looked at each of her family members and took them in. They had all fought bravely in one way or another. They'd each lost something close, sometimes even more than they thought they could handle. The adults had bathed in blood and had been reborn into something stronger, something more cohesive even among the fractions.

They were healed. They were whole.

They were the Redwood Pack.

The End

Coming Next in the Redwood Pack World:

CARRIE ANN RYAN

Maddox and Ellie have another story in Loving the Omega and Emeline and Noah find their happy ending in the Dark Fates Anthology.

Then...

The Talon Pack

A Note from Carrie Ann

Thank you so much for reading **FIGHTING FATE**. I do hope if you liked this story, that you would please leave a review. Not only does a review spread the word to other readers, they let us authors know if you'd like to see more stories like this from us. I love hearing from readers and talking to them when I can. If you want to make sure you know what's coming next from me, you can sign up for my newsletter at www.CarrieAnnRyan.com; follow me on twitter at @CarrieAnnRyan, or like my Facebook page. I also have a Facebook Fan Club where we have trivia, chats, and other goodies. You guys are the reason I get to do what I do and I thank you.

Make sure you're signed up for my MAILING LIST so you can know when the next releases are available as well as find giveaways and FREE READS.

This book was a labor of love. Each time I tried to write a certain scene, I broke down. I've known what would happen to the Redwoods since I first started *A Taste for a Mate* and looked into Edward and Pat's eyes. I knew their children would need to one day become where they were born to be and become leaders in truth. While it hurt to write, I hope you know that this was not a decision that was made lightly. I was up unable to sleep for nights as I wrote this book. In fact, I did the same when I was hinting at what would happen in the previous books. The Jamensons will heal. I hopefully will heal as well. The Redwoods are like my best friends and it is difficult to part with them.

I'm not leaving the Redwoods yet, however. In July, *Loving the Omega*, will be out in the world.

Maddox and Ellie have one more story in them that revolves around Charlotte. It was nice to go back and see how this family is working. There are a few surprises in store as well. Coming in August, I will be in the *Dark Fates Anthology* with my story called *The Hunted Heart*. This is Emeline and Noah's story. You saw hints of them here, but now you get to see where they are now.

Redwood Pack Series:
Book 1: An Alpha's Path
Book 2: A Taste for a Mate
Book 3: Trinity Bound
Book 3.5: A Night Away
Book 4: Enforcer's Redemption
Book 4.5: Blurred Expectations
Book 4.7: Forgiveness
Book 5: Shattered Emotions
Book 6: Hidden Destiny
Book 6.5: A Beta's Haven
Book 7: Fighting Fate
Book 7.5 Loving the Omega
Book 7.7: The Hunted Heart
Book 8: Wicked Wolf

Want to keep up to date with the next Carrie Ann Ryan Release? Receive Text Alerts easily!
Text CARRIE to 24587

About Carrie Ann and her Books

New York Times and USA Today Bestselling Author Carrie Ann Ryan never thought she'd be a writer. Not really. No, she loved math and science and even went on to graduate school in chemistry. Yes, she read as a kid and devoured teen fiction and Harry Potter, but it wasn't until someone handed her a romance book in her late teens that she realized that there was something out there just for her. When another author suggested she use the voices in her head for good and not evil, The Redwood Pack and all her other stories were born.

Carrie Ann is a bestselling author of over twenty novels and novellas and has so much more on her mind (and on her spreadsheets *grins*) that she isn't planning on giving up her dream anytime soon.

www.CarrieAnnRyan.com

Redwood Pack Series:
Book 1: An Alpha's Path
Book 2: A Taste for a Mate
Book 3: Trinity Bound
Book 3.5: A Night Away
Book 4: Enforcer's Redemption
Book 4.5: Blurred Expectations
Book 4.7: Forgiveness
Book 5: Shattered Emotions
Book 6: Hidden Destiny
Book 6.5: A Beta's Haven
Book 7: Fighting Fate
Book 7.5 Loving the Omega
Book 7.7: The Hunted Heart

Book 8: Wicked Wolf

The Talon Pack (Following the Redwood Pack Series):
Book 1: Tattered Loyalties
Book 2: An Alpha's Choice
Book 3: Mated in Mist (Coming in 2016)

The Redwood Pack Volumes:
Redwood Pack Vol 1
Redwood Pack Vol 2
Redwood Pack Vol 3
Redwood Pack Vol 4
Redwood Pack Vol 5
Redwood Pack Vol 6

Montgomery Ink:
Book 0.5: Ink Inspired
Book 0.6: Ink Reunited
Book 1: Delicate Ink
Book 1.5 Forever Ink
Book 2: Tempting Boundaries
Book 3: Harder than Words
Book 4: Written in Ink

The Branded Pack Series:
(Written with Alexandra Ivy)
Books 1 & 2: Stolen and Forgiven
Books 3 & 4: Abandoned and Unseen

Dante's Circle Series:
Book 1: Dust of My Wings
Book 2: Her Warriors' Three Wishes
Book 3: An Unlucky Moon
The Dante's Circle Box Set (Contains Books 1-3)
Book 3.5: His Choice

Book 4: Tangled Innocence
Book 5: Fierce Enchantment
Book 6: An Immortal's Song (Coming in 2016)

Holiday, Montana Series:
Book 1: Charmed Spirits
Book 2: Santa's Executive
Book 3: Finding Abigail
The Holiday Montana Box Set (Contains Books 1-3)
Book 4: Her Lucky Love
Book 5: Dreams of Ivory

Tempting Signs Series:
Finally Found You

Excerpt: Tangled Innocence

From New York Times Bestselling Author Carrie Ann Ryan's Dante's Circle Series

"I'm done with men."

Nadie Morgan barely resisted the urge to roll her eyes at her friend Faith's proclamation. She was pretty sure the woman had said something similar before in the exact same exasperated tone. Faith usually said things like that, considering she was trying to find a man to match who she was and who she wanted to be.

Not an easy thing when Nadie wasn't sure Faith knew who she wanted to be in the first place. Well, Nadie probably shouldn't be casting stones, considering she stood in an eerily parallel place.

Faith ran a hand through her blunt black bangs, leaving them in their perpetual disorder, then curled her lip up in a snarl.

"Don't you roll your eyes at me, Nadie Morgan. If you'd ever get off your virgin ass and actually tell him you want him, maybe you wouldn't be in the same predicament as me."

Nadie froze, the sounds of the bar slowly faded away so she couldn't hear her friends' reactions—if there *were* reactions. An odd numbness settled in, tunneling her vision so all she saw was Faith and her wide eyes set in a pale face.

Out of the corner of her eye, she saw the rest of their friends stiffen as well, then turn toward Faith, their mouths opening, most likely to defend Nadie where they thought she would never be able to defend herself.

In most cases, they'd have been right.

"Well, that was blunt," Nadie finally said, her throat dry. What else was she supposed to say? She was surprised she could speak at all. It wasn't as if Faith was saying anything untrue or far from Nadie's mind. It just hurt to hear it in the first place.

She'd rather have buried it forever and not looked back, but she knew that would have been weak.

Weaker than she'd been acting already.

"Oh crap, I'm so sorry, honey." Tears filled the normally strong-willed woman's eyes, and Nadie immediately forgave her. There hadn't been any true damage, and all Faith had done was tell the truth.

"It's okay." She raised her hands at her friends, and they quieted whatever words they were about to say. "No, really. You just got dumped. It sucks, so you lashed out, and I'm a pretty good target at the moment."

Faith shook her head then got up and walked around the circular table where they always sat when they came to Dante's Circle. Normally, it was a place that had become a sort of home to them, and right then, it was nice to have that familiarity. Faith wrapped her arms around Nadie and Nadie hugged her back. Hard. "No, it's not freaking okay. I'm hurt and in a pissy mood, but that doesn't give me the right to act like a cruel bitch."

"Just a normal bitch then," Becca, deadpanned, then flipped her fiery red curls over her shoulders.

"Hey, don't call Faith a bitch," Lily added in then came up to wrap her arms around Nadie's other side. "Well, she might be one, but we're trying to change that. And Nadie honey, I love you. Don't listen to what Faith said."

Soon, Amara, Eliana, Jamie, and eventually, Becca moved to join the group hug. Nadie could feel

Faith's tears seep into her shirt and knew that her friends weren't there to comfort Nadie, but Faith. The woman wouldn't accept the comfort otherwise, and everyone knew it.

Sometimes she and her friends just had to be sneaky about things like hugs and showing Faith they loved her just as much as they loved the rest of the girls.

"Okay, break it up. I can't breathe under all of you," Faith snapped.

Nadie just shook her head as Faith wiped her tears, straightened her shoulders, and then sat back in her seat on the other side of the circle.

"So, we hate Chadwick," Amara said as she pulled her auburn hair into a ponytail. She smiled prettily at Faith who rolled her eyes.

"His name was Chad, not Chadwick," Faith answered. "Stop making him sound like some dweeb who loves his mom and the country club."

Nadie tilted her head then took a sip of her lemon drop. "Um, but he *did* love his mom and his country club. Wasn't that the whole point? That he wanted to be with mommy and her money rather than stand up for something more? I thought you said something about the snooty mommy and her leech of a son."

Faith narrowed her eyes. "You're not supposed to throw my words back in my face."

"On the contrary," Amara put in. "We're you're friends. If he's a right bastard with mommy issues, that's our job. You're the one who told us that dear Chadwick was a limp neck—and probably had limp other things too—mommy's boy. Or should we call him *mother's* boy. He seemed like the guy who would raise his eyebrows all haughtily and call for his *mother*." Amara tried and failed to use a British accent—which Chad, not Chadwick, did not possess, and the girls fell over in giggles.

"Oh sweet baby Jesus, stop making me laugh like that. I think I'll start leaking," Lily said as she pressed her hands to her breasts. The new mom had control issues sometimes. Lily. A mom. So weird yet perfect at the same time.

"Oh God, you leak when you laugh?" Becca asked, her eyes wide before she turned to Jamie. "That'll be us in a few months."

Nadie just smiled and took another drink of her lemon drop as her now-mated friends talked about babies, leaking, and growly mates. She didn't want to feel jealous, but the little green monster wrapped its spindly arms around her, and she winced. It wasn't Becca's, Jamie's, or Lily's fault that they had met their true halves and something like a perfect life had actually stuck.

So much had changed in the short time since the world had grown around them that sometimes Nadie couldn't run fast enough to catch up.

She frowned and thought about the date then sat straight up. "Well, hell." The other girls stopped what they were doing and looked at her.

"Did you just curse?" Jamie asked, her hand on her baby bump. "You never curse."

Nadie snorted. "I curse, you just never listen. That isn't the point though. Think about what day it is and where we are."

Amara's eyes widened. "Well, hell," she repeated. "It's been two years, hasn't it?"

Nadie nodded then sat back as she watched the reactions wash over her friends' faces. It had been two years since the seven of them walked into Dante's Circle like they normally did, but they'd left with something much more.

Something most of them *still* didn't have a handle on.

Lightning had hit the building, or at least *inside* the building, on that day. Nadie, her six friends, and the owner of the bar...Dante, were struck by that same bolt of lightning. She could still remember the screams, the feel of her body rising from her chair then slamming down to the ground, and the heated sensation of something...else...flowing through her in an arc. It still haunted her nightmares sometimes.

After all of that, none of them had been the worse for wear, just a few cuts and bruises and, of course, Amara's broken arm, but that was it. Amara had healed quickly, as had the rest of them. Too quickly, in Nadie's opinion.

They had been forever changed though.

Lily had been the first to notice—though they all had in a way considering it was weird that eight of them had been struck by lightning and hadn't been killed or injured beyond falling to the ground.

They'd discovered that their human world wasn't quite human.

Every human who called themselves human, Nadie included, were diluted versions of supernaturals, and most weren't in the know about the fact that hundreds of realms existed near and entwined with their own realm.

"I can't believe it's been two years since I met Shade," Lily whispered then gave a little smile.

Shade was a warrior angel and Lily's true half. Apparently supernaturals had another part of their souls out in the world, and they were lucky when they found it. Or at least they were lucky when they found it, and the other half actually *wanted* it, but that was another story altogether.

"And I met Ambrose around that time, though it took another year to meet Balin," Jamie put in.

Jamie had not just one mate, but two. Nadie held back a blush at that thought. What on earth would she do with two men? She hadn't even been with one let alone two. Oh no way, too much for her. That didn't mean she couldn't have her own fantasies though.

"That means it's almost been a year since I met Hunter," Becca said as she frowned. "It seems like so much longer, you know? I mean, Jamie and I are pregnant, and Lily just had Kelly. We're bonded with our mates and have seen so...much."

Nadie nodded, knowing what she meant—at least when it came to what they'd seen. That was the other part of being struck by that particular bolt of lightning.

Each of them had a new energy within themselves. It was as if the lightning had altered their DNA, which the scientist Lily said was possible, considering the paranormal worlds were so much different than the human one. Now, apparently, once one of them met their true half—or the other two-thirds in Jamie's case—they started to grow weak, as if their body was rejecting itself. Then once they made love with their true half, they turned into a paranormal creature.

It was as if she were now in some sci-fi movie that she couldn't quite wake up from. Lily had turned into a brownie; Jamie, a djinn; Becca, a leprechaun. Each of them had met with others of their realm and, in some cases, fell right in step with that part of their lives while others had fought for their right to live—at peace and in general. Not everyone in the realms was happy about the turn of events.

Frankly, Nadie wasn't sure she was either.

The others were talking about how much had changed and how the rest of them still needed to find their true halves. Nadie, though, knew she was in a different place than the rest of them. While the others had hope for a future or were on the bliss side of happiness, Nadie knew she had nothing like that. No, she had nothing. She had a feeling she'd known her true half longer than the rest of them, longer than they'd even known what true halves were, yet he'd done nothing about it.

She closed her eyes, a sudden rush of something more powerful than herself seeming to wrench whatever energy she had left from her bones. Pain arced across her body, bile filling her throat as something clawed at her, her body growing weak. Her hand shook as she set down her lemon drop, but she didn't think anyone noticed. Life was moving on for the rest of them, yet Nadie didn't think she'd move on with her friends.

She swallowed hard, the truth slapping her in the face.

Again.

Her dragon didn't want her.

Well, not *her* dragon, as he never would be hers. He'd seen to that. The tattooed, sexy bar owner, Dante, had known her for years and yet hadn't taken one step toward her beyond being her friend. And he'd started to move away from even that since the lightning. They weren't the friends they'd once been and the loss was almost too much to bear. She'd had a crush on him ever since she could remember and *she'd* never done anything about it, either.

He was a freaking dragon, meaning that even when she'd been human and ignorant of all that went beneath the surface of the human realm, he would have been able to feel her as his true half, would have been able to feel that pull, that deep desire not only to have the other person in his life for eternity, but to have them in all ways possible.

Yet he'd done nothing about it.

Well, that was just fine then. She didn't need him anyway.

Another wave of pain drenched in power washed over her, and she closed her eyes, willing it away. Damn that dragon. No, damn her as well. If she'd had the courage to actually speak her mind, maybe she'd have been able to see what he wanted from her or, rather, what he didn't want from her.

Now she was alone and too scared to do anything about it.

Honestly, she had only herself to blame for it.

She wasn't weak, but she sure as heck was acting like it. Her fingers slid over the smooth wood on the table as she tried to regain some semblance of control. She didn't want this to be the last time she came with her six girlfriends into the bar that had become their getaway, but it was looking more and more like that was what would have to happen.

She couldn't come into the place that called to them and not think about the dragon who filled her dreams. Not that she'd ever seen him in his dragon form, but his human form was exactly what she wanted.

"Hello, ladies," Dante said as he walked up to them. His piercing blue—not that blue was a good enough word for the pools of color she saw—eyes met hers for a moment before moving on to the rest of the girls at the table.

His attention elsewhere, she could do what she loved best—study her dragon. While she was the plain Jane with straight blonde hair and a way-too-innocent face, according to Faith, Dante was the exact opposite.

He'd tied his long black hair in a ponytail so the blue streaks stood out even more. She wasn't sure if he dyed it that way or if black and blue just came naturally. Since he was a dragon, it could just be who he was. He'd chopped off a lot of it recently, something she wasn't sure about, but she thought he was sexy no matter what. So it settled in the middle of his back. She knew that if he didn't keep on it, though, it would grow so long that it touched the floor again.

God, she envied his hair.

He was built, but not too bulky, and wicked tall. At five foot three herself, everyone seemed a bit tall to her, but Dante was a couple inches over six and a half feet. She felt like a tiny fairy next to him, but she liked it.

If she ever wanted to kiss him, though, she might need to stand on a chair to accomplish it.

She blinked away those thoughts, knowing it was a lost cause.

There would be no kissing when it came to the dragon. He couldn't even stand to look at her for too long.

Her eyes went to the tribal dragon-like tattoos running down his arms and the small black hoops in his ears and brow. When he spoke, she could sometimes catch a glimpse of the tongue ring he wore, but he'd never flat out shown it to anyone. Becca thought that Dante might have a few more piercings...lower on his body, but Nadie and the rest of them had never been brave enough to ask.

"Nadie, are you okay?" The deep voice broke her out of her thoughts and sent decadent shivers down her spine.

Nadie look up at Dante and swallowed hard. "I'm fine," she croaked out.

He tilted his head, his penetrating gaze not leaving hers. She needed to stop looking at him because once she left the bar she wouldn't be coming back. Yes, she'd come to that conclusion. She couldn't force herself to live in the shadow of what she'd once been and think she wasn't good enough for him anymore. It would make it only that much harder to leave him if she didn't stop staring at him.

"If you're sure," he said, his voice telling her he didn't believe her.

Well, it was his fault anyway she was feeling like this. He'd ignored her for years, so apparently she wasn't good enough to be his true half. The thought that she wasn't good enough in his eyes burned, but she'd get over it. She had to. Leaving might kill her, but she'd walk out of the bar with her head held high.

She might be rejected, but she wouldn't be kicked while she was down.

"I'm sure. Thank you for asking." She held back a wince. No matter how hard she tried to act cool and unmoved, those stupid manners her parents had droned into her never quite went away.

Dante frowned at her, his eyebrow ring moving delicately as he did so. She didn't like to see him frown, even though she'd noticed him doing it more than usual since the lightning strike.

Not that she'd been watching him or anything.

Much.

Wow, she needed to stop this. Before she knew it, she'd be following him home, climbing through his bedroom window, and watching him sleep.

Stalker much?

She looked up at the man she'd been trying to forget and gave him a small smile. Damn her, she just couldn't stop doing that. His eyes brightened—or maybe that's just what she hoped had happened—and he smiled back.

"Okay then. Well, ladies, you all are closing down the house tonight as the rest of my customers have decided to call it in early. And since I'm closing at ten anyway. Do you want another round, or are you done for the evening?"

The others talked, mumbling their words to each other, but Nadie couldn't keep her eyes from Dante. Something was up with him, but she couldn't put her finger on it. The strain in the corner of his eyes and the firm set of his mouth that he thought he hid so well didn't escape her notice. Before the lightning strike, she might have gotten the courage to ask him as he'd always been a friend and had never made her feel insignificant. Now though? Now she was afraid, too afraid to do anything about it.

And *that* made her feel insignificant.

Something she'd have to change by leaving and never coming back.

She was better than this, better than the empty shell she was becoming.

However, right then, with the slight tension she saw creeping over Dante's shoulders, it wasn't about her but about the dragon who seemed to literally be carrying the weight of the world on his shoulders. She didn't know how to help, or even if she could.

Another flash of weakness—the one that came with meeting her true half but not completing the bond—wrenched at her, and she gasped. Her friends turned toward her, but before she could lie and say she was okay, something odd happened.

It was as if someone siphoned the pain from her, inch by inch, and suddenly, she was fine. Well, not fine, but at least better than she'd been. It made no sense. It shouldn't have been happening like that. Oh, she'd thought it had happened once or twice before, but never to this degree. The pain slid away, and Nadie swallowed hard, able to breathe again.

Dante let out a grunt beside her, and she blinked up at him through clear eyes.

"Dante? You're pale. What's wrong?" she asked as she stood up, worried. She put her hand on his upper arm then froze at her action.

He looked down at her hand then wiped the sweat that hadn't been there before from his brow. "Just a little dizzy, my sprite. I'll be fine." He placed his hand over hers, squeezing, and gave a strained smile. "Thank you."

She swallowed hard at his touch and smiled back.

He slowly slid his hand away and she moved back as well.

He'd called her *my sprite*. Well, that was different. Darn it, she had no idea what was going on with this man, but it was something. Something he was hiding. She needed to gain the courage to ask him. It didn't matter that she was leaving for good. He was her friend, and it looked as though he needed one right then.

But if past experiences were anything, she knew *she* couldn't be the friend he needed.

Not anymore, not with the fact he'd ignored what she was to him for so long.

"If everyone is fine then, I'm off to go to Shade and Kelly," Lily said, and then she said her goodbyes. Faith got up and walked to Dante, whispering something in his ear, but Nadie wasn't sure what it was. Soon the rest of the women left, either not noticing the tension or ignoring it altogether. That was exactly what she needed right then, and she was grateful that her friends seemed to know it.

She followed her friends out the door, letting herself take one last look over her shoulder at the man she wanted but could never have and then went to her car. The others left the parking lot as she got in and tried to start her car.

Try being the operative word.

The car made this annoying chugging sound then ticked before refusing to turn over. She slammed her hand on the steering wheel then cursed when she hurt herself.

"You've got to be kidding me." Everyone had left her probably thinking she'd be right behind them, and honestly, she didn't want to call them back just to leave her car there. She searched for her cell phone and cursed. Damn it. Where had it gone? Nothing was working right. She fought back tears of frustration, annoyed with herself more than anything. They'd all gotten in their cars together, not knowing hers wouldn't start. It wasn't her friends' fault she was stranded, but she still felt alone.

She'd have to go back into the bar and call a tow truck or something. Maybe she'd left her phone at the table. This was not the night of eating chocolate while having a good cry she'd had in mind.

The knock on her half-open window startled her, and the scream that ripped from her throat at seeing the man outside would have made any horror movie heroine proud.

The blond man, his hair falling to his shoulders, held up his hands, his green eyes wide. "I'm sorry, honey. Didn't mean to scare the crap out of you. I was just going to see if you needed help with your car."

The man had to be taller and wider than even Dante, and that didn't make her feel any less freaked out. The barrier of the car door would be nothing to a man like that, and all she could think about, despite his soft words, was an image of him ripping the door off, throwing her over his shoulder, and taking her away.

Damn it. Why didn't she have a weapon of some kind in her car?

And why didn't she know how to use said weapon?

"I'm a friend of Dante's. I won't hurt you. I promise." Hands held out in a surrender position, he slowly backed up. "Why don't I get Dante and get you some help? Okay? I'm Jace by the way."

She blinked up at the man named Jace, unsure of what to do. He might have said he was a friend of Dante, but considering the bar's name was in his line of sight, that could have been a wild guess and a pretty damn good lie.

Nope, she wasn't getting out. She'd just call the bar from her car and have Dante—or the cops—come to her. She reached in her purse and cursed because she'd forgotten she didn't have her phone to begin with. As she had just started to really panic, she let out a breath when she saw Dante himself walking toward them.

"Nadie? Jace? What's going on?" He didn't sound alarmed, more like curious.

"Nadie?" Jace rasped. This time there was something like awe in his tone, and she had no idea what he meant.

Had Dante told him about her? No, that would be stupid. There was no reason for Dante to do so. She was nothing to the dragon.

Dante walked up to Jace, cupped his cheek, and then gave a nod. Nadie felt as if she'd been slapped—she hadn't known Dante had someone...let alone a man. No wonder Dante didn't want her. He already had his mate. Oh Jesus. Fate really was that cruel to her.

Yet something important clicked inside her at the same time at the intimate sight.

"What's going on?" she asked, her throat dry.

Dante moved, pushing Jace a step back then stood by her car door. "Come on into the bar, Nadie. We have a lot to talk about."

She shook her head. "Tell me here. What's going on?" There was something off about this, something she didn't understand. It wasn't fear running through her right then—no, it was something much warmer, something filled with undeniable promise. She needed to put a stop to it before it went anywhere...especially since it seemed Dante and Jace were an item—or something much more.

And once again, Nadie had been left on the outside looking in.

"Nadie, please," Dante begged. "Come inside. For me?"

At that last word, she nodded. She'd never seen her dragon beg, and she didn't want to see it again. He wasn't the type to do so, and that meant something far greater than she could imagine was going on here.

"Fine, but you need to tell me what's going on when we get in there."

Dante nodded. "Yes, I'll tell you everything. Finally."

She got out of the car and swallowed hard. She looked at Jace and blinked. The feeling of being by his side was strangely just as intimate and heated as being by Dante's. That didn't make any sense, and yet she wasn't sure she wanted it to. For some reason she wanted to move closer to them both, hold them and never let them go. The warmth in her belly wasn't a mere attraction, no, it was something far greater.

Something tugged at her heart, her breath, her...everything.

She had a feeling she'd just taken a step toward a future she hadn't thought possible, but this time, she wasn't turning back.

Charmed Spirits

From New York Times Bestselling Author Carrie Ann Ryan's Holiday Montana Series

Jordan Cross has returned to Holiday, Montana after eleven long years to clear out her late aunt's house, put it on the market, and figure out what she wants to do with the rest of her life. Soon, she finds herself facing the town that turned its back on her because she was different. Because being labeled a witch in a small town didn't earn her many friends...especially when it wasn't a lie.

Matt Cooper has lived in Holiday his whole life. He's perfectly content being a bachelor alongside his four single brothers in a very small town. After all, the only woman he'd ever loved ran out on him without a goodbye. But now Jordan's back and just as bewitching as ever. Can they rekindle their romance with a town set against them?

Warning: Contains an intelligent, sexy witch with an attitude and drop-dead gorgeous man who likes to work with his hands, holds a secret that might scare someone, and really, *really*, likes table tops for certain activities. Enough said.

Ink Inspired

**From New York Times Bestselling Author
Carrie Ann Ryan's Montgomery Ink Series**

Shepard Montgomery loves the feel of a needle in his hands, the ink that he lays on another, and the thrill he gets when his art is finished, appreciated, and loved. At least that's the way it used to be. Now he's struggling to figure out why he's a tattoo artist at all as he wades through the college frat boys and tourists who just want a thrill, not a permanent reminder of their trip. Once he sees the Ice Princess walk through Midnight Ink's doors though, he knows he might just have found the inspiration he needs.

Shea Little has spent her life listening to her family's desires. She went to the best schools, participated in the most proper of social events, and almost married the man her family wanted for her. When she ran from that and found a job she actually likes, she thought she'd rebelled enough. Now though, she wants one more thing—only Shepard stands in the way. She'll not only have to let him learn more about her in order to get inked, but find out what it means to be truly free.

Excerpt: Wolf Signs

Need another dose of paranormal? Try *NYTimes & USA TODAY* bestselling author VIVIAN AREND's **Wolf Signs**. Book 1 in the Granite Lake Wolves.

Robyn might be deaf, but she's more than capable of heading alone into the great outdoors. The big, hunky Keil announcing she's his mate, *and* a wolf-shifter? That's a little more unexpected!

Robyn came back into his line of vision and his brother stopped her.

"Good morning, Robyn. How do you say that in sign?"

Robyn paused. She flipped him a thumbs up, and placing her left hand by her right elbow, she lifted her right hand in an arc.

TJ copied her. "Oh, cool, like the sun rising. Hey, Keil, look," and TJ signed good morning to him.

A chuckle from Robyn made them both turn and regard her with amazement.

"You can laugh?" TJ asked.

Her smile fell away and Keil swore inside. She wrote a fast note and disappeared out the door. He checked to make sure she was just headed for the outhouse before reading the message.

I'm deaf, not mute. Lost hearing as a child. Virus. I have an ugly voice. Two sugars, please.

TJ gave a soft whistle. "Man, oh man, is she going

to be a handful. I'm glad she's your mate and not mine. Did you two fuck—?"

Keil hit him. Not hard enough to do permanent damage but hard enough to make his eyes register the shock of it. After picking himself up off the floor, TJ carefully exposed his neck to his brother.

"You will use that brain of yours to remember to be polite when you speak to and of my mate. Understood?" Keil drawled the words as he poured the coffee and prepared Robyn's cup for her. "Even though it's none of your damn business if you were thinking straight you'd already know the answer. Use your bloody nose. No, we have not mated yet. Yet for some insane reason she let me kiss her and hold her, and while I'm pleased to report that yes, she's officially my mate, I have no idea why she doesn't seem to know a thing about wolves."

He sat at the table. "So I don't want you making any stupid remarks until we figure this out. Got it?"

TJ shrugged. "I'll behave. I figure it might be kinda freaky to be told something like 'Hey, didn't you know you're a werewolf and, oh, by the way, you're my mate. Oh, and there's going to be a challenge to the death next weekend for the leadership of our pack and I'm one of the headliners for the match.' I think telling it all upfront might be the easiest way." He turned back and flipped the ham. "Besides, there's nowhere for her to run while we're here. Gives you two time to work it out."

For the second time in as many days, the door behind them slammed open and Robyn charged in, her face red and her eyes blazing. She glared back forth between the two of them, her nostrils flaring slightly.

For not knowing she was a wolf, she had the evil-eye thing down pretty good, Keil thought as a shiver ran down his spine. He watched TJ struggle to keep his feet.

She surprised them by speaking. Her voice was gravelly and harsh but very powerful. Keil had heard a few Alphas over the years and she ranked up there with the best of them.

"Who is my mate?"

Like a flash TJ pointed to Keil. "Crap, has she got my number. I hope she doesn't tell me to go jump off a bridge or something because I—"

Robyn stormed up and grabbed the pad of paper. Keil read over her shoulder as she wrote.

If you don't want to be overheard don't talk where a lip reader can see you.

Werewolf?

Mate.

Challenge. To death.

What the HELL are you talking about?

She pulled away from the table but stopped to add, *Where is my coffee? And it had better be strong.*

~*~

WOLF SIGNS is available now!

Made in the USA
San Bernardino, CA
10 August 2017